HEARTS OF WAR

L.S. PULLEN

Copyright © 2020 by L.S. Pullen

Hearts of War

Text copyright © 2020 L. S. Pullen

All Rights Reserved

Published by: L. S. Pullen

Beta Read by: Kirsten Moore

Edited by: Cassie Sharp

Proofread by: Crystal Blanton

Formatted by: Leila Pullen

The right of L. S. Pullen to be identified as the author of the work has been asserted by her in accordance with the copyright, Designs and patents act 1988

No part of this book may be reproduced in any form or by any electronic or mechanical means, including information storage and retrieval systems, without written permission from the author, except for the use of brief quotations in a book review.

All characters in this publication are fictional and any resemblance to real persons, living or dead is purely coincidental.

DEDICATION

To all of the women who served in uniform or on the home front. Your sacrifice and defiance will never be forgotten.

CHAPTER 1

Sleeping becomes a novelty with old age. It's as though your body knows you're not long for this world—Mother Nature's way of telling you to make the most of today—after all, you may not see tomorrow.

It's lonely without Reuben. There isn't a day that goes by when I don't miss him. And today is no different. I wake, and before reality catches up with me, I reach over only to find his side of the bed cold and empty. It begins again, the physical ache inside my chest. And I know my soul won't be whole until we're together again.

My children meant well when he passed. They wanted me to move back to England, but I couldn't bear to part with our home. He's in the wild lavender which grows, row upon row, in our overlooking field. Woven memories of a life we once had echo in ripples from room to room. His presence is here, and it's where I sense him the most.

I travel back and forth between France and England; however, these last few years have become harder on my body. I'm grateful to my granddaughter, Felicity, for coming back home with me. Her anxiety was palpable, and I worried she might not have been able to make the journey. Fighting her demons has taken its toll on her—dealing with a past she cannot change and yet every day, she carries on. Felicity fights an invisible battle.

She woke in the early hours from another fitful night. I was awake, of course, but I let her be.

I don't want to suffocate her. Healing the scars we carry on the inside can take a lifetime.

I brew some ground coffee for Reuben even though I drink tea and he is no longer here. I still set a mug down beside the cafetière, the smell welcome and comforting. Felicity doesn't question my behaviour. Her eyes are sunken from her restless night. She makes her tea; I give her space.

A familiar ring catches my attention, and I wonder if this will be the news I've been dreading. My chest tight and my limbs heavy, I answer. And my intuition was, sadly, correct.

Lawry passed in the night. The grief his wife, Evie, feels matches my own.

We are the same, Evie and me. Lawry was mine before he was hers—my first love, the man I thought I'd marry.

It's been long enough, and it's time to share the secrets of a past long put behind bars of guarded memories. Few of us remain, and we owe it to their memories to honour them.

After the phone call, I take my photo album to the garden. I stare at the last photo of when we were together. My eyes prick with tears, and my breathing slows as memories take over. How did I survive the war when so many did not?

I fan my face from the early morning summer heat. Bees buzz around the patch of wildflowers. The fresh, sweet floral odour tickles my nose. The overhanging trees are lined with birds as they fly in and out of their nests. Perched on the branches, their chatter is a wild array of happy song. And yet, they have no idea how much grief consumes me.

I grieved Lawry once before, and now I have to grieve him one last time. Death, for the survivors, is a time of reflection. You ache for what you've lost. For what you'll no longer be able to say—the wrongs you'll never be able to put right.

Deep down, we hope they're at peace, free from any wrongdoings or burdens. That their souls are light and full as they pass on from this life.

It's with weighted steps I go through the motions and prepare myself for the inevitable. I open the worn, velvet jewellery box and find the Saint Christopher necklace. It's been an age since I wore it last, and I'm filled with a desire to go back and visit the past one last time. My fingers tremble as I attempt to unclip the clasp. It's the same reaction I had when I first found it waiting for me with a letter from Lawry all those years ago. It was the last gift he ever gave me.

CHAPTER 2

Past – 1940

It was a week ago when Lawry gave us the news of Sami's death. A week of mourning, the grief hardly bearable. I am pacing back and forth, my body heavy with fatigue, my mind muddy with exhaustion. Evie found out she was with child only days before. Never would we have expected such a predicament. Sami's death has shaken us all, but no one more so than her.

Of course, there is a worry of your loved ones and friends not returning from war, but to die during a training exercise is even more tragic. He didn't have a chance. War doesn't come without loss and sacrifice. Evie's inability to openly grieve the man she loves while discovering she's now carrying his baby is unfathomable.

Lawry spent the whole of yesterday going over scenarios to help her best, and his suggestion causes my steps to falter. I'm tired. Maybe I heard him wrong. The words taste bitter and catch in my throat, but I force them free. "You want to marry her?" I ask, bewilderment and confusion clouding my thoughts.

He takes my hands in his, supporting my balance, the pad of

his thumb stroking familiar circles across my palm. His eyes shine with hurt. "No, I don't want to marry her. I want to marry you. But what else can we do?"

And that's what it comes down to: how will she cope being pregnant out of wedlock? Her family will disown her.

"I don't want her to suffer idle gossip of a scandal that never took place." Unwed young mothers have never been treated fairly in this society.

He inches closer, his head bowed, his nose brushing over mine, sending ripples all over my body. I squeeze my eyes closed, wanting to savour his heat. His cologne comforts, easing me into serenity.

"Go, speak to her," I say and step out of the security of his embrace.

He nods and knocks once on her door before entering. My stomach is in knots, I hate this. I sit on the plush cushioned chair in front of the bay window, my eyes scanning the opulence of the room adorned with a black cast iron fireplace, all dark wood furnishings, and a grandfather clock in the corner.

Our dorm is nothing like her parent's townhouse. I mean, Harrods is only walking distance from here. And my parents live in a tiny suburban house in Edgware. Fortunately, her parents are residing in their stately home. They didn't want to stay here with all the bombings. We wouldn't be here right now otherwise.

I glance back to the door, willing Lawry's return.

Please don't do this to us.

Maybe she'll do the right thing by me and say no, if she cares about me at all. Or maybe he'll change his mind and realise how ridiculous this whole façade is.

So, what…she'll be sent away to have the baby. Is that really the worse thing? She can get on with her life, find someone else after it's adopted. That's what they do, isn't it? I can't believe I'm even considering that as an option. I don't even know who I am right now.

I squeeze my eyes closed, willing away the tears. She was the one who wasn't careful. Not me and Lawry. Why should we all have to suffer? My heartbeat is pounding and my jaw aches from grinding my teeth.

Why is this happening to me?

I wrap my arms over my middle. The temperature in the room has dropped. Is this what life will feel like without him— cold, empty? I concentrate on my breathing and keep my eyes closed. Maybe when I open them, everything will be right again.

I hear the creak of the door and the tell-tale sound of his feet as he makes his way over to me. A soft caress from his thumb across my cheek has me blinking up at him. He reaches for my hand and entwines my fingers with his. Our hands fit so perfectly together.

I sit forward. "How did it go?" I ask, my voice hoarse.

His demeanour is now heavier than ever. He shakes his head. I stand, and he pulls me into his body, his strong arms encasing me in a warm cocoon. I always feel safe when he holds me like this.

"I'll talk to her," I say.

Stepping back, I meet his eyes—bloodshot from lack of sleep. I reach out, cupping his stubbled chin softly. The soft whiskers grate against my skin. He leans into my touch, and I hold his stare for a moment before dropping my hand and stepping past him.

I inhale deeply, the air stagnant, as I step into her room. I turn to close the door behind me, my eyes cast down, avoiding Lawry's stare while I close the door between us.

The latch clicks into place, and the wood creaks beneath my feet as I brace myself for what I must do.

"Evie?" I say. Her back is turned to me. I come to stand beside her as she stares blindly out the window. I place my palm on her lower back. "How are you holding up?" I ask.

She shakes her head. "I can't do this without him, Ana. We

talked about all the things we wanted. He *wanted* to be a father. Did you know that?"

"I didn't," I reply honestly.

She nods. "A big family—at least four."

I smile. He was full of dreams of the future, his imagination so vivid. He'd regale us with a new adventure he wanted to embark, and we'd become engrossed. He had a way of commanding attention without even trying.

"Evie, you know you need to consider Lawry's proposition. What other option is there?" I ask, the words thick on my tongue.

She turns to face me. "I'll think of something. I just need time."

I take her hands in mine, leading her to sit down on the edge of the bed. "You don't have time, Evie. You need to act fast."

Her eyes are glistening and puffy from the tears which come in waves. "Neither of you understand the implications of what you are suggesting."

I shake my head. I hate seeing her so flustered, but this is not a fight she'll win—not if Lawry has his way. "Of course, we bloody do. We'll make sure no one ever finds out. Evelyn, please, you have to consider what's best for you and the baby."

Her face contorts, her pain evident. I hate myself for pushing on her vulnerabilities, but what else am I to do?

"Don't you think I *haven't*? My every other thought is about this baby. Samuel will never meet his child, for crying out loud. Our baby will never know the love of its father..."

She begins to sob, a heart-wrenching sound. Up until now, I've never lost anyone I've been close to, and Sami he is—was too young to die.

The saddest part is he'd planned to propose. He wanted to ask her father's permission. He knew by becoming a pilot, it would give him good stead in her father's eyes. Social circles mixing is frowned upon, and her family is very well-to-do. But with all her father's prejudices, he would have consented—as long as Sami could provide for her, of course. He allowed her to attend university when she wanted to find her path. Her circumstances now change everything. I look around her room, filled with such luxury. A four-poster bed, a dark mahogany or walnut carved headboard and canopy. I reach out and slide my palm down the post beside me; it's smooth to the touch. Even her mirrored dressing table is double the size of my small vanity back. She's accustomed to this lifestyle whether she admits it or not.

"Lawry loved Sami like a brother. You're fooling yourself if you believe he will sit back and let you commit social suicide. Evie, your father is a good man, but even he has his limits. This won't fare well for you or the baby if you don't consider Lawry's proposal," I say. I take her by the shoulders, moving into her personal space. My stare pierces into her, pleading with her to listen.

"What would Sami want? You know, if the roles were reversed and it was me in your place, he'd do the same."

She stands and begins pacing. "So, what? I marry Lawry, and then what? You become his mistress?"

I cringe; she makes it sound so sordid.

"This isn't about Lawry and me. This is about you marrying before you begin to show. No one will question the haste. We're at war. You're already well acquainted and more than suitably matched."

She stops mid-step, staring down at her stomach. "You make it sound like a transaction. I'd feel as though I were cheating on Samuel's memory. Like what we had didn't matter. How do I live with myself knowing my child will never understand how much his father meant to me?"

I approach her slowly, dipping my head until my eyes meet hers. "You tell the baby the truth when he or she is old enough to understand. Lawry would never expect you to keep it a secret. Not from your child. You know?"

Exhaustion is heavy in her eyes as she deliberates my words.

"Go, rest, but please think about it."

All fight gone, her shoulders sag and she nods. I wait until she's curled up on the bed before I take my leave.

I pull the door closed with a soft clunk and rest my forehead against the cool wood. The floor cracks and creaks behind me, and Lawry's fresh masculine scent washes over me before his hands cup my shoulders, his breath tickling my neck. "Well, what did she say?" he asks, voice thick.

I turn into him, wrap my arms around him, and bury my face into his chest, sighing.

"She's heartbroken, I've worn her down, though, and I think she'll agree. I mean, what other options does she have?"

His strong hands roam over my back, pulling me into a sense of security.

"I want you to know, no matter what tomorrow brings, I do love you, Ana. Please understand this will be one of the hardest things I'll ever do."

His words do nothing to soften the blow of what's to come. A physical ache forms in my chest as my heartbeat pounds in my ears.

I grip him tighter, never wanting to let him go. Even though he's doing this out of necessity, it makes me question his love for me.

I don't want to be bitter. I don't want to be a woman scorned. I could have demanded he not do this, but then, he wouldn't be the man I've fallen for. "What? Marrying a beautiful woman, you mean?"

He lets out a bemused laugh under his breath. "We'll work something out. I promise to be true only to you."

Tight knots form in my stomach, any words I may have had now stuck in my throat. It's a promise he can't keep. Truth is, he'll honour the vows he makes. If Evie agrees to this arrangement, me and him will have no future.

I can't hold back my silent onslaught of tears. He holds me until they subside, wiping my cheeks with the hankie he always carries. Tilting my chin, he takes in my face, memorising every feature. "I'm sorry you're hurting," he whispers. I place my finger on his lips, and his frown lessens. He takes hold of my hand, kissing my fingertips before his lips move to my cheek. They roam over the corner of my mouth—a feather-like caress—and then his lips cover mine. I open up to him. He kisses me with reverence, and I feel it with every cell of my body—a vibrant kaleidoscope of everything we could have been. Tomorrow no longer belongs to us, and we will have to part with all the memories of yesterday.

CHAPTER 3

Evie took two more days before she conceded. It was like a hot poker searing through my heart, slicing it in two, and then welding it back together all wrong. I've never been so conflicted, my feelings a contradiction. It brings me comfort to know she and the baby are going to be taken care of. They'll want for nothing and most importantly, they'll be loved.

But at what cost to me and my own happiness?

Everyone is dressed in their finest attire. Bright smiles adorn the faces of the guests and there are fresh flowers tied together with pretty bows at the end of each pew. The floral fragrance doesn't quite hide the scent of the aged interior or the smell of the wax candles.

The happy melody coming from the overly cheerful woman playing the organ makes me want to get up and leave. But I remain seated and keep my eyes focused straight ahead.

Everything leading up to today has been disjointed. I've been on the outside looking in while everything was set in motion. I don't think her mother took a breath as she finalised arrangements. And now I find myself amongst a sea of people in a church pew, under the eyes of God as they both say, *I do*.

I notice the figurine of Mary and wonder if Joseph had a woman before he became the surrogate father of Jesus. And I can't help but feel this is some kind of sick and twisted joke. It's as though God is mocking me.

I keep a fake smile plastered to my face, but it's not without effort. My jaw aches and my head is pounding as the Vicar drones on with the wedding vows.

My eyes stray to Evie in her long, white dress. And I envision me standing there instead in my dream dress as I stand beside Lawry. I have to avert my eyes, my throat becomes tight. The urge to cry out or scream is very real.

The crucifix draws my attention and its as though nails are digging into my wrists. And when I look down, I realise it's my own fingernails digging into my skin. But it's all I can do to not stand up and shout when I hear the words.

"If anyone here present knows a reason why these persons may not lawfully be wed, declare it now."

And this is when I allow my eyes to stray back to him, desperate for him to put an end to this façade once and for all.

But he doesn't.

My body sags in a final act of defeat, the weight too much to bear.

I wish I hadn't come, but I wanted to support them, even though no one is supporting me. And worse of all, Evie and I will always have an invisible bond that binds us—we've both lost the men we love. The only difference is, she gets to spend her future with mine.

As soon as we file outside, I take in deep breaths but it's not enough to cover my humiliation and despair. *They're married.*

Everyone cheers and whistles at the bride and groom as they come out hand-in-hand. And straight away, Lawry's eyes seek me out.

I cover my mouth with my trembling hand to stifle the sob as it works its way up my throat. His smile drops, he steps in my direction. His mother catches his arm, saying something to him. But he shakes his head. Her eyes flit to me and back to him. I catch a glimpse of Evie who has a look of pity in her eyes though it's concealed by a smile I know is forced.

I'm crying freely now and drawing attention to myself. There's a soreness in my throat and lungs from trying to keep my sobs at bay. The world is spinning in slow motion, and I know I have to go.

I turn and refuse to look back, my feet hammering beneath me as my legs pick up speed to a beat as erratic as my heart. My thoughts run wild as I think of the wedding gift from her family to a cottage in Scotland. I hate the thought of them alone together.

The image of how handsome Lawrence was in his RAF uniform will forever be etched into my memory. Today, he became a man. Up until Samuel died, there was still an innocence, a boyish demeanour about him. But now it's been replaced with a resigned acceptance of the responsibilities of life.

I'm greeted by a letter upon my return and a blue velvet jewellery box. I sit down on the edge of my bed, not sure if I want to read it. The scrawl clearly belongs to Lawry. I resist the urge to open either—instead, I turn the letter over again and again. The weight of what it might say becomes too much, and I place it next to the box and lay back, staring up at the ceiling.

I never told him I'd signed up to the Women's Auxiliary Air Force. Conscription of women is still relatively new, and there are a lot of people who think women being involved is wrong. But in a time of war, what's right? My basic training begins tomorrow. My case is already packed. And yet I don't know how to tell him.

I roll over and peel open the envelope.

Dear Ana,

I can't comprehend how difficult today will be for you to witness. I know I'll be wishing it were you opposite me. If there were another way, I would have taken it. I don't know what happens here on out. Or what our futures hold. I want to promise you everything will work itself out in time. But it's a promise I can't make. I would never ask you to wait for me or to not follow your heart. If anyone deserves happiness it's you, Ana. I just never envisioned it wouldn't be me in part making that happen. I always promised myself I'd marry out of love, and it should have been us. And although I care for her, it doesn't compare to the love I have for you.

I wanted you to have this, carry it with you. It was passed down from my grandfather and it's always meant a lot to me. He introduced me to all the great books and it's through him I found the love of reading. You remind me of him, in your passion for all things, and I always thought I'd gift it to my son. But it belongs to you now. Carry it with you and you'll always carry a piece of me too.

Yours always,
Lawrence.

I open the velvet lid and peer inside. A silver Saint Christopher coin adorns a glistening chain. He must have changed it. It's too dainty to be for a man. I finger the surface and cover my mouth. I should have told him not to marry her. But I love her too much like a sister to let her befall society's ridicules. The tears continue to stream down my face as I struggle with the clasp before finally managing to secure it.

I finger the pendant and squeeze my eyes closed. Tomorrow, I'll be billeted to The Queen Hotel in Harrogate and for the foreseeable future, my life will no longer be my own. I'll have a purpose, a goal for the greater good.

For King and Country.

CHAPTER 4

After a five-hour train journey from London to Harrogate, I'm glad when I finally arrive. The hotel is larger than I envisioned. I stare at the other women from my peripheral vision and smile in acknowledgment when they notice. Here I am, ready to begin training at the Women's Auxiliary Air Force. It was either this or factory work. I may not be able to serve as aircrew, but I can still make a difference in the auxiliary services.

A couple of women whisper amongst themselves but other than that, the rest of us remain quiet. I wish things would hurry along. I can't stop fidgeting—curling and uncurling of my fingers as my nerves set in.

"Come and collect your irons," says a heavy-set woman over by a long table. We all stand a little straighter and move forward.

"What are irons?" whispers a girl to my right.

I shrug, having absolutely no idea as we both join the queue. We watch the other girls moving off to the side once they have theirs.

When I approach, I paste on a smile in anticipation and almost let out a laugh when I'm handed a knife, fork, spoon and drinking mug.

"Oh, so these are irons," says the same girl, following me off to the side.

"So it would seem," I reply, unable to hide my smile.

"Phyllis," she says, holding out her hand.

I take it in mine and give it a quick squeeze. "Ana," I reply.

"This is Eileen," she says over her shoulder.

Another girl squeezes between us.

"Hi," I say and quickly shake her hand, too.

"Nice to meet you," she replies with a Yorkshire accent.

After we're all issued with our service numbers, we're sent to the mess hall for supper. The noise picks up while we eat—mixed murmurs of excited chatter. I end up sitting with Eileen and Phyllis, grateful for the easy flow of conversation and the company.

I hardly slept last night. I listened to hushed sniffling and crying until it dwindled into light snores and evened-out breaths. Unlike the majority of the girls here, I've already been away from home for school; this is their first time. It's daunting enough for me, no matter how hard I try to put on a façade.

After a hearty breakfast utilising our irons, we're sent for a medical review and a dental inspection. Apparently, we'll be getting vaccinations against all manner of weird diseases. Anything to protect us, I suppose.

Phyllis nudges me with her elbow when a woman steps in front of us.

"You're to strip down to your waist, put your hands on your hips and walk down the length of the corridor."

There's a moment of pause, even from me, before we quickly do as requested.

Phyllis is behind me and Eileen in front as we walk down a double line of orderlies who jab us in both arms with their needles as we pass. My face heats from the embarrassment. It's not particularly dignified but very effective.

"Well that was fun," says Phyllis as she pulls on her blouse and bursts out giggling.

"Don't dilly dally, go get the rest of your kit."

I can't see who just called out, but Eileen is already pushing us through a set of double doors. "Quick, before they try and poke us again."

I hold up a ghastly pair of knickers and immediately drop them as if they're on fire.

"I will not be wearing those," says Phyllis, examining the knee-length ones, otherwise known as blackouts.

I begin to stuff the bland contents into kit bags. The last things to go in are two white hand towels and a first aid kit to be worn in the inner pocket of our best blue tunic.

"Looks like we're leaving our personality at the door," Phyllis says as she swings a gas mask and tin hat in a hold-all over her shoulder with exaggerated force.

"You can say that again," chimes in Eileen.

"It's only while we're in uniform," I say.

As we wait in line to be assessed for our uniform size, the Quartermaster's staff look me up and down.

"I think this will fit," she says, not bothering to measure me. A pile comprising of three long-sleeved shirts with six detachable collars, one cardigan in Air Force Blue, a pair of trousers, tunic, a skirt, and a battledress top similar to a blouse is shoved into my arms.

"Parcel up your civilian clothes and return them home."

I cringe along with the other girls, of being stripped of our attire, too. This just keeps getting better and better.

"You were saying," Eileen says with a frown.

Keeping a positive spin on things, I smile. "Oh, stop. It could be worse." How many times has my mum used the same line on me?

"Your hair can't be longer than your collar, either. You'll have to cut it."

My smile melts, and it's the first time I think I might cry. I grab hold of my braid.

"I'll help you with your hair," says Phyllis.

"Thank you," I reply with a wobble in my voice.

I can't stop fiddling with my ponytail over my shoulder. Granted, I'm not the only one here with long hair, but it still upsets me—the thought of it being cut off and me being powerless to stop it.

"Well, what do you think?" Phyllis holds up a hand mirror so I can see the reflection behind me.

"It's still a little longer than it should be," I reply.

"Don't worry, I'll show you how to style it under, so it still looks short enough," she says with a wink. I let out a long breath and relax into my chair, trying my best to give her a grateful smile.

I manage to keep my tears at bay until lights out. I know my hair will grow back and it's just going to take some getting used to. I can't help but wonder what Lawry will think, and as vain as it is, I miss it already. But I know if it weren't for Phyllis, it would be even worse.

CHAPTER 5

I haven't seen them since I enlisted, but I couldn't put it off forever. The house is almost overpowering in its grandeur, and now, as I approach, I feel small and inferior in its presence. I take the steps slowly and take in a lungful of air before knocking.

I don't know who I'd expected to open the door, but it wasn't Evie. My eyes are drawn to her stomach. The apron she's wearing barely covers her bump. When I look up, her eyes are shimmering, and she lunges forward for what should be a hug, but her protruding stomach makes it an odd affair.

"Lawrence!" she hollers as she pulls away.

It's seconds later when he comes into the hallway sporting a hammer and wearing a tool belt. He drops the hammer on a side table and rushes me. I'm swept into his arms, and for a few seconds, I dare to breathe him in. I hold onto him—this man I wanted to marry—and for a moment, all is right again. I don't want to let go, but I have to.

It's a physical ache when I pull away. There's sorrow etched over his face as he takes me in. He leans down, resting his forehead against mine.

His breath is warm and sweet—just how I remembered. He kisses the corner of my mouth and pulls away, cupping my shoulders.

"You didn't say you were coming," he says.

I clear my throat. "Sorry."

His eyebrows draw together. "Don't be, it's good to see you. I've missed you. We've missed you," he says, waving between Evie and me.

And there it is…the gut-wrenching reality of the situation. It all comes flooding back—the hurt, the heartache. He married my best friend, they're about to become a family, and now, she's living my life, the one I wanted to have with him. Over his shoulder, I eye Evie cradling her stomach with one hand, looking anywhere but at us. She's uncomfortable; I'm the intruder.

I step away from Lawry, he ushers me inside, and then walks further into the hallway. "You look well," I say to Evie. And I mean it—there's a sparkle back in her eyes. It was lost when Sami died, but I see it, though it's faint.

"Thank you," she says. "You're staying for tea?"

I agree. I've come all this way; it would be rude not to. Lawry reaches for my hand and squeezes it once before letting go. We take our tea in the library, and Lawry joins us after going to change. He's no longer wearing the work belt. *Good.* It was an odd sight.

"He was fixing up the old cot. We're making the nursery ready for when the baby comes."

I smile, but inside, my heart cracks. Every time they say *we*, my stomach rolls, and I want to lash out as a flash of anger courses through me. And then I'm filled with self-loathing. I clear my throat and avert my eyes, grateful when Lawry changes the subject and we fall into a comfortable conversation. I begin to relax just a little. I even find myself laughing as I share some stories of when I first arrived in Harrogate.

Lawry watches curiously, but it's mainly me and Evie who talk. A little while after tea, she begins yawning and struggles to her feet. "I'm going to take a nap. Give you two some privacy," she says.

"No, it's fine. You don't have to do that," I say. "I'm not sure I'm ready to be alone with him.

She shakes her head. "I know, but honestly, the doctor advised I take bed rest when I'm feeling tired—even if it's just for short naps." She looks to Lawry and smiles, squeezing my shoulder as she passes and leaves the room.

"You stopped writing," he says. The hurt in his voice palpable. He moves, sits beside me, reaches for my hand. "Why?"

I bring my eyes to his and blink back tears. "You know why…"

"No, I don't. I still write to you once a week. And your letters stopped six weeks ago."

"It's too hard."

"It's my fault. I know this. As soon as I said those vows, I knew things would never be the same between us."

I stand, needing to move, the room suddenly stifling. I walk over to the books and run my finger over the spines, the smell of their leather bindings familiar, the pages musky.

"It's done now," I say, soft.

His footsteps—which always sounded so firm and sure of themselves before—move with trepidation as he approaches me. I turn to him.

"You're right, it is, but *we're* not."

His words, though strong, don't hold the conviction he's trying to convey. He takes my hands, his warmth seeping into my pores. Was I cold? Because when he touches me, there's a heat which wasn't there before.

"But what are we?"

The air around us grows thick with melancholy. I think he's going to answer me, but there are no words to fix this. Instead, he kisses me. I wrap my arms around him and stroke the hair at the back of his neck where it curls ever so slightly at the ends. We're lost in the moment, everything else forgotten but him and me.

CHAPTER 6

I promised him I'd continue to write, but the more we draw this out, the harder it will become. I know this, and yet, I continue with the fairy tale.

"Who you writing to?" Eileen asks, sprawled out on Phyllis's bed. She won't go anywhere near hers when it's made, but anyone else's is fair game, it would seem.

"Lawry," I reply, sealing the envelope.

"You need to let him go. There's plenty more fish in the sea," she says, picking at her nails.

"It's not that simple."

"I know. It never is." If anyone understands, it's her. She's been seeing a married man, a friend of her father. It's why she chose to enlist.

Phyllis walks in with a parcel in hand.

"What you got there?" Eileen asks, scrambling off the bed.

I can't help but laugh; she has no filter. How she keeps her mouth closed when we're at work is beyond me. She never stops…outside of radio communications.

"No idea," she replies, untying the string as she leans back, perching on the edge of the dresser.

23

She opens it, then unfolds some beautiful paper to reveal silk stockings and a bar of milk chocolate.

Eileen blows out a soft whistle. "Someone's been keeping secrets."

Phyllis's ears turn red, her chin dipping down as she clears her throat. "We've only been seeing one another for a few months," she says, the surprise of the token gift evident in her voice while she reads the card, her blush deepening.

"Well, you must be doing something right," I reply, smiling.

She pulls out the bar of chocolate, unwraps it, and passes us each a square. It smells rich, decadent. It snaps as I bite into it and relish the flavour.

"When do you see him next?" I ask, the chocolate melting on my tongue.

"The weekend."

"Be careful, won't you," Eileen says, her voice void of her usual humour.

"What do you mean?" asks Phyllis.

"If you begin to get intimate, just be careful."

I swallow and recall when Evie found out she was pregnant. They thought they were careful, too, but nature had other plans.

"It won't go that far."

Eileen jumps off the bed and straightens her outfit. "Not at first, no. But your urges will increase the more you see each other." She's speaking from experience, and now I'm the one blushing. "I just don't want to see you get hurt, is all." Her words are kind and soothing, her expression thoughtful. She knows about Lawry and Evie—they both do.

"I will," she says, but I hear the uncertainty in her answer.

"Do you want to get some contraception?" asks Eileen. Sometimes, it's hard to believe she is the youngest of us three.

"If it comes to that, then maybe. I'll let you know."

I think she's as ready for this conversation to be over as I am. "Come on, let's get some fresh air and go post this," I say, waving the envelope in my hand, ready to get out of this room that's stifling in the summer heat.

The sky is dark when we go outside; Eileen quickly changes her mind. Phyllis, however, hooks her arm with mine, and we make our way to the post office.

Passing a café, I pause. "Want to grab a cup of tea?" She nods, and we enter. I glance around for a table.

I hear her gasp and follow her line of sight to Roger, the man she's been courting. But it's not him who surprises her...it's the young woman sitting opposite him.

"Hey, you all right?"

"Who is she?" she asks out loud.

I shrug. "Do you want to leave?"

"No, why should we? I've done nothing wrong." She raises her chin, her nostrils flaring as she glares over in their direction with no regard for anyone else.

His head turns, as if he senses something. The smile adorning his face is confusing. He excuses himself and comes over.

Phyllis crosses her arms and looks down at the tablecloth. He clears his throat when he approaches; she looks up. "Oh, I didn't see you."

My mouth gapes open, embarrassed for her since he saw her staring at him. I smile and nod in greeting, but he's hardly noticed my presence.

"Yes, you did," he says. "What's wrong? Did you not like your gift?"

Her cheeks flame, maybe from the conversation we had back at our room.

"Why don't I give you two a moment?" I say, about to stand.

"No, stay," she says, grabbing my hand.

He's completely bemused. What's even happening right now?

"Do you send things like that to all the women you're seeing?"

Her question is brazen, not like her at all. His cheeks glow. "Not at all…what are you insinuating?"

She parts her lips to respond when Roger is tapped on the shoulder. It's the girl who was at his table.

"Roger?"

He turns to her and smiles, his arm going around her waist. My heart stutters. I narrow my eyes, mind racing, thoughts scrambling to understand what is even happening.

"Lily, this is Phyllis—the girl I was telling you about," he says.

She holds out her hand. "Lovely to meet you."

"This is Lily, my sister," he says to Phyllis.

Her mouth drops open, and then she takes Lily's hand, shaking it as she stares between the two.

"You didn't think that I? That she…" he shakes his head.

Tears pool in my friend's eyes, and I know she's seconds away from letting them fall. Roger lets out a belly laugh, and Lily wrinkles her nose at the thought while a soft chuckle escapes her. "He would never do that," says Lily. "He's besotted with you."

Roger nods his head in agreement and grabs hold of Phyllis's hand.

"I'm sorry," she says, her voice weak, her chin dipping down.

"Why don't you join us?" I ask for the sake of Phyllis.

"We'd love to," replies Lily who squeezes around me so Roger can sit next to Phyllis.

He doesn't let go of her hand until our tea arrives, and even then, he cannot keep his eyes off her. Lily is chatty, and conversation moves on to regaling us with stories of his mischievous childhood. And from the way Phyllis continues to stare back at him, I'm sure there may be a need for a trip to the pharmacy, after all. She can get some female condoms just in case.

I'm brought back to memories of Lawry and me when we

first began courting, and a wave of jealously hits me out of nowhere. I hate it. A hollowness fills my chest. I want to hate him for doing this to us, to me. I can't sit back and watch them have the life that was meant for us. But I don't know how to let go, either.

CHAPTER 7

It's been a busy two weeks which has left little room for idle moments. Tonight, the excitement is palpable as we walk a little faster when we near the community hall. In need of entertainment, we couldn't resist when we heard the NAAFI were holding a dance. It's where Navy, Army and Airforce all mix. We pass a large recruitment poster, *Serve in the WAAF with the men who fly*. I push my shoulders back, pleased at how far I've come, and seeing our reflection in a window, I can't help but feel proud.

When we push through the double doors, a thin layer of smoke greets us. The room is alive, music playing and couples dancing. Groups of people sit around tables, drinking and smoking. We find a free table and get ourselves a round of cider. It's not long before Roger arrives and swoops Phyllis onto the dancefloor. And not soon after, Eileen is asked to dance.

I've been asked multiple times, but politely declined...until Benjamin asks, and I accept. I've always loved dancing. He works in logistics in the RAF and thankfully knows I'm not interested in anything, and besides, I believe his interests may lay elsewhere.

Don't get me wrong, he's handsome—tall, light ash blond hair, deep brown eyes—but mostly he's kind and quieter than the other guys who frequent here, which is what I like most about him. We met him and a few of his friends the first time we attended a dance here. Since then, I've noticed the way he watches Eileen, how he goes out of his way to look out for her.

"Why have you never asked Eileen to dance?" The words pass my lips before I have time to stop them.

He pulls back enough to see my face, and with a shy smile, he shrugs. "I don't know."

I think of all the times she's cried over Malcolm, and it hurts her to know she'll always be his mistress and nothing more, and yet she struggles to see it. "You should."

I know he's caught Eileen's eye, but she seems to mirror his behaviour, avoiding excessive conversation. "Maybe I will," he replies, bringing me closer. "But a woman like her is too good for a man like me. She'd break me," he says softly.

I don't know what he means by that. I peer over his shoulder. Eileen is sitting at our table with a cigarette between her fingers, watching us. I wave my hand behind his back for her to get up, but she shakes her head, instead pulling out her compact to check her reflection. When the song finishes, we head back over and join her.

"You look lovely," he says, sitting opposite her.

She pauses, like she's stunned by the compliment and clears her throat before answering him. "Thank you." I've never seen her so unsure of herself.

No more is spoken between them as everyone else joins us— Phyllis and Roger along with his friends, Eric and Nancy. I'm the one carrying Eileen and Benjamin's conversation, though I can't help but notice I'm the odd one out in our group.

We stay for another hour before the girls and I walk back to our lodgings.

"I think Benjamin likes you," I say to Eileen.

She draws back, stilling her steps. "I very much doubt it. He barely speaks to me, and it's not like he's ever asked me to dance."

I grab her arm and pull her between Phyllis and me. "You rarely talk to *him*, either."

"I do, too."

Phyllis lets out a laugh. "You do not. You never shut up any other time, but when he's around, you turn into a mouse."

"Tell me what you *really* think."

The sky rumbles, followed by a curtain of rain, and we all squeal as we crash into the house. We giggle and rush upstairs before our land lady, Mrs. Jones, reprimands us.

Drying the ends of my hair with a towel, I look over to Eileen. "So, do you like him?"

She drops her gaze to her hands, tucking in her upper lip.

"Come on, we're friends," says Phyllis, wiping her lips free from rogue.

"Fine. Yes, I like him. I like him a lot."

I drop the towel and clap my hands, but the vibration of a broom hitting the ceiling underfoot stops me.

"Sorry, Mrs. Jones!" we all sing-song out loud.

"Then why won't you do something about it?" I ask.

She chews on her fingernail—it's rare to ever see her nervous. Even through basic training, she was always so well put together.

"Because of Malcolm," she says, pulling her fingertip away from her lips.

I eye Phyllis; she shrugs.

"Do you love Malcolm? Is that it?" I ask.

She lets out a heavy sigh. "No, I thought I did, but I think what we have is only lust."

I don't know how one would separate the two—love and lust —so I continue, anyway. "Is Malcolm the only man you've ever been with?"

She nods, her eyes gloss over ever so slightly, and then she sniffs as if to clear them. "I was eighteen and flattered by his charisma. The attention he paid me was more than my father ever had. But somewhere, the signals got crossed, and we went too far. I'm ashamed, to be honest. His wife is sweet, a doting mother to their little girl, Ethel."

Lost in thought, she bites on her lower lip. It quivers ever so slightly, and then the tears come. We rush over to the bed and sit on either side of her.

"I broke it off with him. He tried to get me to carry on, but I told him *no*. I even said I'd tell my parents. It was only when I threatened to tell his wife that he finally relented."

I squeeze her hand and rub her shoulder. "You deserve better."

"But *do* I?"

Phyllis leans over her other shoulder, eyes wide. "Of course, you bloody well do."

Eileen's shoulders slump. "I know what I did was wrong, but I didn't understand at the time." She picks at some lint from her skirt.

He did, though.

"You didn't do anything wrong. *He* was married, not you. And he's old enough to know better."

"Here, here. I concur," I say.

Eileen smiles, her features softening. "Thanks, girls."

Once we're all in bed, and I think everyone is almost asleep, Eileen speaks up. "Do you think next time we go out if Benjamin doesn't ask me to dance, I should just ask him?"

"I do," I reply.

"What if he says no?"

I shake my head even though she can't see me. "He won't, and I think he'll ask *you*, anyway."

"Really?"

"Yes. He's just worried you'll break his heart," I say.

"How do you know that?"

"Just something he said tonight. But you'd be good together. He'd worship the ground you walk on."

I hear the smile in her voice when she replies, "I hope so."

I hope so, too.

CHAPTER 8

I've settled into the WAAF way of life even better than I could've imagined. It's kept me busy, and I've forged new friendships, ones I wouldn't have if things were different. The thought brings a wave of mixed emotion. I miss both Lawry and Evie profusely.

Behind a pen and paper, it's easy to believe things are different, that we are two people in love, corresponding while we are apart, but in reality, he's married to my best friend and things will never be as they once were.

I have to read the letter more than once, even though it's as clear as day. I should be happy, and of course, I am, but I am also breaking inside. This is the final piece of the puzzle and only makes it more real. I've been crying for the past hour.

"What's wrong?" asks Phyllis as she rushes to my side, wrapping her arm around my shoulders.

"She had the baby," I reply, taking the handkerchief to blow my nose.

"Oh, Ana," she says, squeezing me a little tighter.

I already told Phyllis everything about my situation after she opened up to me about losing her parents.

"Will you go to visit?"

I nod. "I can't not."

"Maybe you'll feel better when you go."

"It was one of the hardest days of my life, watching them say *I do*. Now I'll be seeing them as a family. I'm happy she has a piece of Sami, though."

"But you're apprehensive about seeing how they are together as a family?"

"What kind of person am I to be jealous of a baby?"

"Oh Ana, stop that. You aren't jealous. You're just grieving over a life—that if things had turned out differently—may have been yours. You'll get through it. Remember why you wanted this for her in the first place. You need to make peace with them. Put it all behind you and move on. Unless you don't want to be part of their lives."

She's right. I need to find a way…otherwise all this heartache has been for nothing.

"I'll find a way," I reply.

"Of course, you will. Come on, let's go arrange your leave."

∽

The house is even more beautiful than the last time I was here. It almost takes my breath away. *Evie's living my life*. I instantly recoil. It's thoughts like these I loathe; I am not this person.

An empty feeling sets in the pit of my stomach, my mouth dries. I don't know if I can do this. I pull in a lungful of air and straighten my skirt while making sure my cap is still pinned in place. I only have leave for the day.

My lace-up shoes crunch beneath the gravel as I walk along the drive and take in the expanse of the property, the fresh green foliage and sweet rose bushes invigorating. The front of the house is wrapped in violet hews of wisteria—wild and free.

Birdsong nearby reminds me of summer days spent in the

country with my own family, and a wave of nostalgia engulfs me. I don't know how long I ponder knocking on the door. I reach forward, the cast iron handle echoing when it meets wood.

It's mere seconds when the door swings open, and to my surprise Lawry, is standing there. Apart from the slight shadows beneath his eyes, he's still my Lawry. His mouth gapes open before he rushes forward and sweeps me up in his arms. I can't hold back my squeal of surprise or the spread of my lips as they form a genuine smile.

I breathe him in so deep, a sharp mix of nutmeg, cinnamon, and musk. A smell only associated with him.

"Lawry," I say on an exhale.

A baby's mewling sound interrupts me, and I pull back. Evie waits in the archway with a bundle in her arms. I give Lawry's bicep a gentle squeeze, and he releases me. Everything slows down as I close in on her. My stomach flutters with foreboding until I'm in front of her.

I peer down. And the wave of apprehension dissipates when I cast my eyes on him. He yawns wide and then suckles on his fist. His eyes blink back at me, his brown orbs just like his father's. My eyes spring to Evie's and without a word, she nods, and I have to sneak another look. He is the spitting image of Samuel.

"Come, let us all go inside," Lawry says. His hand's moving to the small of Evie's back as he ushers us into the house. I pause, unable to ignore the stabbing pain in my chest. It's the simplest of gestures, but it's one which was once reserved only for me.

And then I see it—their lives together laid out ahead of them. Forcing my weighted feet to move, I follow them up the last few steps and over the threshold into *their* home. I feel like an intruder. This is their sanctuary, and I'm invading it.

"Let's go sit," Evie says. I can't see her face, but I hear the smile in her voice.

Lawry slows and takes my hand in his but instinct causes me

to pull away. His eyebrows draw in, and he looks hurt. He mouths the word, "sorry." I look away. He's apologising, but for what? I don't think even he knows.

We all take a seat, and awkward tension fills the air.

"Would you like to hold him?" Evie asks. I can't help but smile with a nod.

I cradle him into my body. I see Evie in him now, too. I don't notice the tears until two land on the baby's blanket. Evie sits beside me and wraps her arm over my shoulder.

"He's beautiful," I say, sniffing back my tears. I'm not even sure where they came from. Lawry hands me a handkerchief. I take it with a small smile and pat at my damp cheeks. Sami Junior begins to fuss and starts sucking on his little fist again.

Lawry comes over and smiles down on us. He watches over him in fascination and awe. And when his eyes roam to mine, he smiles. I don't know if I've ever seen him like this before. I'm caught in a bubble where only we reside. I want to fight for him, for us, and never let go.

And then Sami begins to fidget, his nose scrunching up about ready to cry. Lawry holds out his hands and takes him from me, the action so natural.

"Here," Evie says, gesturing for him. "He's about due a feed."

They share a silent exchange as he transfers him into her arms. She's a natural—just as I knew she'd be—her face content as she smiles softly before she leaves the room. My breath catches in my throat. And that fight I had for us, for him, only moments ago…wavers.

Lawry kneels in front of me, smoothing the hair off my face. "Hey, what's wrong?" he asks.

"Nothing," I reply, trying in vain to avoid eye contact.

He shakes his head and sits beside me. "It's hard for me, too," he says quietly.

It hurts me, knowing this hurts him. "I never said it wasn't."

"We knew this was going to be hard. But what other option did we have?" He squeezes my hand.

"I don't know, but we were foolish to think this would be straightforward," I say, scanning his left hand, the wedding band taunting me.

"Neither of us thought this was going to be easy." He moves closer. "Come here," he says, pulling me into his body.

There was a time when I believed we were a perfect fit, him and I. We were the missing pieces of a puzzle. But now in his arms, I feel out of place. Any dreams I once had of a future with him died with Samuel, and I need to accept it now. I allow myself the comfort of his arms briefly before reluctantly standing and heading over to the grand window that overlooks the back of the property.

"You weren't lying when you said how wonderful it is here," I say, attempting to break the tension.

He comes to join me and stares out into the expanse of the beautiful green pasture and surrounding trees. His description didn't do it justice.

"Why did you not tell me you were joining the Women's Auxiliary?"

I was wondering when he'd ask. It was ignored on my last visit, and I thought he knew why. I turn to face him but maintain distance between us. "I don't know. I needed something just for me. I needed to feel wanted."

He steps closer, his hands in a tight fist. "Ana, I wanted you. I still want you," he says, scanning my face.

"And I want you, but how is it even a possibility now?"

I back away and avert my eyes to the wall covered from floor to ceiling with books. I scan the titles. His footsteps echo behind me.

"I don't know," he replies.

"Sami is adorable," I reply, needing to change the subject.

"He's going to be a handful, I can already tell," he says with a warm smile.

"How are you finding it? Being a father?" I ask.

He pulls one of the books free from the shelf. The War of the Worlds. "I enjoy it when I'm here, but he's still so small. I can't wait to teach him to ride and read—all the things my grandfather taught me." He blows dust off the cover of the book and slides it back into place.

Evie returns without Sami Junior, wringing her hands together. "You'll stay for tea, won't you?" she asks, hope in her voice.

I nod. "I have the whole day before I need to head back."

"Lovely, I'll go get started on something," she says, her movements confident as she turns towards the door.

"Let me help," I reply and begin to follow her.

Lawry grabs my hand as I pass him. "I'm glad you're here," he says before dropping it.

Evie is waiting for me in the hallway. "You could've spent some time together."

"I came to see you both," I reply honestly. "Do you not have a cook?" I ask when we enter the kitchen.

"Yes, but when Lawry is back, and his mother isn't here, we like to let her spend some time in the cottage."

"What's she like—his mother?"

"She's a little hard on the outside, but she's been quite sweet. When she's here, she makes time to talk to me, which is nice. It's been lonely without you and Lawry."

With him being in the RAF, it must be difficult for her out here, without him. I never really gave it much thought before; I was too consumed in how I was feeling.

She hands me an apron, and I tie it around my waist as she dons her own. Then she sprinkles the counter with flour as she begins rolling some dough.

"I'm sorry, Evie, but I just couldn't stay. Everything reminded me of the way it once was."

She points to the apples, and I get to work peeling and slicing. "I understand. I've called Lawry '*Samuel*' on so many occasions. The guilt eats away at me." I shake my head, her words absurd. "He's a good man, Ana. He's been true to you and I would never…"

Dropping the knife, I move around to her side of the counter. "Evie, I never said you would."

She searches my face and brushes her hair out of her eyes with the back of her hand. "Thank you for everything you've done for me, for Sami. I can never repay either of you. The sacrifices you've both made…"

I take her flour-dusted hands into mine. "You and Sami are worth it, don't ever doubt that. It will take time, but we'll work this all out, you'll see."

I don't know if this is for her benefit or mine. All I know is I have to believe things won't always feel so stilted—fractured. I refuse to accept this is how it will remain. But sometimes logic and your heart don't always go hand in hand; they pull, and they push you in different directions.

I'm reminded of the summer spent visiting Bognor Regis, our favourite seaside resort on the sandy coastline. It seemed sunnier there than anywhere else we'd been in England. I couldn't wait to swim in the sea. The waves were calm, inviting even. But the further we waded out, the more erratic and less controlled they became.

I could still taste the rich sea salt on my hands when Papi bought me ice cream after he'd hooked me under his arm and carried me back to the safety of a shallower shore. He had warned me always to be careful and never swim out too far, to respect the ocean, and I still do.

CHAPTER 9

I've been assigned to radio communications for several months now and have enjoyed the work. I felt important, valued. It was the only time I wouldn't obsess over what would happen after the war. Lawry drove me back to the train station after my visit. He was due back himself after his weekend leave and asked if we could continue to write. I'm weak when it comes to him; saying no was impossible.

I saw how he was with Sami Junior—a proud father. He held him even with the fussing. I could see the love and pride in his eyes. But there's also an undeniable bond between Lawry and Evie now. I don't know if they realise it yet. When we had tea together and reminisced, it was almost like old times sans Samuel, of course. Their chemistry was natural, palpable. And because of me, they're refusing to acknowledge it.

They can't fight it forever. Sooner or later, they will give in to the pull. I know this because it was once me holding back with Lawry, and eventually, I let the current take me.

Today, I have a meeting regarding the potential for re-assignment. I know nothing else apart from having been explicitly requested. Curiosity has me intrigued. I am to meet at noon in London, wearing civilian clothing.

London has been transformed into a cosmopolitan metropolis. It's so much busier now, with the large number of commonwealth and overseas personnel. The bus is rammed packed. But I'm upstairs and able to take in my surroundings. I've missed it here. As we pass the theatre, I close my eyes. Memories of my last date there with Lawry flood my mind.

When I open my eyes again, I scramble to my feet, this is my stop. I rush down the stairs and pull the bell, stepping onto the busy street. When I peer up to the entrance of The Ritz, I take a deep breath and straighten my hat as I'm greeted by the doorman.

My eyes roam the expanse of the lobby, the chandeliers, the vibrant red and gold carpet plush beneath my feet. I step up to the clerk and give my name. I'm led into the dining room laid out with tables covered in pristine white linen. He pulls out my seat. I'm transfixed by the silver cutlery sparkling on either side of the plate when I am joined by a tall gentleman.

I stand as he offers me his hand.

"Pleasure to meet you, Miss Dubois," he says in French.

I smile and reply in kind. "Mr Jones, nice to meet you, too."

We both sit. "Please, call me Nigel."

A napkin is placed over my lap as we are served drinks followed by a starter. I stare over the expanse of the room, all the tables are occupied, people smiling and talking as china chimes from the sound of teaspoons and the clatter of cutlery. A pianist plays with ease, lulling you into the opulence of the hotel.

"So, tell me, Miss Dubois, how are you finding Harrogate?" he asks.

I smile. "Please call me Ana. It keeps me busy, but I enjoy what I do immensely," I reply, a hint of pride in my words.

"And your family, do they miss you being gone?"

I ponder this for a moment. "I was already in dorms in university, so this is no different to be fair."

He smiles, bringing his spoonful of soup to his lips, and I mirror him. My taste buds come alive when the rich flavour assaults my tongue. I can't help but close my eyes and savour the taste.

"So, you find you settle into new environments easily?" he asks, breaking off some fresh bread.

"Yes, well I'm here. I never thought I'd see the day I'd be dining at the Ritz," I reply honestly.

He lets out a throaty laugh. "You and me both," he replies.

I find the nerves I had upon arriving have diminished somewhat as we fall into comfortable conversation.

After dessert, we are served with tea. And I'm left wondering how none of his questions have been typical interview ones. If anything, it's as though I am meeting an old acquaintance…except for the fact that our meeting has been carried out in French, which has been easy enough for me since I'm fluent.

"So, tell me, Ana. Are you courting?"

I scramble my brain—it's the most personal question he has asked me—and I wince.

"No, not anymore," I reply.

He studies me before answering. "I'm sorry," he replies.

"It's fine." But truth is, it's not. And saying those words out loud has left me bereft. I take a sip of my tea and hope not to let it affect me too much.

"I lost my wife when the bombings started," he says.

My eyes spring to his. "I am so sorry," I reply.

The Blitz has been relentless since it began with the nighttime bombings. Even with the blackouts. Countless nights so many of us took refuge from the air raids in underground stations. The hardest part was the waiting, listening to the destruction and only seeing the devastation of the bombings the following day—the news of all the casualties and deaths. I can't suppress the involuntary shiver which rolls over me.

"Everyone has lost someone or something." He takes a sip of his tea. "It's why we do what we do. Try to make a difference, even in the smallest ways."

I straighten my shoulders and sit a little higher in my chair.

"But life goes on, we keep calm and carry on." He masks his nostalgia with his comment. It's what we do during times such as these, and I wonder if I'll ever get used to it.

He continues to speak about the war in general but nothing more. When we part company, he shakes my hand firmly. "It really was a pleasure to meet you, Ana," he says.

I give a genuine smile; he reminds me of my father in some ways. "Likewise," I reply. He lets go of my hand and we part ways.

∼

"I can't believe you're leaving us," says Eileen as she helps me pack my suitcase.

"I might not even pass the assessment. I could be back before you know it." It's been two weeks since my initial interview. I've just received correspondence that I am to attend an assessment. If I don't pass, I'll resume my current position in radio operations. Deep down, I hope that's not the case. I want to do more.

"You'll write?" asks Phyllis.

I bite my lip, not wanting to lie. "If I can, of course, I will."

Eileen pulls me in for a hug, quickly joined by Phyllis. We giggle and sniff back tears. It's foolish, really, but we've become so close, and I hate to leave them.

"Does Lawry know?"

The pit of my stomach hollows out from her question. I shake my head and slump down on the mattress. "Not yet, no."

It's not as though I can tell him much, and whatever I do say will likely be censored. I haven't seen him since Sami was born, but we've continued to write. I write Evie, too. She tells me how much he's grown and how alike he is to Samuel. But there are always unwritten questions, ones I'm not brave enough to ask. Lawry has invited me to visit them, but I've continued to make excuses. Why can't I do what I need to do and move on? Why must I continue to delude myself into believing after this has all passed, we have a future? Deep down, I don't know if I believe it anymore. I hope for it though.

"Do you think it's time you decided about your future together?" asks Eileen.

I shrug, Phyllis takes my hand. "I don't know him, Ana, but someone you love should make you happy. Put you first. Sami is here now, and they've been married for over a year. They *could* divorce."

I know she's right. It's the one thing Lawry and I have yet to discuss, but why hasn't he broached the subject? It's expensive, yes, but it's not just that. Sami is his son now, maybe not biologically, but in every other way possible. I'd be asking him to give that up. How could I claim to love him and expect that of him? I can't. It's easier to stick my head in the sand and run like I have been than it is to accept we no longer belong together.

"Once this assignment is over, I'll talk to him," I say. It's all I have right now, and the girls don't push.

The one thing I have learnt is there are no certainties in life. No matter how much we plan for our future, the outcome is not set. When I'm settled, I'll write to him to ask if we can talk. Who knows, maybe my will power will have strength and conviction, and I'll do what I know must be done.

"We just want to see you happy," says Eileen.

Since she and Benjamin started dating, she's a better version of herself. I didn't realise how self-conscious she was until then. Malcolm was not right for her. I know she told Benjamin about him; she felt it was only right if they were to get serious. She told me he was angry, but not with her...with *him*—the same reaction Phyllis and I had when we found out.

"I know. I just don't know how to walk away."

Eileen looks me in the eye. "Isn't that what you've been doing since they married?"

She's hit the nail on the head. It's easy when you're the one giving the advice; it's another when you need to take it. Besides, how do I say goodbye to someone I never wanted to leave in the first place?

"Anyway, enough about that. Let's enjoy tonight. Who knows when we'll be together again," says Phyllis.

CHAPTER 10

Day One

It's official. I've been asked to attend an assessment to become a Special Operations Executive. If I pass, I'll progress to full training. I know nothing about it except it will be an intense four-day course. We've been brought to an RAF base northeast of England, near Bedfordshire, I believe. A large group of us enter an aircraft hangar; it's empty with the exception of tall chalk boards and numerous tables set out around the room.

"Please, everyone, take a seat."

Each table only has one chair. Once we are all seated, I take in the other attendees—fourteen of us in total—and six, including myself, are women. The board consists of three officers and two assistants. We only know this because they introduced themselves, and we're told to call them by their first names. None of them are in uniform, all in civilian clothing, very informal. But it doesn't take away from why we are here. I think they want us to relax, but it's difficult.

"Your first test is your observational skills. In front of you is a layout of a building. You have exactly twenty minutes to memorise the entire layout. Your time starts now."

I peer down at the layout, trying to take it all in one section at a time.

Ten minutes have passed, and I'm no closer to remembering even a third of it. I close my eyes and try to recall one section when there's a barrage of noise and commotion.

Two soldiers' barrel into the hangar. Shots ring out—pop, pop—as they exchange gunfire. The sound ricochets off the metal roof.

The guy to my left ducks under his desk.

I scoot back in my chair, a gasp stuck in my throat.

But just as quickly as they entered, they're gone again.

My pulse is racing, pounding in my ears. My breaths are heavy. Hands trembling, I take a deep breath and try to hone my focus back on the diagram in front of me.

"Time's up," calls William, the tallest of the officers.

Andrew, one of the assistants, has a slight gait to his walk as he comes over and removes the layouts and then replaces them with a piece of paper face down.

"You now have twenty minutes to answer the questions on the quiz. Time starts now."

I turn over the piece of paper and grab the pencil. The quiz is a mixture of questions, not just of the layout, but also of the interruption by the two soldiers. I feel my skin bead with sweat beneath my blouse and swallow hard as I try to recall what colour uniform they were wearing, identifying factors, and also certain aspects of the building.

I already predict I've failed. I was not prepared for that to be part of the test. I hear the scrape of pencils as the others rush to answer their questions, grateful when he calls time.

But if I thought we'd have some time to collect ourselves, I'd be wrong.

"Next is Mechanical Aptitude."

A cart is wheeled inside. We are each handed three model sets—a bridge, a chair, and an aeroplane.

"You have one hour. Time starts now."

I peer up at the others, and their faces mirror my own, complete confusion. I decide to begin with what is likely the easiest and opt for the bridge, thankful I can assemble it quickly.

One of the men to my right went straight to the aeroplane, and the man to my left started on the bridge but is notably slower than me.

I move onto the chair, and it takes me a little longer, but I am satisfied when the final piece is fixed into place. Lastly, the aeroplane. I don't even know where to begin, and it takes me precious minutes as I examine the pieces involved. My heart begins to race harder as time runs out.

"Stop!"

I just finished slotting in the last piece into place.

We all look around to see how everyone else faired, and to my satisfaction, it appears only myself and two others completed all three. I always enjoyed making things with my grandpa as a child; I think it has come in handy now. I wipe my brow and inhale a deep breath, waiting for what comes next.

"Now, you will listen to a song—Morse Code Aptitude Test."

Someone shuffles, and then music begins to fill the space. I pick up my pencil and wait to cypher the code.

∽

Day Two

I stare over the large expanse of the obstacle course laid out before us. And internally cringe. It's too much. How am I supposed to complete this?

"I just heard we need to score at least fifty out of ninety to pass," says Milly, a lovely woman with short, brown hair and light green eyes.

We both watch as one of the men, Fred Lewis, is ordered to

go first. As if it's not bad enough, we all have to watch one another...either at our worst or our best.

"Something tells me I might not pass, but I'm going to give it my all," I say, hoping my words sound more confident than I am.

"What's he doing?" Milly asks out loud.

From here, I can see Fred white knuckling, and I am pretty sure he might have said something about a fear of heights. He bypasses part of the course and continues on.

After someone reaches the section of barbed wire, another one of us is told to begin. Gertrude's turn is next. My mouth gapes open when she refuses to go under the barbed wire. Milly's eyes go wide when she turns to me, and I shrug.

"My hair will get caught," Gertrude says in way of explanation, and I wonder if she's taking this seriously. For the first time since having my hair cut short, I am actually feeling a little smug about it.

Milly goes next, and then it's my turn.

Slamming myself over obstacles and under the wire, I pull my body along, ignoring the ground as it digs into my hip bones.

About halfway, I'm already struggling to breathe. Even with my basic training, this is a test in itself.

I tilt my head back when I come to the ten-foot wall. I gasp for breath as I stare at the monstrosity that has to be the toughest obstacle so far. I am by no means tall, maybe average height. Milly, on the other hand, is the shortest recruit, and she scaled it no problem. I can do this.

Gripping the wall for purchase, I pull myself up higher and higher. I slip, my palms slick with sweat, and my chin grazes the wall. It takes me a moment to get air into my lungs, but the fear of falling urges me to keep going.

Once I'm at the top, I take a couple of seconds to look back down. My vision blurs.

I have to use the rope to scale back down the other side. I

hear a heavy thud as Geoff, one of the strongest, fails the climb. I can't help the elation I feel when my feet touch the floor on the other side.

There is no time to rest when I am ordered to the next obstacle. My stomach drops out at the sight. I have to tilt my head back to look up. Rope ladders hang from thick tree trunks. And then there are rope bridges to cross to the other side.

"You can choose to cross at the thirty feet or sixty feet, but you *will* climb."

I stare in disbelief. Compared to the ten-foot wall, this seems impossible.

"You haven't got all day."

I want to let out a curse, but the longer I continue to question myself, the harder it will be.

I make the vertical climb to the thirty-foot mark and am about to cross... But I don't. I've come this far, I might as well push higher. It's only when I look down that I acknowledge how high I really am. I'm going to fall to my death on a sixty-foot obstacle course.

I step out onto a thin rope bridge. Each side is tethered to the trees behind and in front of me. It wobbles with the contact, and I pull in a panicked breath and hold onto the rope for dear life, trying to keep my balance. If I survive, I know I'll have rope burn. It may take me mere minutes, but in my head, it feels like hours.

Back on the ground, I sit with my head between my knees, trying to control my breathing. A hand rubs my back, and I peer through the crook in my elbow. Milly's face is flushed and damp from the exertion, but she seems satisfied enough.

"How do you think you got on?" I ask breathlessly.

She sits down beside me. "Better than some of the others," she whispers. I say nothing and sip the cup of water, hoping it will stay down as I wait to see if she'll elaborate. "Most only opted for the thirty-foot mark, and Gertrude opted out altogether —complained about some *ailment*."

We both roll our eyes and let out a snort of laughter. It's not hard to like Milly. She's as tough as old boots and doesn't suffer fools gladly, but she's got spirit and clearly cares about being here as much as I do.

CHAPTER 11

Day 3

My body has barely had time to recover from yesterday, and I am being put through my paces. But I don't miss being stuck sitting behind a desk, knowing, if I'm successful, I'll be making a real difference. I'll take blisters and sore hands to get there if that's what it takes.

We're driven to the outskirts of a heavy woodland area, where we have to take a twenty-minute walk. Tall trees cover the trail in shadows, the woods alive. Birds call to one another in song and chatter. Squirrels forage for food, and the crack of a branch breaking from the footfalls of our walk has their claws grappling the bark of the tree trunks as they race to the top when we get too close.

We come through a clearing, and the smell of algae and fresh air hits me as I take in the view of a vast open lake with a muddy shoreline, driftwood at the water's edge, ducks floating amongst the weeds. The sun and the blue sky reflect off the surface like a mirror.

George is the most pensive of the three officers, and hardly speaks but when he does, he commands attention without having to try. "Today, your task is to build a raft as a team. You are all to then use your raft to retrieve the radio on the other side of the pond. You'll be split into Team A and Team B. Each team will take it in turn, and the quickest team will be the winner."

I cross my fingers, hoping I don't end up on the same team as Geoff. Names are called out and I sigh in relief, grateful he's on the opposing team. He'd only weigh us down physically, and he's overpowering. He is already dictating what his team should be doing as our team moves away.

Philip Smith has been chosen as our team leader, but voices begin to grow in decibels, and everyone talks over one another.

"Listen, we need to work *together* if we have any hope of getting across this pond successfully," he says, crossing his arms over his chest. Towering over us, he is easily the tallest of all the students here, and he has a halo of red hair.

I hear a grumble from somewhere in the back of our group, so I step in. "Come on, he's right," I say, scanning my teammates before I look over the supplies we've been provided.

"Thanks," he says, smiling with a wink.

I shake my head, hiding my smile as I pull out the supplies. We line them up on the ground, and then it takes us thirty minutes to assemble.

It's with trepidation we all tackle the task of boarding it.

"We need to even out the weight, so we don't tip over," Philip says, holding onto the end. He lists off who is to board, saving himself for last.

I hold my breath until we're all aboard. Slowly, we wade across to the other side of the pond using our makeshift paddles.

There's a moment when we wobble, and I feel myself tip. I let out a curse, arms flailing, when someone grabs hold of my shoulder and pulls my weight back into the centre of the raft.

When we all step onto dry land, we let out a celebratory cheer.

Now, we sit watching and waiting on the opposing team. I

keep waving my hands in front of me, gnats and midges having their feast. I slap my own flesh more than once to be rid of them.

It's not long before they've assembled something similar to our raft in a fraction of the time. Disappointment floods my thoughts, and I turn away. But the sound of men screaming, grunting, and a spluttering splash cause me to turn back around.

I can't contain my laughter. They are all up to their necks in water, their raft floating away in multiple directions after being split apart.

I'm ready to be away from this gnat-infested pond, and celebrate today's victory with a long, hot shower. I wonder what they'll have in store for us tomorrow...

∽

Day 4

I didn't expect this. Everyone seems to be as surprised as I am, examining the piece of paper in front of us. I peer down at the words consisting of three questions:

Which two recruits would you choose to be on a team with?
Which recruit would you choose as your leader?
Which recruit would you leave behind?

I try to think logically—who is the strongest, the savviest— who showed the most intuition? Who'd slow us down the most in a real-life scenario? I find this test the hardest of all. It's like holding someone's fate in your hands. How many would choose to leave me behind?

How is it that this is both the easiest and the hardest test of all? We each hold the power of someone else's outcome in our hands. *Our* choices will determine *their* future. It probably takes me longer than it should to decide. I turn my paper face down once I'm finished.

Then we wait as we are called out of the room, one by one.

It's my turn.

I force my feet to move, left leg, right leg, left leg, right leg.

I stand in front of my superiors, their expressions void of any hint if they think I'm good enough. What if I'm not? What if this was some stupid delusional fantasy I had? I scold myself; it wasn't, it isn't. I want this almost as much as my next breath. I raise my chin in defiance. Palms sweating, I dare not move to wipe away the evidence. I clench my fists and bite the inside of my cheek to keep myself grounded as my body hums, tingling all over.

"Congratulations, Ana, you passed."

The words are hazy, my ears drumming loudly as the words settle in.

I passed.

I try to speak but words fail me.

Each of the officers step forward to shake my hand and I cringe as my slick palm connects with theirs. But they squeeze with vigour and their smiles match mine.

I did it.

I think of Lawry, yearning to share my news with him, but then I remember I can't... even if I wanted to, even if we were together.

When I'm loaded into a truck, I stare at the other nine people with me. I am beyond pleased to see no sign of Geoff, Gertrude, or Fred. Milly smiles, giving me a shaky high-five. Philip winks at me, and I can't hide my smile. I try to control my excitement, but the energy in the truck is palpable.

CHAPTER 12

Arriving at Wanborough Manor House, I take it in. It's an Elizabethan manor for all intents and purposes. It doesn't scream training school. But that's exactly what it is—hidden in the countryside, surrounded by acres of trees and hilly, rich green fields which continue for miles. This is where I'll be spending the next three to four weeks.

We're split into groups. I'm thankful Milly is in mine. As a security protocol, all groups are to be kept separate, and we are not to mix with any of the other agents being trained. I find it almost strange—aren't we all here for the same reasons?

They have just briefed us on what to expect. This is where they'll train us to become killing machines. Where they'll teach us how to use different weapons, explosives, and silent killing techniques.

I struggle to keep my breakfast down at the thought. Could I kill someone if the time came? I honestly don't know, but I do know that if I hesitate, they could kill me. I try not to let my fear of the unknown show; I don't want them to think they've made a mistake in choosing me.

The trainers begin straight away. They are relentless as they show us moves and have us enact techniques over and over again —until it becomes second nature. I've never had an altercation in my life, let alone seen one. I'm far outside of my comfort zone. This is foreign, and yet here I am, sweating and hurting from being thrown onto the hard ground repeatedly.

"That's it. Use your own body weight as an advantage," says the instructor, getting into position in front of me. "Again," he orders.

There is no room for error. We continue to practice until I finally get it right, and it's only then he calls it a day.

∼

After a long, hot shower, I towel dry my hair and drag myself to bed, too exhausted to contemplate what torture they have for us tomorrow.

"I miss chocolate," Milly says, rolling over on her bed to face me. She still seems wired from today's activities. I don't know where she finds the energy; I am struggling not to ignore her and go to sleep.

"What's your favourite?" I ask.

"Aero," she says, wistfully, rolling onto her back. "What about you?"

"Cadbury's Flake." And just like that, my stomach lets out a growl. We both burst out in a fit of giggles.

"Are you scared?" she asks after our giggles dissipate.

I bite my lip, my stomach uneasy, but I trust her, so I tell her the truth. "Yes. I'm terrified," I reply.

"Me too. When they approached me, I didn't think I'd make it this far."

I shake my head "Me either. I dread to think what else they have in store for us and whether we'll make the cut."

"Same."

My mind slips to Lawry, wondering what he's doing...if he still misses me as much as I miss him. "Are you courting?" I ask.

"I am, but he was drafted. He knows I joined the WAAF, but I won't be able to tell him anything about this. What about you?"

"No. Not anymore." The words get clogged in my throat, and for the first time in weeks, the urge to sob rises in my chest, but I push it away. "There was, but he's married now."

"I'm sorry. He wasn't the one for you," she replies, like it's the most rational explanation, and I let out a snort of laughter.

"He was the love of my life," I reply, turning my back to her.

"Sorry," she replies, covering a yawn.

The training is so physically draining, this is about as conversational as it gets. I squeeze my eyes closed, and it's not long before I succumb to sleep.

∽

There's heavy rain today, but it doesn't deter the trainer as we work in the howling wind, thunderclaps and lightning striking over the fields behind the camp. I want to be inside with a book, by an open window. But that was who I was before I understood loss.

A fist hits me square on the chin, and I go down, my head hitting the mud hard enough to knock the air from my lungs.

"Concentrate!" he shouts, heeding me to listen. Feet move towards me, and I need to try and recover somehow, gain some points for my lack of attention. I kick my leg out and swipe the back of the trainer's ankle, and he goes down with a heavy thud. But he's fast. He rolls to the side, and the weight of his body covers me until I'm sandwiched between him and the thick, wet sludge. "What can you do now?" he shouts over the pelting rain.

I bite down on my lip and try to think. "I'd use any force

necessary," I reply. "Gouging, choking, a knife or anything sharp which I can use as a weapon."

He nods, satisfied, and moves off of me, the pressure on my chest easing. "Enough for today. Everyone, go clean up."

We file out, and I notice Milly is limping. "Are you okay?" I ask.

She nods with a flinch. "I will be."

I've never met anyone with as much tenacity as this woman. She may appear small, but she's not to be overlooked. Two of the men already fell by the wayside today, and I wonder if maybe they are going easier on us because we're women. Once we are in the shower, and I see the bruises coming to life on my naked flesh, I decide there is no way that's the case.

At the back of my mind, I know a man will always outweigh me, that his strength will always be greater than mine. The only way for me to possibly win in combat is to outsmart him and then take him out.

I welcome the heat and steam as the shower soaks me from head to toe. I think of the conversation I overheard today. Never would I have expected there to be resistance from within the RAF and the Navy. I never paid much attention to politics but hearing whispers that the way in which we intend to infiltrate, and fight is thought by some as an illegal form of warfare is daunting.

"What do you think about our activities being considered unlawful?" I ask Milly through the shower curtain.

"It's ridiculous. A madman is trying to occupy Europe—what's lawful about that?"

I give a half shrug she can't see and continue massaging my scalp. "I think God will be my judge when the time comes." And until then, I'll believe what I'm training to do is for all the right reasons. The water begins to cool, and Milly lets out a screech at the same time as I do.

"Would it kill them to let us have a decent shower?"

I can't help but laugh as my skin prickles from the change in temperature. "Probably," I reply, working fast to rinse the suds away before the water turns from tepid to cold. After being here for over three weeks, you'd think we'd be used to it by now.

CHAPTER 13

We arrived at Arisaig House in Scotland late last night, but they waste no time continuing our physical training today with a hard slog over the unwelcoming terrain of Iverness. The wind howls angrily as the cold air attacks my face, finding my most vulnerable points—the flesh I thought was successfully hidden beneath my scarf and coat. But it's the worst kind of interceptor, finding your weakest points and infiltrating them. I can't recall what it was like to feel warm, the harshness of Mother Nature becoming clearer the longer we are all out here in the elements.

I didn't know it could be so severe. I crawl through the gravel and the hard, uneven earth beneath my knees and elbows. I can feel it tear into my flesh, the multiple scrapes, cuts and bruises continuing to cover my body. I don't even have to see them to know they are there. As my breath surrenders to the open space in front of me, it forms a small smoke plume from the exertion. I ache beyond comprehension, the trek up the mountain the hardest for me physically.

The blistering wind whips my hair into my eyes, and I swipe it away. The sting causes them to water. We've been out here for days, training in the rough terrain of the mountains. I've used muscles I never knew existed, my body put through an endurance I wasn't prepared for. I won't give up. Even though I'm screaming inside my head, I keep pushing and moving forward.

The hand-to-hand combat is severe, and it's the part I loathe the most. Up until now, I had never even seen any altercation before, and it unsettles me in a way which I can't articulate.

However, I do appear to be a dab hand with weapon training. My target practice has improved immensely. Learning how to wire explosives had my palms sweating and my hands shaking, but I'm improving there, too. And I'd like to think if I had to use any of this in the field, I'd make my instructors proud.

I propel down the rope, kicking off the rough, jarring edges of the wall and land on my feet before scanning to my left and right. Making a quick decision to take cover, I head for the shrubs, keeping my body low and to the ground, grazing my knees as I go.

I hear Milly let out a whistle nearby, and then she joins me, breathing heavily. We're to remain out here all night—survival in the remote Scottish Highlands. This was where Lawry and Evie spent their honeymoon, and here I am in a bush, trying to remember what heat feels like.

We're allowed to use fire, thank goodness, and as soon as night falls, we get to make our food. We're operating in small teams of four, and I am so grateful Milly is in ours.

Beans and tea—sans the milk—have never tasted so good. It's hot, and I finally feel something other than the empty hollow in my stomach as our last meal was porridge at six this morning. I relish the sensation as it slides down my throat and take my time to chew each mouthful.

"What's the first thing you'll eat when you go home?" Milly asks around a mouthful of food.

"Fish and chips, and a thick slice of bread and butter. What about you?" I ask.

Spoon poised at her mouth, she smiles. "Apple strudel."

"Ale pie," says Mark.

"Nah, fish pie," says Phil. "But honestly, at this point, I'm just glad to be eating."

He's right—anything which fills the void is more than welcome.

I don't sleep well. You're always on alert here, even when you're not on sentry, wondering what's going to happen next.

As the sun begins to rise, the Highlands illuminate in vivid pinks and oranges, reminding me of candy floss. I want to reach out and touch it.

∼

We've been learning unarmed combat for the past couple of days, and I'm relieved we'll be moving over to weapons training today. My body could use a rest from the physical blows and fighting techniques.

"I want you to familiarise yourself with these guns." Mark, our trainer, lays out two handguns on the groundsheet in front of us. "This is the Colt .45." He hands it to me. "And this one is the Colt .38. Both ideal handguns." The metal against my palm is cold but lighter than I might have expected. "I've set up some targets. You will learn how to use every weapon here."

Milly picks up the .38, and her eyebrows rise, but she looks at home holding a gun, and I can't say I'm surprised.

"See, it's a good fit. Sits well in your hand," says Mark. He comes to my side. "Tuck your arm into your hip like this."

I do as I am told. "But wouldn't we take aim and fire?" I ask, the memory of a spy film I saw at the cinema flooding back.

He shakes his head, his brows knitted together. "No, this is a good technique if your assailant is in close range. You fire two shots. This is what we call *the double tap system*."

"Like this?" I ask, tucking tight against my hip.

"Yes. Come on, let's get you practicing on these targets."

Once he's satisfied with our use of both the .45 and .38, he brings over what appears to be some sort of rifle. "This here is a Sten Gun." He passes it to all of us before loading it with ammunition and passing it back round again. It easily weighs around nine pounds. "You'll learn to be proficient using this, and then we'll move onto a bigger target."

So far, we've been shooting at small objects and targets to get used to the weapons. It's my turn to use the Sten, and I already know I don't like it.

"Shit!" I curse out loud from the force of the kickback. It ricochets through my body and down to the ground.

I brace myself again for recoil as I aim, however, this time, the gun jams. And that's pretty much how training goes for the next hour until he is satisfied with our efforts.

Mark winches a life-size figure on the range. Once in position, it throttles towards me with speed which completely throws me. Unlike the other targets, this one is moving. I take a sharp breath, and my whole-body jerks as I attempt to shoot it. And miss.

"Well, damn," says Milly.

"You took the words right out of my mouth," I whisper to her under my breath.

Mark comes over and gives us some more useful tips, but it feels like an age before I manage to hit the target.

"That's it, keep it up," says Mark.

His encouragement gives me the confidence I need. It's not long before all the practice begins to pay off, and we all become more conditioned to shoot anything, anywhere. Then the worry sets in, and I consider this…

There is a huge difference shooting a target and another human being. But I keep these thoughts to myself.

Loading our plates with as much scrambled eggs as it will hold, Milly and I find a table and quickly start stuffing it in. I never was much of a breakfast person—maybe a slice of toast and a cup of tea—but since the training has been full on, I find I am hungry as soon as I wake up.

"Did you hear?" Milly asks before shovelling a forkful of eggs into her mouth. She does make me laugh. My mum would have a fit if she were here.

"What?"

"Philip's gone."

My fork hits my plate with a clank, but I quickly retrieve it.

"What? How? Why?"

She lifts a shoulder in a half-shrug. "No idea."

There aren't many of us remaining from the original team. I wonder why or what reasons someone would fall at the wayside this close to the completion of our training. There's an end in sight; the last three weeks have been intense, but we're so close. We start learning demolition and explosives today. With sabotage being so high on our remit, it's essential.

"Do you think any of us who make it will be assigned together?" I ask.

She shakes her head. "Honestly, I don't think so."

I shrink back. She's probably right. It just seems everyone I've become close with, I end up parting from sooner or later.

"What's the matter? You going to miss me?"

I nod. "You have no idea," I reply.

She grabs hold of my hand and squeezes. "Listen, when this is all over, we'll get together, go dancing. Do all the things girls without a care in the world do." Her eyes glisten, but she blinks the moisture away and gives me a crooked smile.

But I hold onto what she didn't say. *If we are lucky enough to be here when this is all over.*

"Who would have thought it? Women dealing with explosives," she says with mock gasp, clutching her chest. I smile as we work quick to finish our meal. Today, we'll be laying dummy explosives on the West Highland Line...with their cooperation, of course.

∼

"They supplied a train," I say, only loud enough for Milly to hear.

She always seems so excited, eager to get cracking. As demolition and explosives are an essential part of our training, with sabotage being so high on our remit, it would appear they have covered every detail, even by providing a train.

It's real—what we're doing— and now, standing here alongside this metal beast, it becomes even more so. I clutch my hand into a fist at my side to hide a tremble. It's a nervous energy. I want my hands to still, but I know it's not likely, and I worry this could be the difference between me passing or failing.

I don't have much time to over-analyse this as we are sent on our way. It's a long day. We have to keep low and out of sight before we can even lay our dummy charges, and then the most important part—walk away and hide.

And it's during these moments, when I am lying low, that images of Lawry swamp my memories. It's getting more difficult to keep what we have...or don't have...compartmentalised. I thought being busy with training would ease the ache, the longing, but it only hits me harder during these quiet moments.

CHAPTER 14

Scotland seems like a distant memory, now.

I find myself at the Ringway Manchester parachuting school. We're given a tour of the hangars and the ground training, including the large room where they pack the parachutes. There is a large notice hanging from the ceiling, written in large letters. *REMEMBER A MAN'S LIFE DEPENDS ON EVERY PARACHUTE YOU PACK.* My stomach rolls, uneasy, and I worry my breakfast is trying to resurface.

"You okay?" asks Milly.

I nod, then shake my head. Being here brings feelings to the surface of Samuel. So, no. Knowing I am going to have to jump from a plane isn't something I can take lightly. I mean, can anyone? Scenarios I don't want to consider invade my thoughts.

"Do you think they'll let me go wherever it is by sea instead of air?" I ask Milly.

She lets out a laugh, drawing attention but quickly sobers up. I know it was a stupid question; it's not my decision. I'm here to follow orders and successfully do my job wherever they send me.

It's cold today, and I can't ward off the constant chill on my skin, even beneath my clothing. You would think with the extensive training and varying jumping routines—leaping through apertures cut in the bottom of the fuselages of obsolete aircrafts —I'd warm up. But I can't ward off this excess cold.

I take in a gulp of air, looking down to a large coconut matting about twelve feet below me. It's hard forcing myself to fall through. It's why they have us go over and over again.

"Your job is not to think!" shouts the instructor. "This needs to become a core memory. Your job is to follow the motions."

I study Milly as they vary the techniques of the exercise, falling into forwarding and backward rolls. "It's important to keep your knees and feet together!" shouts another instructor. "And your hands head high." He holds his up for emphasis. We do this repeatedly until he is satisfied.

My stomach churns, and I wonder if I might actually vomit. There are four of us seated in a sort of cradle attached to a balloon. A large winch driven by a motor roars as it continues to take us higher and higher. We must be at least eight hundred to a thousand feet from the ground now.

Sitting around the aperture of the cradle with a line attached to bar above us, we wait for the instructor to give the word. I glance at the others with a sickly grin. *There's nothing to it.*

"GO!"

And then in a matter of seconds, I'm plummeting to the ground. A tight sensation grips me in the pit of my stomach, and I want to curl up. There's a mad rush of air through my mouth and nostrils as my body drops like a stone weight. It feels like 125 mph.

I'm going to die.

A harsh jerk suffocates the scream on the tip of my tongue. I look up and see the silk canopy of my parachute overhead. It billows like a colossal grey mushroom, and now I'm floating earthward.

I'm flooded with a beautiful sense of exhilaration. Everything becomes more distinct with every second—the railway lines, roadways, houses, and trees quickly coming into focus. I am strapped into the chute like sitting in a swing, the harness behind and in front of my arms.

I struggle to judge the swing as my body oscillates while descending and the ground rushes towards me. I have to hit the quick release fastening over my stomach to release the straps. Falling, hands above my head, I hit the ground, keeping my knees and feet together and roll.

I made it.

I stand with my hands on my knees and drag in a few deep breaths. *I jumped and didn't die.* All in all, it was a good day.

We are informed the parachute takes longer to open from the balloon than it does from an aircraft and our bodies created our own kind of slipstream for the chute to develop with air. In contrast, in the aircraft, the speed at which it is travelling gives the necessary slipstream for the parachute to develop relatively quickly.

Tomorrow comes the real test—a training drop from an aircraft.

As I lay in bed, exhausted from another day of physical exertion, I also think of Lawry. Would he be proud of me if he knew what I was doing? Would he consider it immoral? Evie, no doubt, would support me. I shake the hypercritical questions from my mind, sleep comes easy, and before I know it, I'm up and sitting on a runway in an old Whitley bomber.

It does nothing to ease my nerves to be sitting in an aircraft otherwise known as a *Flying Coffin*. A shiver rolls up and down my spine, the roar of the engine rising to a screaming crescendo as they build up the revs. The whole aircraft shudders and vibrates, and I'm expecting the bodywork to come apart. The officer says something to me, but I have to shout over the noise to make my reply heard.

The smell of the fuselage from the chemically treated lacquer is disgusting, and I have to try and breathe through my mouth instead of my nose. We're all sitting on either side of the fuselage, and it has a large aperture cut away in its underside for us to jump.

I'm unsettled when the man next to me fails to push himself forward enough for the pack of his folded parachute to clear the edge. He tilts too far forward and knocks his face on the opposite side, and when he looks up, his nose is streaming with blood.

Fortunately for me, I don't have the same problem when it's my turn. I'm smaller in physique, which helps me navigate just enough to jump successfully. There's no time for delays—this could result in some of us missing the drop zone and finding ourselves over a densely wooded area or even water.

Never have I been so grateful for the capabilities of an excellent navigator. I can feel the difference in the jump as soon as I exit the plane, and I guide my parachute as I descend and oscillate by manipulating the harness straps.

There's a lot of confusion and rushing about when we assemble in our landing zone. The euphoria I felt only moments ago from my first jump from an aircraft is marred by tragedy. Two trainees didn't make it—their parachutes failed to open. Otherwise known as a *roman candle*, this has been known to happen when the silk canopy fails to open. Although we are assured it's a sporadic and unfortunate occurrence, it's enough to rattle me to my core. Unlike the Americans, we don't have reserve chutes because we jump from a much lower altitude.

Everything is suspended for forty-eight hours while an inquiry into the tragedy is held.

When we do resume, I am quite surprised by how normal everything is carried out, with, strangely, minimal reference to the accident. It hurts to think that this was what it was like when Samuel died—everyone just went on, business as usual, as though someone's life hadn't just been cut short.

I'm learning the importance of how to compartmentalise. That I have to concentrate on my job at hand, learn to be the best I can, and take it with me wherever I am to go next.

CHAPTER 15

This is all surreal—the equivalent to a finishing school for spycraft techniques. It's just me and my instructor, Argyle. In the large office that's become a classroom, the walls are lined with books, ceiling high with a ladder that slides along to allow access to the ones out of reach. Numerous desks are covered with various items. The light overhead buzzes as I try and take it all in. I feel like a kid again, in a sweet shop.

"Plasticine?" I ask.

"Oh, here." The instructor holds out his hand, and I pass him the square. He pulls a key from his pocket and presses it onto the plasticine and then closes the lid of what looks like an inconspicuous mint box. "It's a great way to get an imprint to get keys cut," he says. "Here." He passes me a fountain pen and a pencil.

I turn them over and try to work out what I'm looking at. I scribble on the pad, and they both work just fine—no invisible ink. He takes the fountain pen and undoes the lid slowly, sliding out a thinly concealed knife.

"Oh," I reply.

"We also have similar lapel pins and hat pins with the same knife."

I nod. The thought of using one as a weapon unsettles me, but it's something I have to push past...otherwise I could endanger myself and others.

"Buttons?"

He smiles like this is his favourite. "There are two different kinds." He picks one up. "Here, this one is a compass."

I take it between my fingers and swivel it to see the dial encased under the dome.

"And this one," he says, swapping the other. "Is a suicide pill."

My mouth dries. You would have to be so desperate to think the only way out is in the form of a deadly pill.

"There are other forms, but that's the best concealment to date," he says proudly.

Placing it back on the table with care, as if it might explode, I move along, picking up what appears to be an ordinary scarf and thumbing the material between my fingers.

"A map," he says.

There's a wire with small rings on either end. He picks it up, sticks his thumbs through each hoop, and gestures to the throat in a strangler motion. "Hand-to-hand combat," he says before he drops it back in the desk.

My stomach drops uneasily; I know there's a very high possibility that I will likely have to use this stuff.

∼

I'm in an average boarding house. Only difference is, I've been kept here, in holding, for four days. I haven't left my room other than to use the shared bathroom across the hall. I haven't even seen anyone. Food is left on a tray outside my door three times a day. The house is mostly quiet, apart from the wireless radio in the evenings, and muffled sounds of conversation. It's just me and these four walls.

After what feels like an excruciating wait, George arrives to give me the final briefing and details of the drop in the confines of my room. I'm presented with a map of where my drop zone will be—France.

There is a sorting of equipment I'll be taking with me. "You'll take these two sets of pills," he says, holding one in each hand. "Benzedrine will keep you awake when necessary."

He shows me the one in his left hand that's in a little rubber cover. The 'L' tablet is the suicide pill. "You bite down, and you'll be dead in fifteen seconds." My hand trembles enough for him to notice, but he is kind enough to say nothing while I take them from him.

"Give me your shoe," he says.

I undo the strap and pass it to him. He pulls out a small pocketknife and lifts the insole. Holding out his hand for the tablets, I pass them to him. There is a small section in the heel with enough room for both. He secures it back in place and I slip my shoe back on.

He goes over the details of my cover. I'm married. Most agents go in alone, without a spouse…but not me. I go over the notes—newlyweds, it's an easy enough cover—and part of me thinks I'd preferred to have gone in alone. But it's not for me to decide.

Mrs. Annalise Delacroix.

I'll have to write a letter to Evie and Lawry. I know regardless of what I write, the majority is likely to be censored, but I can't go without giving them my blessing. I know now I can never be with Lawry, even if he and Evie did divorce. They are a family now, and as much as they are both trying to fight the pull, there is a magnet drawing them together—Sami Junior.

It hurts more than I ever thought possible. I lost him before I even had him. But maybe he was never truly mine. I question his love for me, for us. I've been conflicted over how he could say he loved me, yet he couldn't find any other way to help Evie.

The thought tastes sour. I am not this person, not jealous of a baby.

Dear Lawry,

I never thought I'd be writing to you, not like this. There are things I haven't said and things I may never be able to answer. I wish I could ask you to wait for me, but I can't. The truth is, I don't know what my future holds. Your future, however, is with Evie and Sami, you're a family now. I see how you are with her. You can't see it, not yet, but there are unspoken whispers which pass between you, and you're both oblivious to it.

I can't and will not compete with Sami; the bond you have is unbreakable. And I wouldn't want to tarnish it. Don't be a fool and become an echo of the man I fell in love with. You have so much love to give, and you deserve the same in return.

Lawry, I know you, you'll fight it, but Evie is a good woman. She's a good match for you. Don't deny the spark I see between you. Light it and give yourselves a second chance.

If I thought we could find a way to be together, without tearing your life as you now know it apart, I'd do it. I'm not happy, Lawry. I haven't been since you said your vows. But in joining the WAAF, I found a reprieve. I was able to put my feelings for you into a box. But that's not what love should be.

I've been re-assigned. If I don't return or if this is the last time you hear from me, know that I love you enough to let you go. I want to see Sami grow into the wonderful young man I know you'll raise him to be, but I also don't want to be on the outside, peering in on a life which we could have had.

Maybe one day, when all of this has long since passed, it won't hurt so much, and I'll no longer grieve a love I never really had the chance to explore. Be true to your heart and don't hold back.

All my love, Ana.

I wrote and re-wrote his letter a dozen times before settling with what might be my final words to him. How do I say goodbye when I never wanted to leave him? I know I owe it to Evie to write her a letter, too. It feels like my final will and testament, but I can't go without trying to offer them some semblance of peace.

Dear Evie,

I never imagined it would come to this, me writing to say goodbye. I hope you know I care for you as a sister. When I came to visit, and I saw you with Sami, I knew you were right where you were meant to be. If circumstances were different, you'd be living this life with Samuel, and I can't deny the purely selfish part of me for wishing it.

I saw something pass between you and Lawry, but I don't think either of you is ready to accept it yet. I'm not saying he will in any way replace Samuel; what you two had was irreplaceable. Lawry's instincts are drawn to you and Sami now, like a moth to an open flame. Unbeknownst to him, the small gestures he now shares with you were once reserved for me.

I've been doing a lot of soul searching this past year, and it comes back to this: if you having Samuel back meant you not having Sami, I know you wouldn't change the past.

When you are ready to let love in again, try not to fight the pull between you and Lawry. Embrace it with everything you have. Love him enough for both of us.

If anyone can, it's you. Your soul has always been to nurture, your heart to love unconditionally. You brought out a side to Lawry I never even knew existed. I'd be a liar if I said I wasn't jealous. But it's my burden to bear, not yours. It's a struggle—forcing myself to let go of someone I still believe to be mine, saying goodbye to someone I never wanted to leave. Maybe he was never really mine.

I wish for a day when the war is but a distant memory, and we'll find a new way to be like we once were, without the guilt or self-loathing over the things we cannot change.

None of us asked for any of this. And if I had a choice, I don't think I'd change the path I'm now on.

But, Evie, me and you will always be tied by an invisible bond, an unspoken love for the same man. Be kind to one another and most of all, let him love you.

Your loving friend, Ana.

CHAPTER 16

The fierce roar of the engines are all I can hear. I try to block out the noise by thinking back to the details of the briefing, but at the forefront of my mind, jumping from this plane is one thing, however, doing so in pitch darkness, into the hands of people I am yet to meet, is another. I don't think I've ever felt this apprehensive in my life.

I only know we're nearing our target when we're each handed a hot toddy. I sip, my hands a nervous wobble, the rum doing nothing to settle my already queasy stomach.

I watch as a dispatcher opens a hole in the fuselage and begins to hitch the static line to our parachutes onto a hook inside the plane. He makes a huge fuss to show me I'm attached, but I'm much more concerned by the jump.

Once a red light comes on, I'm ushered forward to stand and wait.

My heart is beating so fast, my breathing is a struggle. I watch the light, waiting for it to turn green. The moment turns eerie as the engine cuts out. I look back to the dispatcher, my panic palpable.

"It's to slow the engine down," he shouts. "You get a better jump in the slipstream. And it quiets the plane for those on the ground."

Moments like these you can't be taught in a training exercise, and I wonder why I am only told this now. I nod, trying to remain confident on the outside.

"*RED LIGHT ON,*" comes a command.

I move, left foot forward, half in and half out of the doorway with one hand on either side.

I hear the shout, "*GREEN LIGHT GO!*"

This is it, my turn to jump. I'm frozen, my limbs not my own, refusing to move. A firm tap on my shoulder brings me out of my momentary haze.

I squeeze my eyes shut, and with a silent prayer, I hold my breath and step out on my right leg into the slipstream and into the unknown.

Free falling with speed, I try to catch my breath as I wait for what seems like an eternity for the static line to open. I couldn't be more elated when I feel the hard, secure tug as the chute releases. The thought of it failing and me plunging to a certain death increases my already rising anxiety.

But as I begin to float softly, it becomes euphoric. I'm able to see some of the others who were on the plane, their chutes opening, too—a group of floating jelly fish in the moon cast sky. I'm caught in the reality and the surrealism of the situation. I just jumped from an airplane, and yet now, everything around me has reduced to a tranquil speed. For the briefest of moments, there is enough break in cloud cover for the moon to illuminate the vast and vivid landscape beneath me. The view catches in my throat. I want to remember this forever.

Until the ground grows closer, and suddenly, I'm struck with how fast I'm actually falling—too fast.

I hit the quick release button over my stomach.

I don't hit the ground; the ground hits me—with a massive thump—and I manage to roll.

I lay, breathing heavily before I risk moving and check myself over to make sure all my limbs are still in one piece.

Grunting, I rush to the canopy and pull the material of the chute into a bundle. Grabbing for a small, handheld shovel, I begin digging. The earth is soft here, allowing me to hide my chute and cover it with a layer of dirt.

A noise nearby alerts me, and I know I am no longer alone.

"Leicester," says a man with a rich, velvet voice. It's a code word used by an ally.

"Square," I reply, confirming I am not the enemy.

A large shadow steps out from the bushes and rushes over. A flash of light to our left signals for us, and the man pushes me forward. I stumble, but quickly right myself, and he grabs my elbow to lead the way with what sounded like a heavy sigh, but I can't be sure over my heavy breathing.

We arrive at a large truck idling in a dirt road, and about six of us are ambled into the back. I'm on assignment with only three people I know from training; the other three are strangers. All I know is I am now behind enemy lines, and under Churchill's direct orders to *set Europe ablaze*.

Rolling to a stop, the engine switches off and everyone is led from the truck towards a cottage. We are taken to some open doors that look like they lead down to some kind of basement, a fact which no one questions as we descend the ladder.

My eyes need a moment to adjust to the light. I'm assessing my surroundings when I come face-to-face with a man, his eyes vivid against his tanned skin. I'm taken aback. His gaze is transfixed on me. I've never had someone stare at me like this—at least not so directly. "You'll stay here tonight."

I recognise his voice—the man who led me to the truck.

"Annalise," I say, expecting him to enlighten me with his name. Instead, he nods and continues to stare for a brief moment. His hand moves, and I think he is going to offer it to me to shake, but he only points to a small table in the corner.

"There's bread, jam, and some milk," he says, then walks away.

I continue to stare after him, but the smell of the fresh bread makes my stomach rumble, and I help myself to some. He leaves us without a backwards glance.

We all set up makeshift beds with blankets, but I'm still too alert from the jump and for the unknown of what's to come to sleep.

CHAPTER 17

It's barely daybreak when we're called upstairs to the cottage. We enter a kitchen where a petite, round woman ushers us to sit at the table.

She loads my plate with fresh eggs and bacon. My mouth salivates; I think I might dribble. I'm so overcome by the aromas, I can hardly stop myself from groaning out loud. I grab for the utensils and try to take my time as I shovel the contents into my mouth, barely managing to do it in a civilised manner.

I'm finishing my last mouthful when the man from last night enters. He sits directly opposite me but doesn't say a word as he gets going on his breakfast. I take him in. His skin is darker than Lawry's, weathered—older than I am but not by much.

I am broken from my observations when his eyes meet mine. He doesn't look away, but I do. I lower my eyes to my plate of food when he speaks with that deep, raspy voice of his. "After everyone has eaten, we'll discuss what happens next. Just remember always to keep your cover. The only place you are safe is within the confines of these walls."

He has an old soul. I don't know how I know this, but there's something...melancholy about him. It's only when his eyes reach mine, and I'm broken from my open observation of him, that my skin heats from embarrassment. He continues to stare, and again, I'm the first to break eye contact.

"Is everyone clear? Any questions?"

I can feel his eyes on me. "No," I say, in unison with the others, refusing to look back up. I'm ready to get on with my mission. "Annalise, when you're finished, Josette will show you to your room."

This catches my attention, and now I'm staring at him. "Pardon...my *room*?"

Everyone else is busy eating, their cutlery chiming with eagerness against the china plates.

He, of course, makes no move to answer me.

Josette comes to clear my plate, and I'm about to help her, she swats my hand away. "Are you full, dear?" she asks. There is no harshness to her voice, only kindness.

I smile gratefully. "Yes, thank you, that was lovely."

"Come along, then, let me show you where you'll be sleeping."

My chair scrapes over the rough wooden floor as I push it back and follow her out of the kitchen.

"You can freshen up in here, and I laid out some clothes on the bed."

"Clothes?"

"For you to fit in. These are better suited as you'll be staying *here*."

"But I was meant to be staying in town... I'm a newlywed."

She smiles. "Yes, you are to Reuben, and you'll be staying here."

"As in the man who asked you to show me to my room? *He's* Reuben Delacroix—my husband?"

She nods. My stomach drops; my cover is being married to *him*.

I take my time to wash in the basin and assess my reflection in the mirror. I dress in the clothes she provided. They fit almost perfectly. I straighten my blouse as I leave the room and bump into something hard and solid.

Not something—someone.

"Clumsy, aren't we?"

I look up. Reuben.

"No, I just wasn't looking where I was going."

I clench my fist and step aside to pass him, but he steps in the same direction. I anticipate yet another snide comment, but he says nothing. Instead, I glance up and am met with his eyes—probing. Orbs of green are even more vivid and intense this close. He tilts his head, eyebrow raised, and then moves to the side for me to pass. But the hallway is too narrow for both of us, so I suck in a deep breath to avoid my body brushing up against his.

I don't look back.

"Much better," Josette says, smiling when I enter the kitchen.

"Thank you."

I go to the basement of the barn and get to work on the radio which is hidden in a small suitcase.

I'm left alone, until mid-afternoon and Reuben comes down. I have no more transmissions, so I pack everything away. "I don't understand…why I wasn't told I'd be staying here? And you didn't feel the need to introduce yourself?"

He gives me a non-committal shrug. "You know now."

"I could have quite easily been a *single* female in town." I don't know why his presence is infuriating me so much.

"No. You are better suited here, with me."

I shake my head. "I don't understand. My French is impeccable. How am I better suited *here* rather than anywhere else?"

"It's nothing to do with your French. If you were to stay in town, you'd draw too much attention."

"Excuse me? How so?" I come to a stop directly in front of him and tilt my head back.

"You're too beautiful. It's a covert operation, and radio operators aren't lasting long. We need this to work."

"It's because I'm a woman," I reply.

He shakes his head and lowers his face to mine. "If I had my way, you wouldn't be here at all."

I cannot believe the audacity of this man. "Oh, I see. Well, it's about time men like *you* get used to women like *me*," I say, gritting my teeth and turn to walk away. His steady hand grips my elbow, pulling me to a stop.

"Men like *me*?" he asks, his voice quiet but harsh as he scans my face.

"Yes—the ones who believe there's only *one* place for a woman."

His expression is perplexed, his eyebrows drawing together. His eyes darken, and I shrink into myself. "You have no idea what kind of man I am." He storms past me and out of the basement.

I am the one who should be annoyed with him.

I head out the basement doors to outside and take a deep breath. Having time to take in my surroundings is a luxury. Lavender—as far as the eye can see. Never have I witnessed a violet this vibrant. Closing my eyes, I tilt my head towards the heat of the sun and allow its warmth to thaw my anger.

"He's a good man," Josette says, as she comes towards me with a basket on her arm.

"Who?" I ask.

"Reuben. Don't judge him too harshly until you get to know him," she says, coming to stand beside me.

"I'm trying, but so far, my first impression of him is he's an infuriating excuse of a man."

She lets out a deep-bellied chuckle. "Come, help me fetch some eggs."

We make our way to the chicken coup, and I watch as she begins to collect some eggs.

"I'm sorry. I don't mean to sound like a child. It's just I'm here for a reason. I have a job to do. Part of that shouldn't involve me hurting his ego."

"Yes, you have a job to do. But this is his life, too. This is our home. No one thought there would be another war to fight, not after the last one, and yet, here we are. And all of this—" she waves her hand, "—is history repeating itself. Life can be a tornado of vicious circles, the wind never relenting."

"I'm sorry, I didn't mean to sound so formal. I'm here because I want to make a difference."

"And I'm sure you will. Reuben is passionate about the cause, too. He may not know how to articulate himself at times, but his heart is in the right place."

She dusts off an egg and drops it into the basket. I reach in and do the same.

Satisfied we have more than enough, she pats my hand before slipping her arm through mine. We head back to the house and into the kitchen. A sweet pastry fragrance floats over me as I walk into the kitchen, and my senses salivate.

"What are you baking?" I ask, licking my lips.

"Apple pie," she replies.

My stomach grumbles, hoping we'll get to have some. A grunt from behind me alerts me to another presence. In the corner is a large dog, sitting on its hind legs, alert and assessing me.

I turn, holding my hand out as I approach. "And who is this?" I ask, my voice jumping up an octave.

"That's Vella," says Reuben from behind. "Careful, she's not very *people friendly*."

I should withdraw my hand if that's the case, but I'm committed, and I want to introduce myself. "Hey, Vella, I'm Ana," I say.

She ducks her head and reaches out with her nose giving my hand a quick sniff before nudging it. I bring it round to the side of her head and give her a quick rub behind the ear before pulling my hand back.

"Well, I'll be…" says Josette, laughing as she retrieves the pie from the oven.

Reuben, however, continues to stare when I turn back towards him. What is it with this man openly appraising me like this?

"She seems just fine with me," I say, and move to help Josette.

He grumbles something under his breath I can't quite make out, and then he leaves just as quickly as he arrived.

CHAPTER 18

Something wet and soft skims across my face, and I startle. I open my eyes to find a damp nose inches from me, and then a tongue darts out and licks my mouth.

"Ewe." I wipe away the slobber and sit upright. Vella is sitting beside my bed.

"Charming," I say, very aware I am talking to a dog. Her tail wags with a thump against the floor, and I slowly reach out my hand and rub her just behind her ear. She appears to enjoy this and rests her head on top of the mattress, her eyes drifting closed.

A noise from somewhere in the house causes her to spring to all fours, and she eases herself back out of my room through the slightly ajar door. I don't know what time it is, but I decide since I'm awake to get washed up and dressed.

I find Josette in the kitchen.

"Morning," I say.

She points to the coffee, and I make myself a cup. I take a sip, the bitterness hot on my tongue.

"There's sugar in the pantry. Breakfast will be ready in a while," she says.

"Thank you. Can I help?" I reply, searching the shelving for the sugar jar. I drop a cube into the mug with a satisfying plop.

"No, thank you, dear. You enjoy your coffee."

I nod gratefully and look out of the window; the sun is just coming up. I slip into a large pair of wellies and step out through the back door.

I hug my mug and look over the fields. The dew-covered grass glistens as the light from the morning sky comes to life.

"It's gorgeous," I whisper.

"Yes, it is."

My coffee spills over the rim of my mug, the hot liquid sloshing over my hand.

"Ouch," I say, shaking off the excess coffee.

Reuben quickly takes it from me and hands me a handkerchief. "Sorry," he says.

"It's fine," I reply and turn towards him. His eyes roam over my body, and I want to shrink into myself. When his eyes meet mine, he doesn't even seem bothered I caught him. I sigh and hold out my hand for him to pass me my coffee.

"We have to go into town later this morning," he says, walking towards the barn without a backwards glance.

I can't take my eyes off him until he disappears inside.

∼

The sky is cloudless today, reminding me of the last time I saw Lawry and Evie. My stomach is tied in knots.

"Are you ready?"

I startle but quickly recover. "Yes."

We climb into the truck, and Reuben is quiet for the most part. I consider striking up a conversation, but honestly, what's the point of even trying? And I am meant to be this man's wife...

"Reach under your seat. There's a small parcel. Put it in your purse."

I rummage underneath me and then pull out a small parcel no bigger than a compact mirror and slip it in the hidden section of my purse.

"What is it?" I ask.

His eyes flick to mine, then back to the road. "You don't need to know. If you're caught, you can't be incriminated."

I let out a huff. "If I am with you, and I'm caught, are we not already incriminated?"

Without warning, he pulls over and comes to a stop on the side of the dirt road.

"Listen, if you're caught and interrogated you can't give them any information if you have none to give."

My throat is dry as I swallow. "I understand, but if we can't work as a team, how on earth do you expect us to pretend to be husband and wife?"

He rubs his face, his shoulders tense and his expression stern. "We will. You have to follow my instructions. We will go to the café for coffee. I'll grab a copy of The Observer. When I open it, you will excuse yourself to use the restroom. Go to the restroom, look for the tile with the emblem of a bird. It's the only one which is loose but only if you know to look for it. You need to swap over the parcels and place it back exactly as you found it. We finish our coffee, and I'll make the remaining of my deliveries. Then we come home."

I make a mental note and my body hums with energy at the thought of my first mission.

"Do you understand?" he asks, no softness to his voice.

"Yes, of course, I understand." Does he need to be so damn obnoxious?

"It's important you do. If there is anything odd or the package looks tampered with, leave it and do *not* swap it for the one you're carrying."

"Of course."

"Good, and whatever you do, don't speak English."

"I won't... I haven't since arriving."

"No, but there is a first time for everything. I don't want it to be in a café occupied by German soldiers." He leans over and taps the glove box. "There's a ring in there, put it on."

I open it but hesitate before reaching out. "It's not stolen if that's what you're worried about."

Why would he assume I'd think that? "I'm worried about the German soldiers...what if they know we aren't together?"

"How will they possibly know?"

"Those who know you...won't they be surprised at you walking in with a wife?"

He shakes his head and grabs the ring as he continues, slipping it onto my finger. His hands are rough but gentle. "No, your fake identification shows you as being my wife. The café isn't somewhere I frequent, and ones who do know me, won't ask questions." I nod and fiddle with the ring while I examine it.

"Something wrong?" he asks.

Did he roll his eyes? "No, it's just a lovely ring. Fits surprisingly well." I hold out my hand and wiggle my fingers as I appraise it.

"You have small fingers like my late wife."

I look up from my hand, wondering if I mistook his words, but judging from the grip he has on the steering wheel when he pulls back onto the road, he's not lying. "I'm sorry."

It hardly seems enough, but I don't know him well enough to offer anything else. I wonder how she died; she can't have been much older than I am. I only ever associated death with the elderly or the infirm before Samuel died, but I understand better now—death doesn't discriminate.

CHAPTER 19

When we arrive in town, we make our way to Au Petit Bistro. The cobbled stone street and shuttered windows are nothing like my father described. What's evident is how much being under German occupation has been harsh on the people. Josette told me the Germans had stripped France for workers—whether voluntary or labelled as prisoners of war.

Then there's the food supply and demand for hefty cash payments. More than half the small businesses here have already diminished. I can see the majority of the storefronts empty, desolate. I know enough but always wondered how much was propaganda. Seeing it like this is heart breaking.

As people queue down the street, waiting for bread, my steps falter, and I have to take a deep breath to steady myself. Reuben's hand moves to the small of my back. He leans down and kisses my temple.

"Are you all right?" he whispers, his voice the softest I've ever heard it. I find it comforting. I smile and nod. His hand remains firm against my back. He buys the paper from a vendor before he opens the door for me to enter ahead of him.

His touch is firm, and heat radiates through me as we walk to the far corner to an empty table. I'm nervous at this moment, but for all the wrong reasons. He pulls out my chair and motions for me to sit. My cheeks heat from the simple gesture. This may be our cover, but it's the first time since losing Lawry and joining the war effort that I've felt at ease.

He orders for us and reaches for my hand. Bringing it up to his lips, he kisses my palm and continues to hold it in his. I glance around. Sure enough, there are soldiers amongst the patrons. One even nods at me. I smile politely in acknowledgement and then focus my attention back to Reuben. His fingers are tracing my hand and the wedding ring. When our coffee is set on the table, he smiles. His face transforms, his features become something of wonder. And I can't help but notice how very handsome he is, how much younger he looks.

My heart begins to beat a little faster when he brings my palm to his mouth again and kisses it before releasing my hand and opening up the paper.

I stand, excusing myself, and he points towards the restroom. Following his instructions, I go to the restroom and study the floor, looking for the tile while I pull out a pin from my hair. My fingers shake as I carefully pull the tile loose and swap the packages. I flush the toilet and check that the tiles look untouched before I wash my hands and leave.

Reuben smiles when I sit back down, and I can't help but return it. His green orbs are bright against his tanned skin, almost mesmerising. I ignore the pull in my lower stomach and finish my coffee. It's bitter and I suppress the urge to cringe. I long for tea.

∽

Back in the truck, we drive without speaking. My heart rate begins to calm. I think it went well... I look over to Reuben who is back to being his stern self. "What do we do now?" It's the only thing I could think to ask in the heavy silence.

"We go back to the farm."

"Yes, obviously, but what about the parcel I collected?"

His eyes dart to mine. "I'll take it, and that's all you need to know."

I cross my arms. "Right, correct me if I'm wrong, but I'm sensing some hostility from you. For the life of me I can't imagine why…?"

Abruptly, he veers off of the side of the road, and the bumpy surface causes me to rock in my seat as he comes to a stop.

He turns, giving me his full attention, his expression stern and a complete contrast to the man who smiled at me not so long ago and escorted me around town. "Listen, we all have a part to play in this godforsaken war. But you ask too many questions. The less you know, the better. Besides, you'll be too much of a liability. Ana, which part of this is hard for you to understand?"

I clench my fist tight. "I understand perfectly, but we are a team, no? But I get it. You think women should be at home—pregnant and looking after the house."

He blinks a few times as if in disbelief. My words must strike a nerve; his jaw ticks. I don't look away as I wait for his retort, but it never comes. Instead, without another word, he pulls back onto the road.

I turn to look out the window, biting the inside of my cheek. Never in my life have I met someone as insufferable as this man.

I remind myself silently why I'm here. *To do a job, to make a difference.* Knowing the atrocities that are going on in the world, I didn't want to sit idly by. This was never about making friends.

Without a word, he parks in front of the barn, and I follow him down to the basement. I remove the parcel from my bag and pass it to him, then proceed to slip off the wedding ring and hand it back to him.

He shakes his head. "No, it's your cover. Keep it on."

I nod, turning away as I slide it back into place. I think I hear him grunt, but I'm not sure. All I know is, I've had about as much as I can stand from him today.

I turn and head back to the main house. It's moments such as those I would likely confide in Evie, but mostly, I'd write in my journal if I were allowed one.

CHAPTER 20

Josette sets the table for dinner. The air around me is crisp, adding to the evening's chill. It's mostly coming off of Reuben.

"Am I missing something?" Josette asks, eying the two of us sceptically.

I wait to see if Reuben will say something, but he doesn't.

"I think maybe Reuben, here, has an issue with a woman who isn't married, pregnant, and at home being the perfect *wife*." The words leave my lips before I can stop them; it's rude. I am, after all, in *his* home, and I wasn't raised to speak with such candour. Maybe I left my manners back in England…with my sanity.

She looks slightly afflicted by this and shakes her head. Her mouth opens, but it's not her voice echoing in the room, it's Reuben's as he holds up his hand to stop her. "Let her think what she wants."

His chair scrapes against the floor as he pushes it back to stand before walking out of the back door.

"Dear, you have no idea." She stares at me with disappointment.

I shrink into myself, feeling like a scolded child, humiliated by my outburst. I drop my spoon into my bowl, no longer feeling hungry. "Sorry, you're right, I *don't*. I've seen tiny glimpses of a man I actually wouldn't mind getting to know, and then in the next moment, he is the complete opposite."

"He hasn't had it easy…" She looks at my hand. I self-consciously touch the ring on my finger, its presence both foreign and yet familiar. "When my Celine died, part of him died, too."

A pressure builds behind my eyes and my chest tightens as it hits me. "She was your daughter?"

"Yes. This was my husband's farm." She waves her hand around softly. "Reuben was a farmhand while at school, and then later, when my late husband, Albert, passed, he was the one who helped maintain it. Celine always liked him, but it took him a little longer to catch up…even though he was a few years her senior. They married six months after I lost Albert. She died less than a year later—a weak heart, the doctors said."

"I'm so truly sorry. I don't know what to say."

She takes my hand in hers. "There is nothing to say. He is a good man. But he has seen and suffered too much loss. He deals with it the only way he knows how. I don't know if he took the time to mourn her passing—the war took that away from him—and then you and so many other brave souls began falling from the sky."

It's silent as I take in her words and stand. "Sorry, excuse me. I need some air. I'm going to take a walk."

She pats my hand before letting go. "Try not to stray too far."

The birds are high in the trees, twittering as I make my way through the woods. I walk for some time, my jumbled thoughts keeping my mind occupied. How can one man infuriate me so much? Slowly, the pinks and reds leaking through the treeline overhead diminish. It's only when the last of the light begins to fade, and darkness rolls in like a rain cloud that the realisation I've lost my bearings hits me. I want to shake myself.

I turn around—an attempt to retrace my steps—but the truth is, the woods surrounding me are closing in the darker it becomes. I don't know how long I've been wandering when I hear the faint sound of a dog barking. I'm about to call out but think better of it, and slink back into the trunk of a nearby tree. I concentrate on listening to the noises around me, but one of them is the overbearing sound of my own heartbeat. Then I hear it—a rustling coming from nearby bushes.

A throbbing begins deep in my chest and ears. I hear the shuffling of feet and a louder bark when a dog rounds the tree trunk, my breaths frozen in place.

I don't move.

It's too dark to make out the dog. It barks, alerting whoever is with it.

I think back to my training of hand-to-hand combat and get my stance ready. There is no sign of aggression from the dog, but that might change.

I see movement out of my peripheral vision but don't have any time to react as a hand covers my mouth.

I'm frozen, contemplating what I should do next.

"It's just me, but you need to be quiet."

Slowly, he removes his hand. I'm about to reply, but his hand returns. His body is flush against mine, pushing me further into the tree. I'm alarmed to feel both frightened and exhilarated. I search his face. He lets out a huge breath. His eyes are dark in this light, and they're locked on me.

I hear a roar of engines, and the thought doesn't escape me that I'm possibly somewhere I shouldn't be. He raises his eyebrows, a silent question, and I nod in understanding. His hand slips from my face.

With his other hand firmly holding me in place, I dare not attempt to move.

We wait and listen. He moves his head so close to mine. I think for a split second that he's going to kiss me, but he whispers in my ear, instead. "It's not safe out here alone in the woods."

I feel stupid for thinking he was going to kiss me, but even more so for the way he just spoke to me like a petulant child.

"Sorry, I lost my bearings."

He pulls back to look at me. I swallow hard. His stare is intense as he reaches his other hand towards my face. I don't move. His fingers gently trail over my cheek. I close my eyes, trying to control my breathing. I should slap his hand away, but it's been so long since I've been touched, I don't want to.

His lips graze mine. My eyes spring open, and I let out an audible gasp, but he's already pulled back.

I'm entirely thrown…it wasn't like it was an *actual* kiss. Right?

He pinches the bridge of his nose, eyes closed. When he opens them, a pained expression crosses his face. I almost feel sorry for him. I shove just enough for him to take a step back.

"Come, let's go."

That's all he has to say? It's more of a command than a request, but I don't retort with a reply. I follow him instead because there's no way I could find my way alone.

Back at the house, I go to the bathroom to wash up before heading to my room. It's dark when I open the door, and I pause in the doorway.

A silhouette stands at the window. He spins around slowly, then stalks towards me, stopping just inches away.

He runs a hand over his face. "Listen, I owe you an apology for my behaviour earlier. I was worried when you didn't come back, and then when I found you… I think I was feeling nostalgic after the talk of my wife. I don't know."

I don't want to see that regret written all over his face. "Listen, nothing happened. If it's all the same to you, I'd like just to start again," I say.

A sigh escapes his lips. "I'd like that." He holds his hand towards me. I look up to his face then back down before reaching out. He shakes my hand with a slow smile before dropping my hand. He walks out and just before closing the door, turns back. "Just try not to wander off again."

CHAPTER 21

"This is Estelle," Reuben says proudly. She's the biggest horse I've ever seen. She may even be a little on the fat side, too. "She's pregnant," he says, in response to my staring at her stomach. His lip twitches. "Don't worry, she still has a few months to go yet."

"Sorry. I know nothing about horses. I'm pretty ignorant when it comes to any animals other than dogs." I mimic what he was doing a few moments ago and stroke her mane.

"The Germans took our other three. We were fortunate to be able to keep her."

She is a rich chocolate brown with yellow and silver dapples, and her lower legs are feathered white. Turning her head to me, she nibbles at my sleeve, her lips wobbling, and I *think* Reuben laughs under his breath, but it's brief and unexpected.

"She's hungry. Here." He breaks an apple in half and passes it to me. "Give her this. Hold it out flat on your palm, like this." He holds out his hand and offers her the other half of the apple. She gobbles it up with her enormous teeth.

I want to take a step back, a little intimated by her if I'm honest, but instead, I stand firm, and when her attention is back on me, I do what Reuben did. Her lips tickle as she takes it from me. I laugh. wiping my palm down the leg of my trousers.

"You'll get used to her," he says, tilting his head towards the basement. "Let's get situated you'll be meeting everyone soon."

It's not long before they start to arrive, but I'm still working the radio, so it's only when they're all here that Reuben starts with the introductions.

"This is André, Pierré, René, Isabelle and Sylvette," Reuben says, pointing to each individual. The women smile. The men nod except for René who comes over and kisses the back of my hand.

"It's good to have you here," says Sylvette. She's tall and slender with luxurious auburn hair and the bluest eyes I've ever seen. Isabelle scans the length of my body, and her expression tells me she's not too impressed. René is still holding my hand.

I pull it away and sit in front of the radio.

André bites into his shiny apple with a crunch and begins talking around the chunk. "Anything?" he asks, the juice from the apple dribbling down his chin. He quickly wipes it away with the back of his hand, his cheeks glowing red.

I shake my head. There's been nothing since this morning.

"So, are you married?" asks Pierré.

I don't know why, but the way he looks me over causes my skin to crawl. I'm about to answer when Reuben steps in. "She is," he replies. I'm about to rebuke his answer, but I refrain when he softly squeezes my shoulder.

"Shame," replies Pierré as he tampers with some wire. He's preparing detonators over on the table opposite side of the barn.

"The last radio operator we had in town didn't last too long," Isabelle says, matter of fact.

I don't know if she's telling me this to see my reaction or because she's trying to make conversation. Either way, it's not something I care to think about. I'm not daft. They were transparent when they briefed me on my assignment—there's less than a fifty percent chance of survival.

"Someone gave her up," says André, with a scowl on his face.

And that's it right there—my fear. Knowing there are still people out there prepared to throw you to the wolves... I try to remain passive and pull the headset over my ears. I wonder how the other agents who I trained with are. If they're safe and fulfilling their missions. I think of sweet, unassuming Milly. Maybe I'll never know, but it doesn't stop me from thinking of them.

∼

Between radio transmissions, I've been keeping busy by working around the farm—something I never imagined finding solace in. But I do.

Reuben and I have fallen into an amicable relationship, and I find myself enjoying our occasional talks and even the silences when we are together. He doesn't fill those gaps with barren words. I'm grateful.

I've come to realize what a good man Reuben is—the way he slips a basket or two to Josette to pass out to neighbours and friends. After he gives what he has to the Germans, there isn't much left for us, but that doesn't stop him doing what he can for others.

"Here," he says, passing me a chocolate bar.

"What's this for?" I ask, unable to hide my smile. It's been so long since I had chocolate.

"You deserve a treat," he replies before walking away. I slip it into the front of my apron.

After I finish my chores in the barn, I wash up and return to the basement. There's news of a convoy on route, and we need to disrupt it from arriving at its final destination.

CHAPTER 22

René left the latest copy of *The Observer* today. I read the one page that's in French; my German is sketchy, and I'm only able to translate basic words. But this one page is full of anti-British, pro-French and antisemitic propaganda. It's the way the Germans are twisting this to appear as though they and the French are complimentary of one another. An appalling anti-British cartoon is included, too. I don't need to know German to figure that one out. I look for anything I can relay in my transmissions—even the smallest detail I think may be of help.

The weather is beginning to turn, and the nights are drawing in earlier. There's a tap on my door, and I rush over to open it, the wood cold beneath my feet.

"Hi," I say, surprised to see Reuben standing there. "Everything okay?"

"Yes. I thought you might want these." He passes me a ball of wool.

"Thank you," I reply, and unfold it to find a pair of thick socks. I rush to the chair and slip them on.

He moves inside the room and looks around. He meanders to the book I left on the nightstand and picks it up.

"Sorry, I hope you don't mind... It was on the shelf."

"It was only collecting dust. My wife loved to read," he replies, thumbing through the pages, careful not to lose my place.

"Me too," I reply. "How about you? Do you read?"

He nods. "A little." He places the book back where he found it.

"How did she die?" I ask and regret my question. "Sorry, none of my business."

He shakes his head. "Would you like a drink?" he asks, and I'm taken aback by his question, so I nod.

I follow him into the kitchen, the heat from the agar welcoming. He goes to the cupboard and finds a bottle of claret. He pops the cork and pours us both a glass. We sit at the table—him at the head, me just to his right.

He clinks his glass with mine, and we both take a sip.

"I didn't mean to pry..." I say.

"It's fine, I don't mind." He says nothing more for a moment, and I think that's the end of that, but then he begins to speak, his eyes growing a darker shade of evergreen. "We were friends before we were lovers."

My cheeks begin to warm, and I take another sip of my wine, hoping it's not light enough in here for him to notice.

"She was younger than me—about your age. We were married less than a year when she passed. A weak heart, the doctors said. She hadn't been sick or anything...just collapsed one day out in the field. It happened so quickly."

I cover his hand with mine when I see the pain etched on his face. "I'm so sorry," I say, even though it doesn't seem enough.

"It's okay. I still have Josette, but I know she wished we would have given her grandchildren."

"My best friend just had a baby before I was assigned here," I say—no idea why I just divulged that with him.

"Boy or girl?" he asks like he's interested.

"Boy. She named him Samuel Junior, after his father."

"Strong name," he replies.

"He was."

He puts his glass down and turns his hand over with mine, his fingers caressing my palm.

"He died?" His eyes probe.

"Yes, before he was born. She's married to his best friend now."

His touch is both unexpected, yet familiar. "You don't approve?" he questions.

I free my hand from his. "It's complicated."

He pours himself some more wine, then holds the bottle over my glass. I nod, and he fills mine, too. Silence falls between us, but unlike other times, it's weighted. I know I owe it to him to elaborate. "Lawrence and I were courting before Samuel died. He offered to marry Evie out of loyalty to our friend. To take care of her and the baby."

His eyes are all over my face now as he takes in my words. "The man who married her was your lover?"

No amount of dim light can hide my blush now, and I cough to cover up my slight unease with his assessment of the response. "We were courting, yes." I take a large gulp of the wine, grateful for the warmth as it helps to ease my embarrassment.

His hand covers mine. "He sounds like a fool to me." I go to pull my hand away, but he holds it firm and leans closer, his breath tickling my skin. "A fool for letting you go."

I close my eyes, refusing to let the tears come. I feel pressure on my lips, and my eyes open to Reuben searching my face. My lips part, and he leans in, planting a soft, chaste kiss.

"You deserved better," he whispers against my lips before he pulls back.

"There was no other choice," I whisper back.

He shakes his head, and a sad smile adorns his face. "There's always a choice," he replies. He leans away from me and collects our glasses.

"Maybe," I reply, getting to my feet.

His back is to me when he speaks next. "Good night, Ana."

"Good night, Reuben."

Without another word, I turn and head back to my room. I pause when I see a dark shadow in the corner but am relieved to see it's Vella.

"Hey, girl, are you staying with me again tonight?"

She flops to the floor and drops her head over her paws—all the answer I need.

I climb into bed, my feet grateful for the warm cotton covering my toes. Reuben's words echo in my mind as I close my eyes.

There's always a choice.

The saddest part is I agree with him, and deep down, I wish Lawry had chosen me, too.

CHAPTER 23

Today, we made the trip into town, and I exchanged parcels exactly as before. Only this time, I am to pass it over to someone else.

"Okay, so you need to collect the sheets. In exchange, you need to hand over the envelope," says Reuben.

I nod and make my way into the laundrette. It's warm in here, and I unbutton my coat as I look around. It appears empty except for me and a large woman behind the counter.

"Good morning," she says with a smile.

"Morning," I reply.

"I've been expecting you. Your sheets are ready."

The woman behind the counter produces a large bundle and hands it over. I pay her and slip her the envelope.

"Thank you."

"Au Revoir."

Once back in the truck, Reuben drives away.

"What was all that about?" I ask

"Oh, the envelope? It was a powder," he replies. "Itching powder."

I watch him, waiting for him to go on. "For the soldiers'

uniforms." And then he does something which shocks me—he laughs. The sound is rich and velvety like his accent, and I can't hold back a small laugh of my own. He appears younger, less weighted with the responsibilities of war, and it's a reprieve to see him this way.

"Isn't that a little risky?" I ask.

He shakes his head. "No more than anything else during these times. Besides, they will use it sparingly and sporadically."

I've read the reports and heard the rumours of the repercussions of being involved in anything like this. The thought makes me sick to my stomach; you put everyone at risk—yourself, your family, your friends.

Reuben eases off the accelerator, and I follow his line of sight to an additional checkpoint.

"Do you have your ID card?" he asks

"Of course."

Once we reach the soldiers, they signal for us to stop. One with a rifle in hand comes to the window to peer inside before ordering us out of the vehicle.

There is an Alsatian barking aggressively to my left, causing me to flinch. The soldier holding the leash begins to walk around the truck while another lifts the canopy and checks our contents.

Reuben and I are told to stand on the side of the road. My heart kicks up a beat, and my hands begin to tremble. The dog's barking is relentless, unsettling.

"Papers?" demands the soldier who told us to get out of the truck.

He studies them and us before he searches us. His hands go to my shoulders and down my arms. Reuben fidgets beside me, and I catch his eyes with mine. I shake my head just enough for him to notice.

The soldier's hands skim over my body. As he slides them up between my thighs, I want to gag or better still swat his roaming hands away, but I don't. I hold my breath. Seconds feel like minutes. He releases me with a smirk but doesn't check Reuben, whose fists are clenched so tight, his knuckles turn white.

There's a crack of thunder followed by a bright flash of lightening, as if the weather is picking up on Reubens mood. An involuntary shiver rolls over my body. We are allowed on our way and climb back into the truck.

We've only been on the road minutes before hailstones begin crashing down and Reuben has to pull over as there is no visibility. We sit in silence, the windows fogging up.

"I should have stopped him," he says through his teeth.

I cross my arms. The thought of that man's hands over my body makes me nauseous. "It's fine," I reply, but it's not, and there's nothing we can do about it. The hailstones stop as quickly as they began, and he pulls back onto the road.

"I'm sorry," he says, without looking at me.

I look out of my window and say nothing.

We pull up in front of the barn. Rain is coming down fast and heavy. He climbs out of the truck, and just as I'm reaching for the door, he pulls it open and ushers me out.

He covers our heads with his coat, and we run into the barn. He shakes it out, hangs it over a hook. I wipe my hands down my thighs and Reuben steps in front of me. He tilts my chin up towards him. "Are you all right?" he asks.

I nod.

He steps so close, I can feel the heat from his body. "I should have stopped him," he says again.

I touch his bicep—it's firm and stable from years spent on the farm. I squeeze it. "It's done now," I say, remembering how a stranger's hands lingered on my body. Even though it was only seconds, it makes me itchy.

His hands cup my face, and he rests his forehead against mine. I inhale, licking my lips.

My body sways into his.

And then he kisses me.

It's not chaste this time. It's full of something I've never felt before—need.

I move my hands to his shoulders and grip the back of his neck. I'm lost in a moment I didn't see coming...but it's one I've been longing for.

My stomach clenches with desire, but I pull back, breathing fast, not ready for where this might go. He nods like he understands and kisses my forehead.

Instead of stepping away, he pulls me into his chest and holds me in his arms. I'm more shocked by this than the kiss, and it's something I didn't realise I needed. The last time I was held was by Lawry, but not even *he* made me feel this way.

That thought scares me.

CHAPTER 24

Isabelle has been unusually quiet. She's not the loudest of people, I've noticed, and even though I've only known her a month, I can tell something isn't right.

"Hey," I say.

She turns her face towards me and smiles, but it's forced. She looks back over the field.

"You feeling okay?" I ask.

"I'm fine," she replies.

I tap her on the arm. "It's all right if you're not. I'm here if you want to talk. Us girls have to stick together."

The corners of her mouth raise ever so slightly. "I was just thinking about my mama," she says. "I miss her…especially today."

"What's today?"

"My birthday," she replies.

I surprise her when I pull her in for a hug. "Happy Birthday." She lets out a giggle. When I pull back, she has a small smile. "Come on, let's go make sure the men aren't causing trouble." I link my arm with hers and head back to see what awaits us today.

I manage to slip away back to the house while everyone is busy going over a failed sabotage attack in Paris.

"Josette?"

"Off my floor," she says on her hands and knees, scrubbing.

"Sorry." I step back into the doorway. "I need your help."

She turns her face up towards me, wiping the hair from her temple with the back of her hand.

"It's Isabelle's birthday. I think we should celebrate."

Josette gets this look in her eye—one only a mother can muster—and slowly pushes herself to her feet. "It just so happens I've been saving some stuff. I could whip her up a cake."

I go to step forward, but her eyes shoot to the floor. "That would be perfect. I'll try and let the others know—"

"Know what?"

He is so close, I startle and spin on him, slapping his solid chest. "Reuben, don't do that!"

Josette chuckles to herself. "Away with you both! My floors do not want you here."

I push past him, a little flustered.

"Well?"

Darting my eyes around, I make sure no one else can hear as I step close to him. "It's Isabelle's birthday, did you know?"

He shakes his head.

"Josette is going to bake a cake. I thought we could have a small celebration."

He licks his lips. I notice how full they are and immediately avert my eyes, heat seeping through my blouse.

"Why not?" he replies. "What can I do?"

"Maybe let the others know…but have them keep it a secret. I wish I could give her a gift."

Tapping his chin, he thinks for a moment. "I might have something that could work."

"Oh, no, I didn't mean to imply—"

He holds up his hand. "I never said you did. Come with me."

I follow him to the side of the house and into the back living room. It's cosy with a stone fireplace and two comfy looking chairs. He heads over to a small wooden bureau and opens the bottom drawer. I notice how well defined he is as he bends down and have to reprimand myself—*what is wrong with me?*

"Here it is." He stands and brings over something wrapped in a muslin cloth. He unfolds the material to reveal a hand mirror with wildflowers painted on the back.

"This is beautiful," I say in awe and take it from him, looking it over, the wooden handle so expertly carved.

"Will this make for a good present?"

I try to hand it back. "Yes, but it's too much."

"No, please. I made it for Celine's birthday, and it was only sitting in the drawer."

I shake my head. "It is beautiful, Reuben. You're very talented."

He coughs. "I'll go and carve her initial onto the handle," he says.

Momentarily speechless, I stare at him. He brings his finger to my chin and closes my gaping mouth. Heat fills my cheeks, and I stumble over what to say. "I have an extra scarf I brought with me. Maybe we could wrap it in that."

He nods, but neither of us make a move. The room grows smaller and becomes almost stifling.

"Right, okay then," I say. I make a move at the same time he does. It reminds me of the first morning in the hallway. A smooth laugh breaks free from him. The sound is mesmerising. "Wow."

"What?" he asks, tilting his head to the side.

"You don't seem as mean when you're laughing." With that, I turn to leave.

"I wasn't always this way," he says to my back.

"It's a shame," I say, leaving him behind me. "I'd like to get to know the man behind that smile."

Rummaging through my drawer, I find the silk scarf and know straight away Isabelle will love it.

I head outside, stopping at the rose bushes. Picking the yellow and white ones, I reach for one more just at the back, and as I snap the stem, something sharp digs into my thumb. "Ouch." I pull my hand back and drop the rose to the ground.

I squeeze my thumb, something sharp digs into my flesh.

"You okay?" Reuben kneels beside me, grabbing my hand.

"A thorn," I say hissing through my teeth. "I think it's still in there."

He examines it, and then before I can stop him, he quickly pulls out the thorn. Blood trickles over my skin. He lowers his face and licks his lips right before his wet tongue applies some pressure as he sucks the pad of my thumb into his mouth.

His eyes dart to mine through thick lashes, and an audible gasp escapes me. Teeth graze over the sensitive area as he releases it. My body becomes tingly all over, and a deep warmth builds in my lower stomach.

Entranced by him, I can't move. He leans closer. I'm heady from his proximity and the sensations he's just evoked in me.

"I think you'll live," he says with a crooked smile. He hands me the rose I dropped to the ground, and I add it to the bunch in the basket.

"Thank you," I breathe out.

Getting to his feet, he holds out his hand for me. I take it. My legs, however, do not feel like my own, and I have to remind myself to keep my balance.

He turns to walk away and I call out, "Reuben, wait!"

I force myself to catch up with him. "Here, for the mirror," I say, holding out the scarf. He nods, and it slides smoothly from my hand as he takes it from me. When he walks away this time,

I'm breathless and utterly confused. I am entirely affected by him, and I think he knows it.

CHAPTER 25

"Surprise!" we all yell as Isabelle comes into the kitchen. She covers her chest with her hand, as her eyes flicker between us all. "What's going on?" she asks.

I go over and wrap my arm over her shoulder. "We're celebrating your birthday," I say, guiding her to the table where a cake sits beside the flowers and her gift.

"Come sit," says Josette, ushering her into the chair.

"I don't know what to say."

"You don't have to say anything, my dear."

Josette lights the candles, and we all stand around singing her happy birthday.

"Make a wish," says Reuben, and my heart turns to liquid.

She smiles and blows out the candle, squeezing her eyes closed. She looks so young when she opens them, unshed tears pooling around her lids before breaking free.

"Don't, dear," says Josette trying to hide her tears.

"Here," I say and push the gift towards her.

With a delicate touch, she unwraps the mirror and gasps. Her reaction is as priceless as mine. Her finger traces her initials, and she sniffs loudly. "It's beautiful," she hiccups.

I catch Reuben's eye and mouth, "Thank you." I'm rewarded with a smile.

André adds a record to the gramophone. The atmosphere light, Isabelle wraps the scarf around her shoulders, and Sylvette begins cutting the cake and passing it out.

René opens a bottle of claret, and we all raise our glasses in a toast. André bows and offers his hand for Isabelle to dance; she laughs and gladly takes it. Sylvette forces Pierré to his feet, and although he acts like it's a chore, you can tell he's enjoying it.

I'm swaying on the spot to the music when I hear Reuben's voice. "What the heck…" He pulls me into his arms. I stumble and tread on his foot. "Sorry," I say. "I'm just nervous." I want to berate myself. Why did I say that? It's the wine, it makes my lips loose.

"You're fine," he says, showing his perfect white teeth as he smiles.

My entire body heats like I've been laying in the summer sun. My palms become slick, and I worry Reuben will notice, but he says nothing as he holds me against him. He dances like he does everything—without fear or consequences. I can feel him everywhere.

I try to step back, but he holds firm. "What? You don't like my dancing?" he questions playfully, a glint in his eye.

"I do, but I think you should ask Josette," I whisper.

His eyes soften, and he lets out a heavy sigh. He's about to let go when André beats him to it, taking Josette in his arms. We must dance at least five songs before we part.

"Sing, come on Sylvette," asks André loud enough for us all to hear.

She shakes her head. "No."

"Come on, Reuben will sing with you," says Josette.

No one seems to have the heart to say no with that, and begrudgingly, Reuben goes over to Sylvette. "You can play then," Reuben says to André, pointing to the piano.

I always wanted to learn to play.

When Sylvette begins to sing, the room falls silent, everyone enamoured by her voice. The melody, the notes—she hits each one so perfectly. She smiles wide and elbows Reuben to join in, and he does. His voice carries a rich baritone. I shake my head.

"Of course," I say, laughing.

"He's good, isn't he?" says Josette.

"Why am I not surprised?"

"Sylvette used to sing professionally before the war," says René with a gleam in his eye. "But she stopped when her husband died after the war broke out."

We break into a round of applause, and Reuben and Sylvette exaggerate a bow each.

Isabelle hugs her mirror to her chest. "Thank you, this has been the best day," she says, sniffing back tears.

I pull her in for a hug. "Happy Birthday, Isabelle."

"Come on, let's get out of here before Josette kicks us out," laughs René. She swats him with a tea towel which he successfully manages to dodge.

After everyone has gone, I catch Josette in the kitchen. "Bed," I say. "Let me do those."

She takes my hand in between hers. "Thank you, dear." She leans up and kisses my cheek.

I'm washing up when Reuben comes back from checking the farm for the night. He picks up a tea towel and begins to wipe at the dishes. "You don't have to do that," I say, looking at him from the corner of my eye.

"What? Do English men not know how to do domestic chores?"

An un-lady like noise escapes my nose. "Something like that. You sing wonderfully."

He shrugs it off.

"I can't carry a tune for love nor money," I say.

Leaning his hip against the sink, he turns to me. "I very much doubt that."

"It's the truth."

"One day, Annalise Delacroix, you'll sing for me."

It's not *what* he says so much as *the way* he says it that causes the plate to slip from my fingers. With quick reflexes, he reaches out and manages to catch it before it hits the floor…but not before I cover my skirt in soap suds.

"Is that so?" I force out. When I take the plate from him, his fingers brush over mine.

"It's a promise." His eyes are smouldering, and I don't know what this is—this pull I feel towards him. As much as I try to tell myself why I'm here, this attraction doesn't fade. Then there's Lawry. I remind myself Lawry is no longer mine, not really.

I turn back to the dishes and concentrate as I scrub them clean. He remains quiet until our task is finished and everything is put away. Disappointment washes over me; I've enjoyed seeing this side of him.

"Goodnight," I say as I go to pass him.

He leans down, pressing his lips against mine. As quickly as they are there, he pulls back with a smile. "Goodnight, Ana," he says and walks to his room, the door closing softly behind him.

I blink and bring my fingertips to my lips.

Sleep evades me for a while, but when it does come, my dreams are of Reuben's lips on mine.

CHAPTER 26

Reuben has been even more irritable than usual, and I don't know why. He grunts whenever he is spoken to or asked a question.

"Is everything okay?" I ask.

"Yes." His reply is curt.

I'm tempted to push, but I don't. Instead, I turn and walk away. I decide to go towards the meadow instead of the woods. I learnt my lesson and don't fancy getting myself lost again, especially not when he's in an insufferable mood.

I pass a beautiful array of wildflowers, the colours so vivid. I decide to pick some and take them back to Josette for the kitchen. When I bring them to my nose, the soft floral scent is warm and fresh. She'll love them.

Vella brushes up against my leg, and I give her ear a rub. She's my shadow, following me most places now. I don't mind, I enjoy the company, and besides, she may not say much, but she's a brilliant listener. She already knows all about Lawry. I wonder if she could talk…would she tell me to get over him? To move on?

I find a soft patch of grass and lay down, staring up at the clouds as they play in the baby blue sky.

"Dragon," I whisper, laughing to myself. I point up until I find another cluster. "Post box."

"Do you always talk to yourself?" a gruff voice says, standing over me.

"Do you always creep up on people?"

Reuben sits down beside me, surprising me when he lays back, too. "Touché."

I eye him as he rests his head, his arms in a makeshift pillow. His biceps fill out his t-shirt, and I can't help but appreciate his physique.

"What do you see?" he asks.

Swallowing hard, I feel my cheeks heat. "What?"

He lets out a soft laugh, the corner of his mouth raising. "In the clouds..."

"Oh," I say and play with a blade of grass between my fingers, watching the clouds until I see something familiar. "A horse," I say and nod my chin towards its direction.

"Looks more like a cow to me."

"Well, it's up for interpretation," I reply.

He turns his head towards me. "Tell me about where you're from."

I bite my lip, thrown by this; only moments ago he was obtuse. "I grew up close to the city of London, but I've always dreamed of living in the country." I watch to see his expression.

He continues to listen intently, his eyes going from me to the sky. "Rabbit," he points out, smiling.

My heart stutters, a deep warmth spreading through me as I remember the way he kissed and held me after our trip into town. But lately, he's become a little frosty, and I didn't know why.

I've been staring at his lips. I don't notice he's no longer searching the clouds; he's searching my face.

He rolls onto his side, facing me and rests his elbow into the grass leaning his chin against his palm. I can't break away from whatever hold he has over me as he watches me, watching him. My arm is between us, and he turns it over, so my palm is facing up. "Close your eyes," he says.

"Pardon?"

"I want you to guess when I reach here," he says, his fingers tapping the inside of my elbow. My body tingles.

He's almost playful when he says it with a glint in his eye. I'm unable to resist. "Hmm, okay," I reply and close my eyes.

At first, I feel nothing and think he isn't touching me. I can hear the sounds of our breathing, of Vella humming a soft snore not far from us, and the birds tweeting up a storm in the tree line. Then I feel it, the faintest tickle and laugh.

"Eyes closed," he says, close to my ear. My belly flutters uncontrollably. "No peeking."

He continues his ascent, and when I think he's reached the crook in my elbow, I say, "stop," and open my eyes. But he is nowhere near my elbow. "What?" I ask.

"Ha, see," he says with a boyish expression. "Do you want to go again?" he asks.

I nod my head, refusing to accept defeat. The pad of his index finger goes back to the palm of my hand. "Ready?"

"Yes," I reply and close my eyes.

I don't understand how someone who works the land and is twice the size of me can have such a cashmere touch. I try to block out everything else. But as he continues, my body comes to life, every nerve alert and wanting.

"Breathe," he whispers.

I let out a gasp and my eyes flutter open to his face inches from mine. He stares at me and bites down on his lower lip, and I pull mine between my teeth. A sound escapes me as I swallow.

"Do you give up?" he asks, his voice smooth over my skin.

"Yes."

His head lowers until his lips are almost touching mine.

"Good."

And then they are probing, and his tongue sweeps my upper lip. I part them, inviting him in for a kiss.

I become heady as the intensity increases, and my entire body hums like a bee to a wildflower. I grip his bicep.

He is the one who pulls away. My eyes scan between us, and I see why, his arousal evident. I blush profusely, and then a giggle escapes me.

"Oh, you think it's funny, do you?"

I both shake my head and nod. His eyes squint, and then he lunges, tickling my sides, causing me to let out a surprised squeal. I reach for his waist and tickle him; he rolls onto his back, and I find myself straddling him, digging my fingers into his sides. It's only when I feel him between my legs where the warm throbbing is that I stop, stunned.

His eyes widen, and then he pulls my face down to his. My body rubs against his, over and over again.

Something builds.

I know I should probably stop, get up and walk away. But I can't find the strength. I need to satisfy this urge.

His hands go to my hips. His tongue is doing something to mimic the movement of our gyrations.

It's too much; I want to burst.

His fingers dig into my skin.

I let out a strangled sound of pleasure when I find my release.

I rest my forehead against his shoulder and say nothing, trying to control my breathing. The thrum continues to pulsate between my thighs. When I muster the courage, I push my hands against his chest and stand to remove myself from him, his arousal even more prominent now.

Reaching for the handful of flowers, I snatch them up, and without saying a word, I whistle for Vella and walk back to the house, leaving a bemused Reuben laying on the ground.

CHAPTER 27

I don't know what just happened. Okay, I know what happened, but I'm shocked I let go like that. Every time I think about it, my entire body breaks out in a blush.

Josette cried when I offered her the flowers and helped redirect my thoughts. "What's wrong?"

She wipes at her face. "It would have been Celine's birthday today."

The revelation hits me like a physical blow. *Celine's birthday.* And there I was, kissing Reuben. A wave of shame coats my skin, and then I hear his weighted steps approach.

I turn to him. "Is that why you've been insufferable today?" My words come out cold, bitter, even to me.

Josette watches the exchange, her tears suddenly forgotten.

He nods, and I see something pass his expression. Wait…was that regret?

I nod and turn back to Josette. "How about you let me make the tea today. Maybe you and Reuben could take those to her grave."

She smiles gratefully.

"Only if you don't mind." She wipes her hands on her apron

and then begins to untie the knot. "If that's all right with you, Reuben?"

"Of course," he says from behind me, clearing his throat.

"I'll go quickly change," she says with an eager spring to her step.

I walk to the sink and hold onto the edge for stability.

"Back there had nothing to do with Celine," he chokes out. "The kiss in the meadow—it was only you and me."

His words are full of honesty and hurt. But I wish I had known; it taints what we just shared somehow. I eye the gold band on my finger and for the first time since I put it on, I have the overwhelming urge to remove it, so I do.

"Don't," he says, hurt in his voice.

I place it on the windowsill, dip my hands into the soap suds, and begin to wash the dishes. The slosh of the water lapping against the basin takes away from my heavy breathing. I don't know why I am suddenly so mad at him.

"You should have told me," I snap in a whisper.

"What? And have you feel sorry for me?" Now he is the one who sounds mad.

"No," I say.

"Sometimes...don't you just want to be? Don't you want to forget about all of the bad and just concentrate on the good?"

I turn my face and see him staring intently at his feet just as Josette enters.

"Ready?" he asks, his face now melancholy.

"Yes," she says and wraps a lilac ribbon over the stems of the flowers before exiting the back door.

I wait for Reuben to leave, but instead, he walks over to me. "I would never compare the two of you, Ana. Whatever this is —" he points between us, "—was not to disrespect her memory or you."

He turns and leaves me completely bewildered.

I make a broth my Grandmother taught my mum and try not

to over analyse what happened between us. But I can't help it. Was I a substitute? When he kissed me, was he wishing it were her? I don't understand where this level of jealousy is coming from. We have no agreement between us. We've made no promises. And yet...*I* did, didn't I? When I told Lawry there would be no one else for me but him.

I leave the broth covered on the stove, no longer hungry and not wanting to see him when they come back.

I force my sluggish body to the bathroom and draw a bath, sprinkling the water with lavender salts. As I soak, my body begins to relax. I continue to slip in and out of thoughts of the way I felt earlier in the meadow, and throbbing builds between my legs.

I reach down and close my eyes, but quickly pull my hand away.

And then I realise what's wrong. This feeling I am ridden with...it's guilt over Lawry—nothing to do with Reuben or Celine.

How can I be mad at him?

The only one I should be mad at is myself.

I sat there and, in my mind, condemned Lawry for marrying Evie. I've kissed another man and been intimate with him and rather than admit this, I used his dead wife as a tool. Shame washes over me.

When I fall into bed, the dreams come in waves of flashes of loss and grief. I calm in the early hours when Reuben's familiar scent washes over me but don't know why.

I wake at dawn and stretch. Running my fingers through my hair, I still when the strands catch on something. I stare in disbelief; I never put the ring back on.

Vella comes over and yawns, pawing for attention. I stroke her head. When I smelt him last night, it wasn't a dream. He calmed me from my restless thoughts.

Filled with self-loathing, I know I need to apologise, but

when I go to the kitchen, Josette informs me that he's gone away for a day or two.

A pang of uncertainty rattles in my chest, and I try to push it away but know it likely won't leave me until I see him again. I wonder if I've given him a reason to question it... Did I make him feel guilty over Celine?

CHAPTER 28

A rustle catches my attention, and I turn to find Vella following me. I smile and whistle for her to come over. I've noticed she's never far away.

"Hey, girl. What you up to?" I ask, tickling her behind the ear —the spot she loves the most. I continue towards the barn with her hot on my heels. A rumble of a growl escapes her, and I turn to see what has her on guard. Stepping out of the shadow of the barn is…Pierré.

"Morning," he says, eyeing me as he chews on a piece of hay.

"Morning," I reply. Vella lets out another growl.

"What's the matter with the mutt?" he asks.

"She's not a people person," I reply, repeating the words Reuben said to me when I first saw her.

He moves closer, and Vella comes up to my leg, the hair on her back rising in a warning.

"I didn't know you were coming today."

"Just dropping by," he replies.

His eyes scan my chest, and now *I* want to growl. I turn to go back towards the house when he grabs my elbow. "Where are you off to?" he asks.

I shake my elbow to free it, but he grips it harder. "Let go," I say, my adrenaline spiking the longer he remains touching me.

"Come on. I've seen the way you look at me."

If I do stare, it's not intended as a form of want or admiration. "I think you're mistaken. Let go." I shake my elbow again. His grip tightens even harder.

Vella is growling now, and I don't know who will attack first—her or me. But I don't have time to think about it when she goes for his ankle. Baring her teeth, she locks on until his hand releases me.

He falls to the floor, kicking her with the other leg but she's strong and shaking him fiercely.

"Get your mutt off of me."

I go to grab her collar, but she's latched onto him with determination, and there's blood seeping through his trouser leg.

"VELLA!" shouts Reuben, and I startle, turning towards him.

He's been gone for three days, but my relief in seeing him brings an unexpected wave of emotion.

"Heel!" Vella lets go, but doesn't stop growling.

"What the heck? That mutt should be shot," Pierré grunts, grabbing at his ankle.

"What happened?" Reuben asks, his eyes trained on me.

"We were coming to the barn. He came out of the shadows, she went for him," I say, omitting some of the truth.

Reuben kneels and examines his leg. "She barely broke the skin. You're lucky. It could have been worse," he says.

"Fucking stupid mutt," Pierré says, eyeing Vella with disdain.

I shake my head. "She was being protective," I say.

He knows why she did it. She likes him less than I do.

"Go on, Josette will see to it." He holds out his hand, but

Pierré knocks it away and grapples to his feet. He spits on the floor and then limps towards the house.

Once he's out of earshot, Reuben turns to me. "What happened? She would never attack someone for no reason."

"He grabbed hold of my arm. Misconstrued my watching him as some sort of invitation."

Now he is the one who seems annoyed.

"It's fine. If she hadn't, I would have," I reply. "Something about him I just don't trust."

"You and me both," he replies.

I kneel and kiss Vella on the nose. "Good girl."

Her tongue lulls out of the corner of her mouth, her tail wagging.

When I stand, Reuben moves to my side. "Are you all right?"

"Of course, I'm fine."

"I hate the thought of anyone putting their hands on you without your consent," he says, grinding his jaw.

I cross my arms. "Believe me, so do I."

His hands hang beside him. His fingers twitch before he reaches for my face. "About what happened between us… I'm sorry if you thought it was a ruse—me using you to replace Celine. I would never do that," he says.

"I was angry with myself, Reuben, not you. I'm the one who is sorry."

He shakes his head. "Neither of us have anything to be sorry for," he says.

At the back of my mind, a niggle of guilt tries to surface, but I push it away.

"Tell me what you want," he says, his eyes probing.

I don't know, and yet at the same time, I ache to feel his lips on mine again.

I don't think, I act. I go on my tiptoes and pull his face to mine.

Our kiss is full of heat, want, and a desire I didn't know I possessed. His hands remain firmly on either side of my face. Mine, however, roam over his back. A feral noise comes up from his throat, and Vella lets out a loud bark. He pulls back and then kisses me one last time. "I should go make sure he's not causing Josette any trouble."

I nod with a smile and watch as he walks away. *What is he doing to me?*

CHAPTER 29

I wasn't prepared for what would await me when I came to France, and I don't mean the war. I mean the man.

Reuben continues to shed layers. The more I get to know him, the more I'm drawn to him—not just physically but emotionally. We find ourselves talking so much more now, and as much as I hate to admit it, he's not as condescending as I once thought.

I pay attention to the way he is with Josette; he dotes on her as if she were his mother. He never talks of his parents, and I wonder why that is.

"You don't see your parents?" I ask one day as we are mucking the stable.

He pauses what he is doing before he continues raking over the straw. "Not for a long time," he admits, and I wonder if that's the end of the discussion, but then he continues. "My mother once told me my father wasn't the same after the war. He tended to use the belt... I don't know why she always made excuses for him." He drops the rake and wipes over his brow with his sleeve. "That belt killed her," he says it so matter of fact.

A gasp falls from my lips.

"She was protecting me like she always did, only this time, she fell and hit her head. She never got back up again." His eyes go distant.

I flinch. "I'm so sorry, Reuben."

He shakes his head, his eyes coming back into focus. "It was a long time ago. If he hadn't died, I would've probably killed him myself."

A shiver rolls over me. He means it. "How old were you?" I ask.

"Eleven. My aunt took me in. My uncle worked for Josette and her husband. I started odd jobs around the farm and never looked back."

I reach out and touch his bicep.

"What about you and your parents?" he asks. "Do you have siblings?"

"No siblings. My mum tried a dozen times after me, but it wasn't meant to be. I think it's why we were so close when I was growing up…like they were trying to compensate for not having any other children. It's why I want a big family someday," I say.

He smiles just as the sunlight breaks through a cloud and enters the open barn door. His features are so decadent. I never thought a man could be beautiful until now. His eyes brighten against his tanned skin, a compliment, and the rarest colour I have ever seen. Growing up, yellow was always my favourite colour, but now it's most definitely forest green.

"I'm sure you will," he replies. But this time, his eyes are smouldering as they do a sweep down the length of my body. A pulsing weight comes to life between my legs. I want to look away, to hide my reaction, but it's almost impossible.

He comes towards me with purpose and takes me in his arms, my back against the barn wall. I taste the sweet salt on his upper lip from the heat of working most of the day. And then he kisses me. He's an elixir, and I am the afflicted.

CHAPTER 30

I've sent over a hundred transmissions since I've been here. The French resistance is relentless in their pursuit to cause as much mayhem and destruction to the Germans as possible. And as I've been ordered, I'm here to help *set Europe ablaze*.

But it doesn't come without reprisals. They will retaliate and arrest family or people of interest they believe to be affiliated. Those they arrest are interrogated, shot. Some become prisoners of war.

We continue to sabotage transport, even factories. But we try to do this without implicating others, try to cover our tracks. Rumours are rife that speak of prisoner of war camps—even death camps—but the thought of this is one I dare not allow my mind to consider.

My new transmission is of a train transport. We are to intercept by blowing up the tracks. This one is a big deal, and it's crucial we hit our target. I've grown quite fond of the guys… except for Pierré, who gives me a wide berth, but his eyes still linger.

"Ignore him. I do," says Isabelle

"What is his deal anyway?"

She shakes her head. "I have no idea, but he doesn't take orders well. A true communist if ever there was one."

We each have our reasons for being here. But I've noticed how lately, she always kind of targets him, and he responds to her in kind. I don't know what is going on between them. I can't put my finger on it.

"Okay, so here's the plan," Reuben says to us all, beginning the detailed brief for our mission.

∼

Dinner is quiet. It's only the three of us—Josette, Reuben, and me. The atmosphere is palpable. When we finish, Reuben leaves Josette and me alone, and I offer to help her clean up.

She waves me off. "I know something is on the horizon and whatever it is, it's bigger than normal—" I interrupt her, but she cuts me off. "I don't want to know. I want you to be careful. Take care of my Reuben." She gets to work on scrubbing the pan, and I see the torment of worry in her eyes. She and he have a bond; she loves him like a son.

"He doesn't need looking after," I say, hoping to reassure her.

"Oh, but he does. He won't admit it, but after he lost Celine, he lost a part of himself." She stops what she's doing and turns back to me. "I see a renewed strength in him since you arrived. He cares for you."

I cough to cover my blush. I don't even know how to respond.

"Just be careful, okay?"

I nod. "I will," I reply and it's the truth.

"Go on, go get yourself ready. Leave me be," she says, shooing me away.

I wash up and change into the warmest clothing I own. It's bitter now that winter is here, and the temperature continues to drop with each passing night.

There's a knock on the door, and before I reach it, Reuben steps into the room, closing the door behind him.

"Is everything all right?" I ask.

His face is a mask, not giving anything away. "I wanted to make sure you're all set for tonight."

"Of course, this is what I'm here for, after all."

He nods. "But I wish you weren't..."

I cross my arms. "Not this again," I reply, thinking we were past this.

"I don't mean it like that," he replies, uncrossing my arms and taking my hands in his.

"Then what do you mean?" I ask.

He pulls me with him and ushers for me to sit beside him on the bed. The mattress dips with our weight.

"It's not because you're a woman, or because I think you aren't capable. War is woven into wrongs that can never be made right. You deserve better than this—" he waves his hand around the room, "—I don't want to see you hurt."

My breath catches in my throat. It's the closest he's come to admitting having feelings for me. He doesn't have to, though, because it's reciprocated.

"I don't want you to get hurt either," I reply honestly and raise my hand to his cheek. His five o'clock shadow scrapes over my palm, and I welcome the sensation.

"Promise me you'll do as I say, and you won't do anything stupid."

I want to strangle this man, but I know if I don't appease him, he'll be worrying about other things he has no control over. "I'll do my best," I reply honestly.

He searches my face, and I'm rewarded with a rare smile. My stomach jumps to life, and I clench my thighs together.

His lips cover mine. Every kiss with him is different and yet familiar, and each time it says something else. His tongue dances with mine and a whimper escapes me.

Never have I ever been entirely consumed by another. I didn't know a kiss could be like this. He pulls away first, and I'm left bereft from the broken connection. He looks pained like it physically hurts him, too. He helps me to my feet.

"Ready?" he asks.

"Yes," I reply, with more confidence than I feel.

I gather my coat and scarf and examine the room with one last, wistful look. Vella follows us to the door and refuses to leave my side even when we arrive at the truck.

"Stay," Reuben says, rubbing her behind the ear.

I kneel and kiss her on the nose. "See you later, girl."

Reuben opens my door, and I climb in. When we pull away, I stare back at the house as it disappears behind us in a blanket of darkness. It has strangely become a home away from home. A wave of nostalgia hits me as it fades away to nothing. I hope this time we make it back.

CHAPTER 31

He drives in silence until we pull up along a brook. He then drives us just off-road enough so that the truck is hidden in brush away from the dirt road.

"We go the rest of the way on foot, but it's important you remember the way back if for some reason something goes wrong. Do you understand?"

I nod; he grabs my elbow.

"I'll be sure to pay attention." I can understand his apprehension. I did get lost in the woods when I first arrived, but I wasn't on a mission then—I was a silly girl stuck inside my head.

This is different.

This is what I've been training for.

He whistles, and then there's a flash of light barely visible that is gone as quickly as it is seen. We head in that direction while I look around for something significant. There is a peculiarly shaped tree that's near where the truck is hidden.

At the tracks spreading out, we take our positions of setting the explosives and the wires. Then we wait, laying low on the grass verge, eyes and ears alert.

Reuben appears beside me and settles in close. I can feel his heat. "Are you holding up okay?"

"Fine. Just it's colder than I imagined."

"Temperature has dropped." He reaches over to my hands. Taking them in his, he rubs them and blows on my fingers. It sends a warmth through me but in all the wrong places. If my face wasn't so cold, I'm pretty sure it would flush with colour and give me away.

"Listen, once we hear the train, only three of us are staying back to blow the traps. I need you to head back to the truck and wait for me."

"What? Since when?" I pull my hands from his.

"Since you are the radio operator. We can't risk you getting caught."

"I'm no more important than the rest of you."

Before he has the chance to reply, we are flashed from the other side of the tracks.

That's when we hear a sound in the distance.

"That would be the train." His eyes dart to the tracks and then back to me, and I think it's the first time I've seen fear in them.

"No, we'll both go once our target is hit." I turn my attention back to the tracks; the train is almost upon us now.

And then it's only a hair width away, and I plunge the handle down, but nothing happens.

There's a few second delay, and then a massive boom.

The earth moves under my feet, and I am thrown into the air from the force. Debris and dirt explode into a fireworks display; I try to shield my face.

There is a brief moment when the only noise I can hear is an excessive buzzing. Flashes of light slipstream through plumes of smoke. Disorientated, I blink, clearing my smoggy vision.

A figure is kneeling in front of me. Hands cup my face.

"Reuben," I say on an exhale.

His lips are moving, but it takes a moment for my ears to catch up. "You have to go now. Run!"

He pulls me to my feet so fast, I struggle to catch a breath.

"Go," he says, placing a chaste kiss on my lips before he turns me and pushes me in the direction I need to go.

I try to run, but my footing is off, and it's more of a wobbly stagger. I keep stretching my mouth and jaw, hoping to release the pressure in my ears, wanting the buzz to subside. I keep going, bumping into branches of the overhanging trees.

Shots ring out in the distance, and I know my hearing hasn't been completely damaged.

I find my footing, and my running isn't so off-kilter. I rush past a holly bush, catching my hair on its limbs and scratching my face in the process.

And then I see it—the truck.

I dive in and start the engine, then jump back out. I run to the edge of the bushes I came through, straining to see if I can hear anyone coming.

And I do. Only…the voices are German, not French.

I recoil. I need to turn off the ignition, I think, sure they can hear the sound of the running engine.

I reach my hand in and turn the motor off, staying crouched down beside the driver's door.

I hear approaching footsteps on the hard ground. I wait. One of them comes around to my side of the truck.

My reflexes are quick enough to kick the rifle from his hands, and then I kick out with my other leg, swiping the back of his ankles. He hits the floor with an *oomph*.

I scramble for his weapon, jam the butt of the rifle into his head hard enough for his head to lull and him to be knocked out cold.

My hands shake—cold or adrenaline, who knows? I grip the rifle.

I don't know what comes first—the crack against my skull or the sheering, ice-cold pain.

The rifle falls from my hands, and my body is now flush with the ground. I push myself up.

Blinking, I try to right my vision, but it's no use. I'm either going to vomit or pass out.

What just happened?

I grip the dirt between my fingertips and drag myself towards the arch of the wheel to push myself to my feet.

And that's when I feel it—the metal hilt of a gun at the base of my neck.

CHAPTER 32

I think I'm told to turn around, but I can't be sure; my hearing is as blurry as my vision. I swallow the foul taste of bile.

I make slow work of moving until I'm facing a soldier, grateful his gun is no longer touching my flesh.

He points the gun at me and motions for me to raise my arms. I do. His eyes roam over my body and then past me to the other soldier who I knocked out. He calls out to him.

"Hemmich," he shouts. He motions for me to move to the side.

There's a low grumble and a grunt before I hear the rustling sound of the soldier righting himself, then coming towards his comrade.

"Turn," shouts the uninjured soldier and I do as I'm told, but keep my face angled towards them as I do it.

One of them pushes my body up into the truck with such force, the wind is knocked out of me.

Hands quickly work up and down my legs, around my waist, and up to my arms.

Shots fire out over my head.

The soldiers yell in German.

The one who hit me turns and shoots into the darkness, the other looks at me and then to the ground where his rifle lays.

Another shot whizzes past his ear and ricochets off the tree trunk.

He ducks.

It gives me just enough time to grab the rifle. When he rights himself, he steps towards me. My finger pressing down on the trigger, I shoot—a bullet straight in the chest.

He stumbles towards me with a gurgled sound, his mouth gasping for air before his eyes roll into the back of his head and he sinks to the ground.

A hand latches onto my shoulder, and I turn quickly, nauseous. My finger presses the trigger.

It's Reuben.

His hand slaps the gun to the side, offing my aim, but not enough—the shot hits his arm.

I can hear screaming, and then Reuben is cupping my face. It's me, I realise. *I'm screaming.*

I clamp my mouth closed so tight, my teeth knock together with force. Reuben is speaking, but I can't understand what he's saying. Maybe it's from the blow to my head.

Then he's hauling me into the cab of the truck.

We're driving. *I shot a man.*

The thought catches up with me, everything is so distorted, nausea takes over.

I begin pulling at the door handle. "Please stop, stop the truck!" I try to shout over the roar of the engine, but my voice is weak.

Reuben's eyes dart to my face, and then in one fell swoop, he veers off the dirt road almost into a ditch.

I scramble out with a thump, and my body slumps to the cold ground as I expel the contents of my stomach until I'm dry heaving.

He scoops me into his arms when I'm done, and then puts me back in the truck.

"We need to get off this road," he says, running back to the driver's side. "It's not too far, I promise."

I lean my forehead on my window as he drives over crevices and bumps. The bed of the truck rocks up and down, jarring my teeth together. The image of the dying man falling to the ground keeps playing on repeat over again in my mind—whether my eyes are open or closed. Something wet trickles down my temple, and I gingerly move my fingers into my hairline. It's soaked and sticky with blood.

CHAPTER 33

I'm jolted into consciousness when the truck stops abruptly. I think I've slipped off into a weird daze.

Reuben opens my door, reaching out for me. He guides me inside a small, secluded house.

He ushers me to sit and then runs back outside. The sound of the engine is moving further away.

I jump to my feet, but it makes me want to vomit. I rush to the door anyway, scramble to pull it open, and peer outside.

The humming of the engine cuts off, and then I see a shadow —Reuben jogging back towards me. I step back, finger my necklace when he comes inside and closes the door behind him.

I grab his arm; he winces. My hand coated in claret.

"It's just a graze," he says as if the fact I shot him is no big deal.

"It could've been worse. I killed that man, he didn't even draw his weapon, and I pulled the trigger. I'm a murderer." I cross my arms and begin to pace, my entire body trembling.

When I turn again, Reuben is toe-to-toe with me. "You need to listen to me. It was them or us. You did what you had to do."

"And my shooting you?" I ask.

He wipes matted hair away from my eyes. "It was an accident. I shouldn't have approached you from behind."

"That's not the poin—hold on, you're speaking English," I say.

He nods and smiles. "Yes, you need to calm down. I thought this might help."

I want to smile, but instead, a strangled sound escapes my throat, and I can't stop the onslaught of tears. I try to step away, but he pulls me into him.

"It's okay," he says, but this only makes me cry harder, and the effort hurts my head even more.

He leans down and kisses the edge of my mouth, whispering for me to calm down.

And that's when I remember he's still bleeding.

"We need to take a look at where I shot you," I say on a hiccup and swipe under my nose. What on God's green earth must I look like?

"Come on, there's a bathroom through here." He leads us into a bathroom, shining the torch in front of us.

"What is this place?" I ask.

"I was fixing it up. Decided it would prove useful. I store provisions here." He ushers me to sit on the edge of the bath.

I rub at my arms, unable to stop the vibrations running through my body. Reuben notices and goes in a cupboard to pull out a sweater. "Lift," he says. I stare up at him. "Your arms, lift your arms."

He drops the sweater over my head and pulls my arms through. "I need to take a look at your head."

Balancing the torch on the edge of the sink, he pulls out a box. The inside is full of bandages and other medical supplies. He washes his hands and then soaks some gauze with water and brings it to my scalp. It takes a second or two before my brain catches up, and I flinch at the sharp pain.

He begins cleaning the area, but I see the way he's working his jaw. This is just as unpleasant for him as it is me.

"I've never shot anyone before, and now I'm a murderer."

"Listen, you know what the implications would be if you were arrested? There was no other choice."

I know he's right, but when it comes to my day of judgement, will God see it that way? 'Do to others as you would have them do to you.' – Luke 6:31 –

I can hear these words in my head; my mother used to recite passages from the Bible to us growing up.

"I spent many weeks training, learning hand to hand combat. They even interrogate you, but nothing prepares you for this."

"No. None of us should be here," he says while he finishes cleaning up my scalp.

His shirt is caked in blood. I need to see his wound, too. I stare at my own blood-soaked hands, then I move beside him and begin scrubbing them. No amount of soap or water will ever make these hands feel clean again. I sniff back the overwhelming urge to cry.

Refusing to be beaten, I scrub my hands one more time. He stops me, takes my hands in his, and gives them a gentle squeeze before letting them go.

CHAPTER 34

"Let me take a look at your arm," I say.

He nods, and I watch as he pulls one arm through the sleeve but struggles with the other. I move to help him, and it's then I see the extent of the bullet wound.

"Reuben, you foolish man. This is more than a graze."

He shrugs. "It's not that bad."

I reach out and prod the area. He lets out a curse word. I turn him around to see the exit wound—it went up and out.

"You'll need stitches," I say.

He points to the box, and I see there's everything I'll need. I have to keep blinking to right my vision, and no matter how hard I try to tame it, the tremble in my hands remains even as I apply the stitches.

It's quiet—just the sound of our breathing—until he speaks. "Why are you here?"

Taken aback by his question, I tie off the stitch and stare up at him. "I wanted to help."

"But you could have done other things to help that wouldn't involve you coming here and getting caught up in this mayhem."

I bandage his arm, his skin warm to the touch. Him talking to me has somehow managed to calm my nerves. Maybe because he went out of his way to speak to me in English, and I am nostalgic as I think of home, but these past few months here in France have become like home. "It's an amalgamation of reasons. My dad is French. We don't even know if his family is safe."

He grabs a towel and runs it under the tap, ringing it out. He brings it towards my face and wipes it gently. He's so close, his breath floats over my skin.

"My father's brother died in the Great War, and yet here we are...history repeating itself."

"Maybe we'll never learn from our mistakes."

He drops the cloth into the sink before he looks through the vials of liquid and finds two syringes.

"Penicillin," he says.

My eyes widen, I hate needles, but he's right. He fills one and takes hold of my arm. Needle poised, he asks, "what was your other reason for coming?"

"Love," I reply honestly just as I feel the pinch of the needle entering my skin.

He rubs it once it's done and hands me the other syringe. I inject him. "The man who married your friend?"

I nod, and my stomach drops but not in a good way. When I used to think of Lawry, it fluttered wildly with excitement. Now it's with a sense of dread. "Yes. I thought it would be easier the further away from them I was."

I clean up the soiled gauze and let out an exhale.

He pulls himself out a sweater and slips it over his head with a grunt. "And is it?" he asks.

I shake my head. *No.*

"Come." He holds out his hand to me, and I take it. He leads me into the front room. "I don't want to risk starting a fire. I'll get some blankets," he says, leaving me standing in the middle of the room.

He returns with blankets over his arm and a lit lantern. He lays them on a rope twist couch, which I can't help but admire now that the room is no longer in semi-darkness.

"I was re-upholstering it for Celine," he says. "Before she died."

My stomach twists uncomfortably. "It's beautiful," I say, stroking the velvet cover. I sit down, kick off my shoes, and pull my legs up under me, wrapping myself in one of the blankets, the smell of them familiar, oaky—*Reuben*.

"Thirsty?"

I nod, licking my lips, parched now he comes to mention it.

I lean my head back, the throbbing a constant, and listen to him rummage in the kitchen. He returns with two mugs and a bottle under his arm with a plate of what smells like cheese. My stomach grumbles.

He pours us both a drink and passes me a mug. I sniff—alcohol. I take a sip, the warmth welcome as it cascades down my throat—a rich, velvety claret. He hands me a cracker topped with sliced cheese. I take it gratefully, his fingers brush against mine, and he smiles. His eyes come to life under the light of the lantern, and I have to force myself to look away.

"Thank you." I nibble at the cheese, the creamy texture attacking my taste buds. I all but groan as I savour the flavour.

"So, tell me about this man."

The love of my life. "What's there to tell? Sometimes we lose in love."

He nods, gazing into his mug, and I watch as his jaw ticks. "Yes, we do," he replies, and although my loss is unlike his, I still empathise with him.

"She didn't leave you out of choice," I say.

His eyes rise to mine. "If it's any conciliation… If it were me and not him," he says, his stare unwavering. "I would have chosen you."

It's not the first time he has said that to me, and his response

—without a hint of hesitation—has me believing him. I'm glad I've already swallowed the last bite of cheese because his words cause my throat to tighten with a mixture of surprise and…something else.

I don't know how to respond; his words carry a heavy weight in the air, the room almost stifling.

"I'm not saying what he did wasn't noble—it was. But I would have found another way."

I go to shake my head, but the throbbing stops me. I raise my fingertips to my scalp, prod the area gently. Reuben moves from the floor and sits beside me, then he softly moves my hand away to have a look. "It's stopped bleeding, but you likely have a concussion," he says and drops his hand to his lap.

I watch him for a moment, and then he reaches his arm over my shoulder and pulls me into him. I don't resist. I need this—*him*.

I yawn, and close my eyes for a minute, just for a minute. And then I ask him the question swirling around in my hazy mind. "Do you think things happen the way they're supposed to…that everything happens for a reason?"

He squeezes my shoulder just a fraction. "Maybe. I think every man has his own destiny."

"I guess we all have our part to play," I say, mirroring his own words back to him from our previous conversation. I'm hit with yet another yawn, exhaustion taking over.

His words, although distant, still reach me. "And mine is with you," he says before his lips meet mine.

My heart squeezes in satisfaction, but I'm too far gone to reciprocate as I drift into darkness.

CHAPTER 35

I startle awake, dazed and confused by my surroundings. Breathless, I clutch my chest.

"You're okay, you had a nightmare," Reuben whispers into the room beside me. His hand finds my back, and he rubs it in small circular motions.

"I… and you…so much blood." I bring the back of my hand to my brow and wipe away the sheen of sweat.

"It was just a nightmare," he says, his voice comforting.

"But it wasn't. I shot you," I say, unable to ignore the reality of the situation.

"I'm fine. Come on. You need to go to bed."

He gets to his feet and holds out his hand. I wrap my fingers with his and stand, but I'm light-headed. He takes me under my arm and walks me to a back room where he points over to a bed and turns to leave. I go and sit on the edge.

"Here." He sits beside me and hands me a mug. "It's water," he says.

I take the mug from him and hold it between my palms, sip the contents slowly, the cold, refreshing liquid welcome. When I'm finished, he takes it from me and places it on the floor.

Crouching down in front of me, he takes my chin in his hand and looks me over. "You're bruising," he says.

I cup his face with my hand. "So are you."

Tilting his head, he moves his face into my palm, and plants a soft sweet kiss. A warm feeling explodes at the bottom of my stomach. He leans his forehead softly against mine. "I'm just glad we're both alive," he says.

And that's when it hits me—either one of us could have died, and he wouldn't know how much he means to me.

I kiss the corner of his mouth. He turns his head, and his lips meet mine. My face in his hands, he kisses me with reverence. His tongue dances with mine—all-consuming.

I move closer, and a rumble escapes him.

My hands reach for his body. It's not enough. I slide them under his sweater—I need to feel him.

He pulls back and swiftly removes it, followed by his t-shirt. My fingers dance over his bare torso in wonder.

Reaching for the hem of my sweater, he tugs it up and off, careful as he does. He's less forgiving with my blouse—ripping it open, a couple of buttons popping off. He trails kisses along my throat and down my chest.

His hands are skilled in their pursuit. He slides down the strap of my brassiere and takes my breast into his mouth, sucking hard on my nipple.

I flinch from the sensation, but it's not painful. My senses are heightened with every touch, every kiss. He does the same with my other strap until it's pooled at my waist. He cups both my breasts in the palms of his hands, then his face dips as he trails his tongue between the two.

My hands move to his hair. I massage my fingers into his scalp until they reach his neck, and I pull him closer. His lips find mine again, eager, full of want. He pulls away, causing me to whimper.

He strips out of his trousers and underpants. When he takes

himself in his hand, I can't look away, I'm mesmerised by his manhood.

Softly, he kneels on the bed and pushes me down until my back is flush with the mattress. He releases himself to work my trousers and my undergarments free, and the fresh air shocks me. I sit up onto my elbows.

I'm wet between my legs. His hands stroke my thighs, and with thick eyelashes, he stares up at me. "Okay?" he asks.

I nod, heart racing, body quivering.

His fingers trail up between my legs. I jolt when he spreads them before taking himself in his hand between my legs as he moves over me. There isn't time for me to catch my breath as he pushes his way inside me, and I let out a pinched squeal of pain, gripping his arms in alarm.

He freezes, looks between us at his body connected with mine and then back to my face.

I scrunch my eyes closed and turn my head to the side. I can feel him. The sensation is unfamiliar, full.

He drops his mouth close to my ear, his breath tickles. "You've not been with a man before?" he asks.

I shake my head and bite my lip.

"Do you want me to stop?"

The question causes a tear to break free, and I turn to face him and open my eyes. He brings his thumb to my cheek and wipes it away.

"No," I whisper, my skin flushing with embarrassment.

He cups my face with one hand, holding his weight off me with the other. He twitches inside me, and I fidget ever so slightly.

"I promise to be gentle. To make this good for you, but you need to relax," he says.

Letting out a breath, I nod, and his lips catch mine for a slow, torturous kiss, sending warmth to my stomach again. And then he begins to move in slow, controlled movements as my body becomes familiar with his.

I gradually begin to relax and adjust myself when he increases the tempo with each thrust. When I mirror his movement, something profound begins to build.

His hand that was holding onto mine releases, and he works it between our bodies, his fingers now working circular motions on my most sensitive spot.

"Ahh," I sigh, unable to keep quiet. The sensation rocks through me. He speeds up, and my hands slide down to grip his rear.

I pull him into me until there is no space between us and then something happens—a drawn out release followed by an explosion of pure euphoria.

And then I'm falling.

CHAPTER 36

When I begin to rouse, there's a warm weight over my body. I open my eyes to find Reuben's injured arm slung across my waist. Memories of last night come flooding back, and my stomach stirs. I wrap my fingers around his wrist to release his hold from my body, but his grip tightens. "Stay," he says, muffled into the pillow.

I can't control my smile. "I need the bathroom," I say.

He releases me with a huff. Naked, I bring the blanket closest to me up to my chest and sit up. Reuben raises himself to his elbow and reaches for my chin, turning my face to the side. He leans up and kisses me before laying back down. His erection is standing to attention. I grip the blanket tight and rush to the bathroom.

Once I relieve my full bladder, I take stock of myself in the mirror. Do I look different? I touch my lips and my face. I can't stop smiling. I make quick work of cleaning myself, and though I'm tender, surprisingly I'm not sore. There's a faint show of blood but nothing more. Evie warned me how the first time would hurt, and it did, initially, but after that, it was more uncomfortable than painful.

Reuben said he could make it good for me and he did. My stomach jerks. The pulse between my thighs is an indication of just how good it was. I finger my hair as best I can and return to the room.

He passes me, naked, on his way to the bathroom. My eyes follow, and I gulp down my appraisal of him until he's out of sight. I am trying to piece together my clothing when he approaches me from behind. His body is warm pressed against my back. His arousal is evident, too.

His lips graze my ear and my neck. He sucks gently and kisses my skin. "Why did you never sleep with him?" he asks.

I tense, his question catching me off guard. His hands massage my shoulders, and I start to relax. "I wanted to wait."

He blows a soft breath over my neck before his lips and teeth sink into my skin. My head tilts back. His hands trail to my stomach, and he pulls the blanket from my grasp. Then, his fingers move lower, but he stops below my belly button.

I close my eyes and take a deep breath. "And why did you sleep with me?"

I shake my head, his fingers dipping where I want them the most. I spread my legs just a fraction. "Because I didn't want to wait," I say honestly.

He spins me to face him and cups the back of my neck, tilting my head towards his, searching my face. And then he kisses me with a desperation like one of us can't breathe without the other.

His hands cup my rear and his fingers dig into my flesh before lifting me from the ground.

"Wrap your legs around me," he says into my mouth.

I do as he instructs and he backs us up against the wall. It's cold against my bare flesh. He adjusts himself. I watch as he slides me down the length of him. I can't look away as he begins to move. I've never experienced a want like this before, and the more he moves, the harder it is for me to control myself.

He backs us towards the bed, still rooted inside me, and sits with me straddling him. He coaxes me to move, so I do until it becomes too much, and he rolls me underneath him—this time, it's hard and fast. My nails scratch his back as the same sensation begins to build, and we climb together, higher and higher, until we both surrender to the inevitable.

∼

We drive back to the farm, both consumed with our thoughts, mine of wonder and bliss…and then of guilt and shame. Not from being with him—but for killing another. How do I overcome that?

"Do you think everyone else got away unharmed?" I ask.

His eyes move to mine and then back to the road. He shrugs. "I don't know. I hope so."

I'm so overwhelmed as we pull back up to the farmhouse, I could cry. This place is like home.

Vella jumps up at me, licking my face in a frenzy. Josette rushes out to see us, grabbing hold of Reuben, who winces slightly. She shakes her head but says nothing as she comes around to greet me with a hug. She searches my face, and I am sure in the light of day, the bruises are on show.

"Come, I got supper ready just in case," she says, pulling on my hand and wrapping her arm around Reuben as we head to the back of the house.

The rich smell of broth greets me in the kitchen, and my senses come alive. Neither Reuben nor I say a word as we get to work on scarfing down our supper.

It's just beginning to get dark, and my body is aching now, the aftermath of last night and probably this morning catching up with me. I blush, embarrassed, wondering if we smell like lovemaking.

"Would you have any objections to me drawing myself a bath?"

Josette waves me away with an annoyed expression for even asking.

I slip into the bath with a sigh and hiss slightly once I am fully immersed. I'm bruised in places and sensitive in others—a mixture of both pleasure and pain.

I think of Lawry, wondering if we would've been that magnificent together. Not that I have anything to compare it to. Who knows? Reuben isn't new to it, so maybe it wasn't as good for him as it was for me...

A knock on the door startles me, and my hands cover my chest.

"I'm just in the bath, I won't be long," I call out.

"Can I come in?" It's Reuben. The door doesn't have a lock, just a latch.

I know he's seen me naked, but I feel like it wouldn't be appropriate. "Can you wait until I'm finished?" I ask.

The latch lifts and in walks Reuben. I sit up and pull my knees to my chest. He raises an eyebrow, a silent question: why did I cover myself?

"Why couldn't it wait?" I ask.

Walking towards me, he says, "I wanted to check you were all right."

"Of course. Why wouldn't I be?"

Saying nothing, he reaches over me for the soap and dips his hands into the water, rolling it over in his hands. He comes behind me and nudges me gently. I sit forward, and he begins to wash my back.

"I crossed a line, being with you," he says. "I wouldn't have been so forward if I had known."

"Known what?" I ask as his hands massage my shoulders, my body wholly pliable and at his mercy.

"You were waiting," he replies.

"I *was* waiting. Now I'm not," I say.

"So, you don't regret it?" he asks as his hands stop moving.

"No, I wanted you," I say over my shoulder. He leans down and kisses me. When he pulls away, I turn the question back on him. "Do *you* regret it?"

"No, it was one of the best days of my life," he replies, his voice low as he rinses my back.

"I wasn't a disappointment?" I ask, self-conscious.

"Not even possible," he replies, kissing my ear. His candour never ceases to amaze me. "If you want me to come to you tonight, leave your door ajar," he says, handing me back the soap. His eyes roam over my body. The look in his eyes makes me wish he were in the bath with me.

Just as he goes to slip back through the door, I call out, "Reuben?" He pauses. "It was one of the best days of my life, too," I say.

I'm rewarded with one of his rare smiles before the door clicks closed behind him. I dunk myself under the water and come back to the surface, hissing. I'd forgotten about my scalp. I wince and carefully shampoo the ends as best I can.

I don't know how long the war will continue, but while I'm here, I'm not going to live in fear of the things I cannot change. Instead, I want to embrace the things I have control over in the moment, and that means giving myself to Reuben without doubt or guilt. After all, we do not know what tomorrow will bring.

CHAPTER 37

We've been monitoring this factory for weeks now. With thousands of employees, it was easy for André to go in and keep under the radar. It was initially targeted for a bombing raid, but somehow, only a dozen bombs hit the factory, and it only sustained minimal damage.

A nearby village suffered from a high number of civilian casualties. And these will likely increase in number if the bombing raids continue. Although the work in the factory is still supervised by the owner, it's to the service of the Nazi regime. They churn out large volumes of war material at the hands of their many skilled workers.

It's imperative the factory be taken out of action—preferably with the least amount of civilian fatalities possible.

André was the one who suggested we reach out to the owner, Luis. It was risky, but we had little choice. He explained who he was and that there were two choices. Either the factory plant would continue to remain a target, with the likelihood of civilian lives continuing to be lost, or he was to work with us to sabotage his machinery.

This didn't go over well with him; the last thing he wanted to do was to be an accomplice to sabotaging his own plant. He was also dubious in case this was a set up by the Germans, leading him into a trap. It's why Reuben and I find ourselves having to meet with him and André at a safe house with the radio—so we can contact London and he can liaise with them. Luis agrees.

We have to stay the night. We cannot afford to be caught on the road. When we are on a mission, we avoid drawing attention at all costs. Once Luis leaves, André offers to take the front room so Reuben and I can take a bedroom each.

"No need," replies Reuben, who wraps his arm over my shoulder. My cheeks heat, and I can't even make eye contact with André.

"Night then," he says and takes himself off into the nearest room.

I step out from under Reuben's arm.

"What?" he asks with a smirk.

I swat his arm. "You know *what*."

A laugh rumbles from his chest. It's such a rare sound, I'm taken aback.

I wouldn't class myself as a prude, after all, I'm the one sharing my bed with him. I never thought I'd be with any man out of wedlock. Maybe it's why I was so insistent on waiting when it came to Lawry and me. But coming here…and after everything that happened back in England…I guess I just decided not to spend what life I may have waiting.

He pulls me into his body, and my stomach flutters to life like it always does when he touches me.

"Come, let's go to bed," he says, bending down to kiss me.

His lips are always so full and wanting, his tongue probing. His strong hands find their way south and cup me firmly. He lifts my feet from the ground. I wrap my legs around him. His arousal pushes up against me and makes my knickers damp.

He kicks the door closed behind us, a giggle escapes me, and then before I know it, I break out into a laughing fit.

His eyes are amused, but his voice is gruff. "What are you laughing at?"

I shrug, truth is, I've never been with him with someone so close by, and it makes me both nervous and excited.

"Is it because Andrè is just next door?" he asks in a whisper.

I nod, wondering when he began to read me so well.

"We don't have to be together, we can just sleep," he says.

I'm sure my teeth light up the room when I smile. "Thank you," I say, but I'm also a little disappointed.

We strip down to our undergarments—me in my slip and him in his pants—and climb into the bed.

The frigid air causes my nipples to harden. Reuben rests on his elbow, his face in his palm as his eyes roam over my body. His fingers move to my breast, and he circles my areola. I can hear my breathing increase in the quiet of the room. His fingers make their way to my stomach, to the hem of my slip. Then they slide up my inner thighs.

He moves until he's at my damp entrance, his finger circles me, and I twitch a little. The whole time, his eyes remain locked with mine. And then his finger, no, *fingers* are inside me, and my mouth falls open as my eyes close.

"Look at me," he says, his breath blowing softly against my cheek.

I do, and his fingers work me harder. I have to bite my lip, worried André can hear the erratic sounds of my breathing. Reuben's arousal is hard against my leg. I reach down and grab him. I guide my movements up and down the way I've briefly seen him do. His breathing accelerates.

We both ask the same silent question. I let go of him, and his fingers withdraw from me. Covering my body, he aligns himself with my entrance, and with ease, he slides into me. We both sigh in satisfaction. I wrap my legs around him, my ankles digging into his backside. Every movement he makes is measured.

Each time I give myself to him, I lose more of myself.

CHAPTER 38

After weeks of planning, tonight is the night we are sabotaging the factory. We've all memorised the plans and know exactly what our jobs are. The air is charged with invisible energy. We had to wait for the right moment to sneak inside past the guards.

I'm over on the east side with Pierré. René is on the north side with André, and Reuben is the west side with Isabelle. Sylvette is on the south with two others who I've never met before.

I know Reuben wasn't pleased about me being with Pierré. Still, he couldn't bring this to everyone's attention without a reasonable explanation, and his relationship with me is hardly cause to be questioning our assignment.

Pierré stays close to my side but otherwise doesn't do anything untoward as we quietly navigate to the areas we need to plant our explosives. When I reach mine, he stops and looks at me. "Be careful, and if anything happens, you get yourself out, okay?"

I'm a little taken aback. Is he saying that like he doesn't want me to get hurt? Or because he thinks something is going to go array?

"And you," I reply.

"And feel the wrath of Reuben... or worse, Vella?" He smirks. "No chance." Then he walks away.

I stare at his retreating back, left a little discombobulated. I can see him when he reaches where he needs to be. It's not entirely dark in the plant, but there are enough shadows and recesses in the building for a guard to lurk or saunter by.

I get busy taking everything from the canvas bag, and as instructed, I connect it to the machine. I don't even know how this will turn out. The factory is enormous; we'll be lucky to make even a dent with the majority of them.

I'm just setting the last one when I hear a *creak*. I scan around me, seeing nothing, but then I hear the unmistakable sound of footsteps.

I freeze.

I listen to the weight as they connect with the floor though I still can't see anyone. I slowly step back into the shadow of the area I'm in when the sole of my shoe squeaks against the ground.

The footsteps falter.

I reach into my pocket for my gun, then pull it out with my finger poised over the trigger.

The wind is howling outside, rattling the walls, making me jittery. I remain still and wait. The sound of the footsteps continue, and this time, I notice they seem to be moving away from me.

I sigh in relief, but in doing so, I lean into something hard. It rattles.

I can barely make out Pierré, but it looks like he's frozen, too.

He must be able to see whoever is out there because he does something completely unexpected—he rolls something in the opposite direction from me, and the guard rushes over to see what it is.

I can see the guard's silhouette now. He's looking in the

direction of Pierré. But I can't see him at all; he must have hidden.

A voice from behind me startles me. "Rats again?"

"I think so," another replies.

"Coffee?" asks the guard from behind me.

"Thought you'd never ask," the other says over a yawn, walking back out of my line of sight.

I don't dare move until the sound of their retreating footsteps have disappeared from earshot.

When I'm finished with the last explosive, I meet back up with Pierré, and we move to our exit.

Once we're outside, we make our way to the meet point and I can see the others waiting. Reuben's posture is stiff and rigid until I come into view.

"Thank you," I say to Pierré before we reach them.

"No problem," he replies.

He gives a nod to the group, and with that, we all go our separate ways.

I don't mention what happened to Reuben as we drive away. But I'm surprised to feel the rumble of the earth and the night sky light up behind us once the charges detonate and we have been on the road for at least ten minutes. We spend the night at the cottage and head back to the farm at dawn.

Then the news comes flooding in.

Steel doors were blown off their hinges, leaving areas in darkness and charred remains of machinery.

Some equipment was ruined beyond repair, whereas others with the right parts could likely be fixed.

But we hit our target and hard.

This should take them out of operation for a few months, especially if we can continue to intercept the replacement parts, making it harder for them to continue manufacturing for the Germans.

It's satisfying to know our covert operation has meant the air raids in the area will cease. London knows bombing is not the only option. The more lives we can save and still not implement others is a small victory.

It's rare to have time out from radio transmissions, trips into town and local villages, or working on the farm. But after weeks of hard work and such a fantastic result, tonight we celebrate.

"Don't you think it's interesting how Pierré's section, although damaged, survived?" asks Isabelle in a whisper.

I shrug, and my eyes find him. To be honest, her question before last night might have made me consider something untoward, but now I'm not too sure. Besides, even Vella seems to tolerate his presence now.

"Maybe," I reply. "I never really thought about it."

She gives me the side-eye but soon moves onto another topic. I'm grateful. For one night, I want to pretend I'm just socialising with friends—no war, no ulterior motives.

Sylvette finds some music, and we drink the claret André brought. We have cheese and crackers, grapes, and even chocolate.

Reuben stands and offers me his hand when a slow song comes on.

I don't question this or worry about what anyone else thinks as he pulls me to my feet. It's not long before Pierré has Sylvette up and dancing. Isabelle practically forces André, his cheeks pink. He keeps pushing his glasses back up his nose, but all in all, he is a good sport about it.

We play cards, tell jokes, share stories. I can't remember the last time I laughed so much my face ached and my stomach hurt. It's late, so wooden crates are pulled out along with some blankets, and everyone makes up a bed.

Reuben and I retire to the house after he's changed. My door creaks and he joins me in bed. Exhausted, he wraps me in his arms. I don't recall what life was like before—when I used to sleep alone. Vella snores quietly in the corner, and a sense of dread washes over me.

How am I supposed to leave when this is all over? If I'm one of the lucky ones who makes it out alive, how do I say goodbye?

CHAPTER 39

It's been over two weeks since Sylvette checked in and it's worrisome. The longest we go is a week, but this is too long, and we all know it.

André has been asking around, but no one seems to know anything. It's why we are so shocked when Josette comes rushing over to us when we return from working the fields.

She fidgets, wringing her hands together, her face contorted with worry. "It's Sylvette," she says.

"What about her?" Reuben takes her elbow and ushers her to sit down, her body visibly shaken.

"She's been arrested."

"What?" I exclaim.

Reuben's eyes spring to mine.

"Marguerite was in town, queuing for bread and she overheard some talk, and that's when she found out."

"But how…why?" I ask.

"I need to try and find out what's going on," Reuben says and gets to his feet. I go to follow him, but he stops me. "No."

"Bu—"

"No, Ana. I need you to stay here and radio it in. I'll reach out to one of my contacts. See if anything can be done."

I nod. As much as I don't like it, he's right. He rushes inside to get ready.

"Come, Josette, let me make you a coffee," I say.

She gets to her feet, unsteady, and I link her arm with mine. "I think it might be cause for something stronger," she replies.

I hunt around in the cupboard and find her stash of sweet sherry and pour her a glass. About to put the bottle away, I backtrack and pour myself one, too.

We sit in silence opposite one another until Reuben enters. He walks over and kisses the top of Josette's hair. She reaches for his hand and gives it a squeeze. I stand when he comes to me, giving me a chaste kiss, his fresh scent lingering long after he's left.

I don't leave Josette. She's known Sylvette a long time, longer than me, but we share a mutual fear for her well-being.

"What do you think will happen?" she asks me, sipping her drink.

I shrug and try to ignore the prickling of my skin at the thought. "I have no idea…depends on what they arrested her for." It's a ridiculous response. They can arrest you for just walking past if they want to. It's almost as if they are throwing their weight around to prove their power.

She grabs her knitting. The *clank-click* of each stitch is welcome. Vella circles at her feet and curls herself into a ball. Although Reuben said she wasn't a people person, I think she was grieving the loss of Celine.

"I'm going to head down to the basement. I won't be long."

Her eyes slide up from her stitch work, and she gives me a sad smile. It haunts me until the radio is put together and I send some transmissions.

The news comes back; they're concerned about informants.

Ever since the hit on the factory, the Germans are even more forceful than ever. I've heard of double agents, but the thought of our own turning on us causes the sherry lining my stomach to roll over.

Soon, René arrives. His eyes are heavy with worry. Word got around quickly.

I stand, greet him, then sit back at the radio.

"Where's Reuben?"

"He went to see what he could find out."

"I hope he fares better than me," he replies.

"What happened?"

"All I know is she was stopped at a checkpoint and there was scrutiny over her papers. Then she was being herded into the back of a truck and taken to the police station."

I bite my lip and begin to pace. "But when was this?" I ask.

"Thursday," he replies.

I wonder where she'd been until then. "Do you think she was keeping a low profile, and when she did venture out, they pounced?"

He shrugs. "Probably. We all know the drill. She would have avoided us at all costs if she thought her cover was blown."

André and Isabelle turn up sometime after. I keep checking the radio, and we work on some detonators. When Reuben comes down, his face has aged since I saw him only a few hours ago.

He sits, and André reaches for the wine to pour him a mug.

"She's been moved to a detention camp."

I let out a rush of breath at the weight of his comment.

"What, why?" asks Isabelle, chewing her thumbnail.

"Something to do with her heritage." He gulps his drink. "It came to light she's Jewish on her mother's side, and because she didn't declare it, they arrested her, and she's been moved to a camp."

I cover my mouth. There's been rumours. And we've seen

what's happened in town. All the businesses owned by Jews have been relinquished to non-Jewish residents, but this is getting worse."

"That's ridiculous."

"Pierré tried to get her out, saying it was only a quarter and she wasn't aware she would be implicated for not volunteering the information. But he was threatened with arrest himself. It was only because one of the French soldiers knew him, that he was allowed to leave without a scene."

I can't believe this.

"Is that true? About her being Jewish?" I ask.

"Yes," Pierré says. No one even heard him arrive.

"It just seems ludicrous they would arrest her over that. And how would they even know?" I ask to no one in particular.

"People are fickle. I've seen neighbours turning on their friends in the hopes they will profit from their indiscretions."

Pierré scrubs his palm over his face, his usual arrogant expression somewhat sombre.

"How did *you* know?" Isabelle asks him accusingly.

"Because I am, too," he replies. His eyes lift to her. "As do you. We talked about before. You were there, Isabelle."

The room falls silent. The weight of knowing we can't help Sylvette curdles my stomach. But we all know how dangerous what we do is, and yet, we do it anyway.

"At least she wasn't accused of being a spy," André says.

He, of course, is correct. She could have been interrogated or executed if that were the case. A camp isn't great, but maybe we can send her a food parcel…see if we can get some correspondence back and forth to let us know if she's all right.

"We need to be more careful. Especially you, Pierré."

André pours Pierré a drink and hands it to him. "I have no family left, and those who know me have no idea of my Jewish heritage. Except for those in this room."

The air grows thick as his words float over me. We're all in danger, him even more so. As arrogant as he is, he's a conundrum to me, but at this point, I still don't know how well I can trust him.

CHAPTER 40

Sleep evaded me throughout the night. I clung to Reuben like at any moment he would disappear. I continue to think about Sylvette, how easily it was for them to send her to a detention camp. I wonder how she's being treated. If they hurt her. Does she know we tried to look for her?

I can't seem to comprehend the fact that friends and neighbours are turning on people they have known their whole lives. And for what? Greed? Reward?

Careful to not disturb Reuben, I leave him sleeping and slip into some clothes. I pull on my wellies, needing to be outside, to breathe. Vella comes with me without me having to coax her. She's become a friend, as strange as that may sound. I feel safer for being in her presence, and if she felt half this way about Celine, I can see why she mourned her so deeply when she died.

I never gave much purchase to how a dog may pick up on the humans around them, not until Vella. Her loyalty is stronger and greater than any human I know—unwavering, really. She puts humankind to shame.

We walk for a long time until we come to a meadow. I need to stop and rest. The heels of my feet are rubbing in my boots. I didn't slip on my socks; I'm sure I'll pay for that later. I can already feel the blisters forming. I consider slipping them off, but it's too cold, and what if I can't get them back on? I don't fancy walking back to the farm barefoot.

I sit down on a soft patch of dew-covered grass and Vella lays on her stomach spreading her legs behind her like a frog. I close my eyes and tilt my head back, the fresh breeze rippling across my face. My eyelids flicker as the sky rolls overhead and the sun begins to rise. The nearby trees come to life with bird chatter, and in the distance, a rooster crows.

The air is fresh and sweet as the wildflowers begin to open after an evening enclosed in their petals. Everything here is peaceful and gentle. It helps me forget the harsh reality of what waits for me back at the farm. Shafts of golden orbs light up the meadow in halos.

Crunching leaves alert me to another presence. Vella's head raises and her tongue lulls out, but she doesn't move. I already know it's no one to be worried about. I smell him on a breeze, whispering past me before he sits beside me.

"Here you are," he says.

I turn to him and smile. He pulls me into his lap, causing me to squeal.

"I missed you this morning." He rubs the tip of his nose with mine, the faint smell of coffee on his breath.

"Sorry," I reply and give him a chaste kiss on his lips. I rest my cheek over his chest, and the familiar beat of his heart drums a staccato rhythm with mine.

"Are you thinking about Sylvette?"

I pull back and look at him. "I hate not knowing if she's all right."

He rocks me softly in his lap. "I know," he says. "Me, too."

I never thought I'd feel at home in another man's arms, least of all his. It's easy to separate what I have with him and what I had with Lawry, but I know at some point, I need to face facts.

I'm holding onto the thread of a promise—one I haven't kept. I still love Lawry. I don't think that will ever go away, but it's not the same.

I gave him my word in my letter, which I now know was a contradiction. I'll be true to him and yet if he wants to move on, to do so. There was never any real closure with us, and if I get the chance, I know I need to give that to him, if not for him but me.

"Shall we go into town? Maybe see if we can find out anything else?"

I move from his lap and get to my feet, wiping my hands down my trousers. His smile is warm at my quick response. "I'll take that as a yes."

He jumps to his feet and grabs hold of my hand. I hiss through my teeth after we begin walking.

"What is it?"

"I didn't wear any socks. I'm pretty sure my heels have blisters."

He steps in front of me, his back facing me. "Jump on."

I let out a childish giggle.

"Come on," he says, exasperated.

"You're going to give me a piggyback?" I ask in disbelief.

"That or I can sling you over my shoulder," he says, turning his head to the side so I can see his face. The thought stirs something in my stomach, and I blush. Doing as he says, I hop up and he cups his arms underneath my thighs.

When he deposits me at the front door, Josette manages a smile at the sight. "What happened?"

"Blisters," I say.

Gingerly, I sit on the step and pull off my wellies. My blisters have blisters. Josette insists I let her see to them before we go into town—no room for argument. I'm grateful she manages to cover them so I can still slip into my shoes.

Its eerily quiet today as we walk through the cobbled streets. I pass a young girl with some sort of yellow badge on the left of her chest. But she scurries past me, so I don't get a chance to see it.

As we approach more people, I see what it is... A yellow star the size of my palm with the inscription, "*Juif.*"

I cover my mouth with my hand, overcome with light headiness. I heard about an ordinance being issued, but it was speculation. Reuben's arm wraps around my waist, and I drop my hand. A young girl no older than six, wearing a pretty white dress that's ruined by the yellow star haphazardly sewed on... She's being persecuted for being Jewish, nothing more.

Already, I can see the divide, the segregation as fellow French civilians avoid them or worse—force them into the road and off of the pavement. I'm not wearing one, and yet I feel every ounce of humiliation. I watch as a young boy no older than twelve spits on the path right in front of a woman, her head bowed over the stigma of what her badge represents.

All because she is Jewish.

CHAPTER 41

We found out Sylvette, along with her two siblings, her mother, and grandmother were sent to Drancy internment camp in the north-eastern suburb of Paris. Just for being of Jewish descent. It also houses undesirables…whoever they may be.

We've been busy getting together a food parcel. I've spent hours writing a letter on the inside of the wrapper of canned prunes, asking what we can do to help, if she can get word to us to let us know she's okay.

The thought terrifies me that she's being treated like a criminal over something she has no power over—no more so than someone with brown hair or green eyes.

"You know it was originally police barracks before the war," says René.

"What was?" asks Isabelle.

"Drancy," he replies. With that, she bursts into tears. René's face pulls into a grimace, and he coughs out an apology as he pats her arm.

I widen my eyes at him and take her in my arms as she cries into my blouse. He exits the room very quickly, leaving us alone.

"It's my fault," she mumbles.

"Don't be daft," I say, stroking the length of her hair.

She hiccups on a sob. "She was the closest I had to a sister. You're like my family."

An ache builds in my chest. It's worse, not knowing if or when we might see her again.

"And why do you think she was doing all of this?" I ask.

She pulls back, embarrassed by the wet patch her tears have left on my blouse. I wave it off and pass her my hankie. "For the same reason as us?"

"Yes. For a free France. A free Europe."

"Do you think if they were to find out who she was, who she was helping…she'd use her capsule?"

I sit down, caught off guard by her question. "Honestly, I don't know." The thought hangs in the air.

"I wouldn't be able to survive interrogation. You hear awful rumours of what they do. Especially to women. I wouldn't be able to handle that," she says, her usually sun-kissed face taking on a pale tone.

Taking her hand, I squeeze it hard between my fingers. "If you ever find yourself in a position where you know there's no other way out, you use the capsule. Do you hear me?"

The thought of Isabelle—the youngest and sweetest of us all—being at the mercy of monsters is something I couldn't bear.

I think if Sylvette had no choice, and it was there, she'd use the cyanide. She is the most tenacious person I have ever met. She wouldn't give them the satisfaction of breaking her. But I pray it won't ever come to that and she can serve out her time in the detention camp with her family until this ghastly war is over.

~

Days turn into weeks.

One day, we receive a postcard from Sylvette. It's short, much shorter than I would've liked, but she's okay and if we can send her another food parcel, she would be grateful. That's all it says.

Reuben eyes it suspiciously. "What? It's her handwriting," I say, agitated by the way he is studying it.

"Yes, but I think there's more," he replies, holding it up to the light.

I take it off of him and study the piece of card, and that's when I see the corner. It appears tampered. I ask him to grab my manicure set, and carefully, I pull back the edge. He's right. Inside, there's more.

I don't know how long we have.

We're to be relocated in the coming days.

Destination unknown.

BE CAREFUL.

"Relocated?"

"I need to see if there is any way of us getting someone to try and bribe the guards for more information," Reuben says, studying her postcard. Clearly the inside was meant for us; the outside to get past the guards.

It all makes sense now why the Germans were so intent on setting out the ordinance in September, forcing Jewish citizens to register their information at a police station. They could then go ahead with a mass round-up. The resistance tried to warn some of the Jews, and somehow, some managed to get away or hid with their neighbours.

And now they've rounded them up like cattle.

The thousands arrested in Paris have been confined to the Vélodrome d'Hiver. We've heard of only a few doctors and nurses being allowed to visit, and anyone caught trying to escape have been shot. They are only allowing the Red Cross to take them food and water. From the numbers, I don't know how long that will sustain them.

They've already been there for five days, all their rights wavered. And just like Sylvette's last correspondence, there's rumours of transport and them being moved to internment camps, too.

"I don't understand why the police are complicit," René says, his voice full of anger.

"Apparently, they are all foreign Jews or something like that."

René raises his arms and drops them back to his sides, clearly as bewildered as we are.

CHAPTER 42

Since the roundup, everything has become dire. The resistance is becoming more restless, and we are ramping up our efforts.

I'm exhausted from the worry of it all. Reuben barely stops. I've never seen someone so determined to make a difference. At night, I'm restless, my sleep sporadic. And when I do finally succumb to it, the nightmares are vivid tendrils, dragging me into my version of hell:

Reuben being ripped away from me. Or the face of the soldier I shot through the chest. Other times, it's Evie and Lawry cowering in a basement, Sami Junior crying as they wait out an air raid. Then always, just as I'm about to wake up, their shelter explodes into millions of fragments and they all evaporate before my eyes.

Sometimes, Reuben will be the one to pull me out of them. But the worst ones are when I wake, paralysed with fear, unable to separate my dreams from reality.

I know my time here is becoming more compromised and I may be ordered somewhere else or to return home, but how can I even consider this when there is still so much for me to do here?

I catch Reuben watching me as I tend to the stables or the fields. When we're both here, he's never far away. I've become accustomed to his presence. I do not recall what it was like before we met. He was always meant to be in my life—I know that now. The worst thought is if the war had never happened, would I still have met him? Deep down, would I have always felt this thread of tiny disconnect where something was always missing but unable to pin what it was?

Josette has become weary of late. Sylvette being detained seemed to snuff out a fire she always carried. I know Reuben sees it, too—he doesn't miss much—but how do we possibly make this right? We can't get to her, it's near on impossible. All we can do is hope she can wait it out, that good will prevail.

The SS is a reckoning. They loiter around villages and towns, scoping out civilians and businesses, looking for a way to infiltrate our network.

René had a close shave during a meeting in the local church; a man of the cloth doesn't even deter them from throwing their weight around. They beat an older man in the street, and we don't even know why. Not that there should ever be a reason, but what was it that he had done to deserve such hatefulness?

I spin the ring on my finger and notice the tan line. I recall seeing a similar one on Lawry's finger. This is the first time the thought doesn't become overbearing. My broken heart has been slowly mending. Sometimes, I wish this wasn't all just a ruse, that the ring I wear didn't belong to his late wife. I feel like I am cheapening her memory.

On occasion, Reuben will talk about her, which brings on his rare smiles. I remember when he told me he likes to speak about her, and I wonder if it's easier to do so with me because I never knew her. He doesn't tell me she was the love of his life or anything overly sentimental; his recollection of their time together is wistful.

I'm broken from my thoughts when I hear a commotion of

voices and rush back towards the house, Vella not far behind. I don't know what's going on; there are three people I have never seen before and one appears to be hurt.

"Quick, down to the basement," orders Reuben.

I follow, bewildered, the man grunting from the pain as the other two hold him up between them.

"Grab the medical box," says Reuben.

I do as I'm told, and they lay the man onto a pallet. "What happened?" I ask.

The man grabs my ankle. "Am I dying? Are you an angel?"

I almost laugh but manage to restrain myself as I look to the other two men.

"I'm Claude, this is Vince," says one man, pointing to himself and the man next to him.

"Ana," I reply.

"Friends of mine, from the Resistance," says Reuben, as he rips open the man's shirt. I smell it before I see the pool of blood in the centre of his stomach.

I immediately fall to my knees and offer my help to Reuben. I know basic first aid, but the sight of blood makes my pulse race and my palms sweat.

"Through and through," he says.

"He was in hiding, but word got out they were searching properties, so he had to leave. He was meeting with us when he was shot. I don't know how they didn't catch up with him."

The man who's bleeding continues to slip in and out of consciousness.

"What's your name?" I ask him and take hold of his hand.

"Samuel," he replies. His face holds a sheen of sweat, his eyes struggling to focus.

I swallow down roughly, and my nose twitches. "One of my closest friends is called Samuel," I say, my voice slightly choked. I clear my throat.

His eyes stay on mine, and his panic recedes a fraction.

"He has a son, Sami Junior, looks just like him."

His hand squeezes mine. "My wife is with child," he says, gritting his teeth.

My eyes roam to Reuben who nods at me and continues with what he's doing.

"What do you want?" I ask. "A boy or a girl?"

His smile widens. "A girl, so she looks like my wife, but as long as the baby is strong and healthy, I'll be happy."

"What's your wife's name?"

I keep eye contact with him while he speaks. "Ruth."

"That's a beautiful name."

He nods his head, and his eyes shine a little. They flutter closed, and I worry he may fall asleep, so, I continue. "What about names for the baby?"

He squints his eyes open, lets out a chortled laugh, and then coughs, the pain evident. "If it's a girl, I get to name her. I like Sara, it means Princess."

"And if it's a boy, who gets to name him? Your wife?"

I look to the other men who are busy helping Reuben.

"Yes, she wants David."

I wipe his brow. "And what does David mean?"

"Beloved—" his eyes flutter closed. I squeeze his hand firmly in mine.

"Come on, aren't you going to tell me the meaning of yours and Ruth's names?"

Licking his cracked lips, he barely nods.

"Mine means 'God has heard' and Ruth's, 'friendship'."

My chest tightens. I dare not tell him how my Samuel has passed, but I feel he was sent to us for a reason, and I refuse to give up on him.

When the doctor arrives, he confirms the bullet missed any major organs. If his fever breaks, he'll likely make a full recovery but the next day will be critical. I only leave his side to relieve myself, and even then, there's no argument from Reuben. If it were my Samuel and he had lived, I'd want someone to stay by his side and nurse him through.

CHAPTER 43

Later, we hear those confined to the Velodrome were moved to several internment camps—some to Drancy. The conditions in the drome were appalling. The glass roof was painted blue to deter bombings. But that made it three times as hot inside. Some tried to escape but were shot. It's been heard some couldn't bear it and ended their own lives.

There was only one working tap. From the ten toilets available, they only had access to five—the other ones had windows, so those were closed off. The ones available were backed up and became unusable. The Red Cross passed this to a Secret Agent who fed it back to London.

I can't even begin to imagine those horrors, and I wonder what London will do. Will they send in more agents?

The situation has become precarious. Even in parts of France that aren't occupied, they targeted Jewish civilians and Gipsies—categorising them as undesirables. What does that mean?

It's almost two days until Samuel's fever breaks, and he comes through the worst of it. Having him here is a risk, but it's only until he is well enough to be moved.

"How are you feeling?" I ask, helping him to get comfortable so he can eat some of Josette's broth.

"Better, thank you."

"What happened? How did you get shot?"

"I was informed the police were doing a mass roundup of Jews. I'm Jewish," he says, almost ashamed to admit it.

"I thought you might be. Your name is Jewish," I reply with a warm smile, letting him know he has nothing to be ashamed of.

He smiles back. "My friends took me in, but it wasn't safe having me there." He winces slightly and adjusts himself. "So, I left, and when I refused to stop at a checkpoint, I was shot."

"You were lucky you had help," I reply.

He nods. "I know."

"Where will you go once you're well enough to travel?" I pass him the bowl and spoon, which he holds under his chin.

"To join my wife and her mother. They left on a ship to America. We have family over there. Once I have my papers, I can join them."

I nod and let him eat. I am hoping more than anything he finds his way back to them.

～

It's five days before he's well enough to leave. Claude and Vince arrive after dusk to help transport him to his next rendezvous point.

"Thank you for everything," he says as he pulls me in for a hug.

"You're welcome. Stay safe."

Josette hands him a food bundle and pats his cheek affectionately.

He tries to offer Reuben money, but he refuses.

"You'll need it for your new life in America," he says, no room for argument.

"I'll never be able to repay you," he replies.

"It's only what you would have done if the roles were reversed," he says.

We wave them goodbye and Josette has a newfound spring in her step. Maybe it's because in a time where she was unable to help Sylvette, at least we were able to help Samuel.

Reuben grabs a blanket from inside and wraps us beneath the thick wool as we stare up at the night sky. The moon is full, and the sky is littered with stars. He points out the North Star and constellations—some I think he makes up. But I don't rebuke. I enjoy the sound of his voice.

"You miss Samuel, your friend that died?" he asks, his lips brushing against my ear.

"I do, very much," I say, and look over my shoulder. "I miss the life I used to know."

He kisses my neck just below my ear.

"I feel like I lost three people, not one," I say, and it feels good to say it out loud.

His tongue darts out, causing my thighs to clench.

"I can't imagine seeing the woman I love with another man," he says, heat from his lips warming my skin.

"Evie did what she had to do."

"And now she's with Luis?" he asks, but he knows this already.

I can't hide my giggle. "Lawrence—Lawry, not Luis."

I see the corner of his mouth raise. He knows perfectly well what his name is. "You still miss him?" he asks, curling a strand of my hair around his finger.

"Of course, I miss them all."

I don't know if he specifically meant Lawry or Samuel, but my answer is the truth. I miss them all.

"I know you once said Josette would've liked grandchildren. But did you want them?"

He tenses behind me. Maybe I've overstepped, but he replies

anyway. "She was pregnant once, but she lost the baby. But I wouldn't have wished a life for a child without a mother."

I turn in his lap, wrap my arms around his neck, then say the only thing I can. "I'm sorry. I know you'll make a wonderful father."

His face brightens at my words, and he pauses, seemingly contemplating my comment, but he doesn't reply. Instead, he stands and wraps his arms beneath my buttocks. "Come, let's try to get some rest."

From the way he's staring at me, I don't think we'll be doing much sleeping. Excitement shoots through me.

CHAPTER 44

Moving freely through town has become increasingly difficult. Patrols have increased over the past month. We've made a few trips since then, but they've been sporadic, so not to arouse suspicion.

"I don't have a good feeling about this," Reuben says, reaching for my hand.

"Me either," I reply.

My stomach has been in knots all morning, and I don't know why. "You still want me to get the parcel?" I ask as his finger lightly rubs over the band on my finger.

"We have to try," he says. Leaning over in the cab of the truck, he kisses me softly.

I run my fingers through his thick, caramel hair. It's longer than when I first met him and curls just at the ends.

"Just be careful. If anything happens, you go to the safe house."

I nod. We've discussed this before. Only me, him, and Josette know about the other cottage.

I've also been storing the radio somewhere different after each transmission—just as an extra precaution since we have news of several sightings of insurgents being arrested or worse… falling off the grid completely.

I know as soon as we enter the café that something is wrong, but we'd seem suspicious if we turned around now and walked back out.

Reuben orders us each a coffee, and once we're seated, he takes hold of my hand and smiles. But it's forced. Our fingers linked, I take a quick survey of the room without lingering.

One of the officers who searched me sits in the far corner. His lips curve into a devilish smirk. My stomach rolls with unease.

I don't want to be here longer than we have to, so I excuse myself to use the restroom. I make a point to relieve myself as I train my eyes on the tile which lays perfectly in place, but it's the wrong way round. Even if whoever left something there was in a hurry, they managed to put it perfectly flush with the other tiles…the direction would have been correct, too.

I think it's a warning.

I still pull the hair grip from my bun and pop the tile up to peer at the small parcel. Immediately, I drop it back into place exactly as I found it.

Adjusting my lose hair, I take a deep breath and return to Reuben. He takes my hand under the table and squeezes. *Are you okay?* I squeeze back twice for *no*.

I reach over for the paper and accidentally (on purpose) knock over my coffee. It pools on the surface and runs off the table into my lap. I stand and quickly wipe with a serviette.

He rights the cup and apologises to the waiter who comes over to clean the table. "Let's get you home and cleaned up," he says.

I nod and apologise for the mess.

Reuben leads me out with his hand firm on the base of my back.

We step onto the cobbled sidewalk when we hear it. "Halt!"

We do—even if it's not intended for us, you never assume—and slowly, we turn to see if the order was for us. I clutch my bag tight to my body, knowing in the hidden compartment at the base is the parcel I wasn't able to swap over.

It's the same leery soldier as before. His eyes roam up and down the length of my body. A shiver rolls over me, and Reuben rubs my back once before dropping his hand.

But it's not him who is my leading cause for concern.

It's the soldier beside him and the insignia on his collar and sleeve—SS.

"Where are you going?"

The SS officer watches as the other soldier steps forward, waiting for a response.

"My wife spilt her coffee. We're going home so she can change."

"Papers?"

I fiddle inside my purse and produce mine. Reuben removes his from his wallet, and we pass them over. He takes his time to look them over before passing them to the SS officer.

He assesses them and then says, "search them both."

Internally, I recoil, the memory of his hands on me before bad enough, but the way he approaches like I'm his prey makes my skin crawl and the hair on the back of my neck to prickle.

Reuben stiffens beside me. I can sense the tension rolling off of him.

Don't do anything stupid.

The soldier reaches out for my purse, and then he searches the contents. Finding nothing of significance, he hands it to the SS officer who rummages through it.

"Arms up!"

I hold my arms out, and then his hands begin their search. His eyes are fixed on mine, and he's so close—too close. His hot breath slivers over me, reminding me of a snake I once saw at a reptile exhibit, and I can't control my shiver.

I can feel eyes all over me as he moves to my stomach, then he touches my buttocks, making a point to squeeze me once. I try to remain still. Every part of me wants to remove his hands from my body.

But when they move down my legs and then up and under my dress, my stomach rolls. Bile works its way up my throat. I swallow hard and try to breathe through my nose. His smell alone is repulsive.

He cups me where no other man has touched me but Reuben. I squeeze my eyes closed and retreat inside my head until his hands leave me.

I have the urge to throw up but refuse to give him the satisfaction.

He is rougher with Reuben as he searches him, and when he comes up empty, he takes a step back.

The SS officer tosses back my purse and our papers which land at my feet ungracefully. The other officer is about to say something when the earth vibrates, and his voice is drowned out by a mighty *boom*.

CHAPTER 45

Reuben acts fast, pushing us both the to the ground with such force, the air is knocked from my lungs.

He covers my body with his. An ear splintering explosion erupts. And the seconds that follow are silent.

I peer up from where I lay, a thick, smoking dust cloud filling the sky until it covers us. A hacking cough escapes me, and I struggle to catch my breath. My eyes water mercilessly.

I reach for my scarf and cover my mouth.

There is a commotion, and when I peer up, bullets are raining in the direction of the blast.

The man who had his hands on me is shot in the face. As he falls to the ground, his body turns enough for me to see half of his head blown off.

Soldiers assemble and launch an assault.

A man—not much older than Reuben—is dragged through rubble piled up in front of the shop, and slung at the feet of the SS officer, followed by another man and a woman.

They're forced to their knees. There is shouting.

The officer pulls out his sidearm, walks up to the woman,

and shoots. The man screams and launches himself towards him, but another soldier shoots him before he can do anything.

The remaining man, who they dragged out first, keeps his head cast down, waiting for his turn.

"Seize him," the SS officer says. His eyes assess the area for any other act of rebellion. Hissing and burning can be heard from the aftermath of the explosion.

Everything is now covered in a cloud of grey smog.

Reuben pulls me to my feet and runs his hands over my hair and my face. "Are you hurt?" he asks.

I don't have an answer because at this moment, the only thing I feel is numb.

He bends down, grabbing our ID and my purse and stuffs it into my hands. Then with one look in the direction of SS officer, he waits as if asking for permission to leave.

The SS turns his back and walks away. It's all the confirmation Reuben needs.

He grips me with an arm around my waist, and we make our way back to the truck. He says nothing until we are out of town and back on the road to the house.

I pick at the dirt from my dress, noticing the runs and holes in my stockings. My knees are grazed from the cobbled street. I reach down and slip them off and hold them over my knees to wipe the surface blood from larger gashes.

Reuben eyes me and then the road. "Are you all right?" he asks again.

"I'm fine," I reply.

"Did you get the package?" he asks.

I shake my head and turn to him. "No. It had been tampered with, so I left it."

"Are you certain?"

"Yes, whoever left it wanted me to know something wasn't right without giving themselves away."

He looks perplexed as he mulls this over in his head. "It's why we were stopped and searched," he says.

I shudder, crossing my arms.

"He got what he deserved for putting his hands on you." The way he says it riles me up.

"Since when am I your property?"

His head whips to mine, and he slams on the brakes, veering the car onto a grass verge.

I pull on the handle and leap from the truck, storming towards the direction of the house. His heavy footsteps are loud behind me. When his hand reaches for my shoulder, I swipe it away and turn on him, lashing out.

His eyes go wide, but he tries to grab me again. This time, I push him with enough force that he stumbles back.

I slap him hard across the face. I am so angry. But not with him. I don't even know who I am in this moment.

He stands in shock as I turn and start running, pumping my arms with as much energy as I can muster, digging my feet into the ground as I run into the lavender. Purple flashes past me.

My heart races so fiercely, I don't hear him run up beside me, cutting off my path.

I plough hard into his chest, and he takes the brunt of my weight as we fall to the ground. I scramble to get up, but he has hold of me—my back to his chest—his heavy breathing in my ear matching mine.

I try again, but his arms remain solidly wrapped around my upper body, and I lose my will to try again. He's not the one who I should be fighting in the first place.

A chortled sound works its way up my throat as a strangled sob escapes me.

His arms ease off their grip, and he turns me into his chest, holding my head under his palm, rocking us. "Sshhh, it's okay," he breathes into my ear. "We're okay."

He knows—how close we came to being caught, how close

we were from being killed in a crossfire. And worst of all, how that man's hands were over my body.

I reach for his face and pull it to mine. My lips crash against him, teeth knocking, but I don't care as he plunges his tongue into my mouth.

I scramble for his trousers, but his hand stops me. He links his fingers with mine, almost painfully, and his mouth doesn't leave mine as he slows down our kiss.

"I want you," he says, breathlessly, when we come up for air. "But not like this." I hear the hurt in his voice. "Not out of anger," he says.

He wipes my face, eyes boring into mine. "I'm glad he's dead. Because no matter what you may think, *you're mine*. And I would have hunted him down and killed him myself if it meant him never laying eyes on you again."

I feel the tension in his body, and I hear the truth in his words. He would have done it. I grab hold of Reuben's shirt in my fist. "I just want to forget," I tell him.

Reuben leans down and kisses me slowly. His hands roam over my back, down to the hem of my dress, trembling when they caress the bare skin on the back of thighs. His lips mould with mine—it's slow and sensual.

But he takes it no further. Instead, he holds me until my breathing settles and my anger dissipates.

CHAPTER 46

After the sun sets and the house falls quiet, I wrap a blanket over my shoulders and step outside. I stare up at the moon, the sky bright with stars. I've never seen them look as beautiful as they do here.

The smell of firewood mixed with pine needles and fresh hay floats over me. The door behind me creaks as Josette steps out.

"What is it dear? Is something wrong?" she asks, saddling up beside me.

I rock on my heels and let out a sigh. "Sometimes I forget who I am," I say.

She nudges me, walks over to the bench, and sits, waiting for me to join her. "What do you mean?"

I shake my head, wondering how to explain it. "Before I came here, I thought I knew who I was. What I wanted. I never wanted any of this," I say, waving my hand out in front of me, struggling to find the right words.

She pats my knee, her hand knotted at the knuckles from working with them all these years. "It's taken me a lifetime, and I wonder if we ever truly know who we are. When my Celine passed, I thought the part of me that was her mother died, too.

But it didn't. My need to nurture, protect, to care—those feelings never went away."

She reaches for my hands and takes them in hers. "And as for what you want and what you need…they are two different things entirely. You sparked something in Reuben when you arrived. You breathed life back into him, and whether you see it or not, you two need each other."

I want to deny this, but with Reuben it's a need, a necessity. He pays attention and he knows me. But my life's in England. This is a cover, a ploy. I have a job to do and what happens after the war if we both make it out alive? What happens then?

"Maybe, but my life isn't here—" I don't finish my next sentence because out of the shadows steps Reuben. He walks past us towards the barn. Josette lets go and stands up, her knees cracking with the effort.

"Go on. Go to him," she says.

I follow in his wake and make my way into the basement adorned with lanterns. He's working on something in the far corner. His face is cold, impassive. I approach him, and his eyes rise to mine.

"I don't know what you heard, but it's not what you think," I say gently.

"I heard enough. But this right here *is* my life." His hand circles the room.

"I know and my life is back in England—"

He cuts me off. "You don't owe me an explanation. It doesn't change anything," he says. I don't know what he means by this and he doesn't give me a chance to find out. "I think it's worth finding out what happened today in town, don't you?"

I nod. He's right, I need to check and see what's been reported.

When I finally make contact, I'm informed that two operatives are unaccounted for and there's definitely an informant. It's why I am given a date and a time for a rendezvous with a new source.

And I'm to go alone.

Reuben doesn't like this any more than I, but what can I do? They're my orders. We receive some other intel about a factory that we need to pass on, but other than that, there's not much else to report.

I turn off the radio and pack it away, hiding the parts separately.

It's quiet at supper and it's not long before everyone retires for the evening. Vella follows me like she does every night to sleep on the floor at the foot of my bed on an old blanket.

I leave my door ajar for Reuben, but wonder if this will be the first time he won't use it. I'm exhausted from the events of today. I try to hang on in the hopes he will come, but by the time I succumb to sleep, he doesn't.

Something warm and heavy fills the mattress beside me, and I roll over in a sleep induced haze, reaching into the darkness, wrapping my arm over Reubens waist. When I wake later, it's still dark, but the sound of a steady heartbeat beneath my ear lets me know I wasn't dreaming—he came to me.

I sigh in relief and kiss his chest beside my hand, his soft hair so familiar to the touch. His grip on me tightens.

For the first time in my life, I realise a home isn't a *place* so much as the *people* in it. And right in this moment, I know my home is right here, in the arms of Reuben.

CHAPTER 47

I stand with my back to Reuben's chest, his chin resting over my shoulder, taking in the sight before us. I smell the dew-covered lawn as roosters call out to the rising sun. Oranges, reds and pinks make waves in the sky. It's the most beautiful sunrise I've seen, each one spectacular but different in their own right.

And for a brief moment, I allow myself to imagine a life without war. I'm Reuben's and he is mine—together.

I turn in his arms, searching his face. He doesn't want me to go today, but he respects me enough to know this is why I am here.

"If anything happens, you make your way to the cottage. I'll come to you."

I nod and rest my cheek against his chest. *Thump, thump, thump, thump* it beats in sync with mine. He lets me stay as I am, content in his arms, as the farm comes to life and a tractor starts up in the distance.

I peer up, the light illuminating his eyes as he leans down to kiss me slowly. I grip his shirt in my hands, pulling him closer, needing to feel all of him against me. He picks me up, and I wrap my legs around his waist as he walks us back into the house and to my room, not once removing his lips from mine.

~

I'm seated at a table, and I place my purse beside me. It's the first time since arriving in France that I've needed to dress up. When Reuben saw me with my lips painted and blush on my cheeks, I knew he didn't want to let me go. I'm wearing my one pair of silk stockings and a pair of earrings Josette gave to me.

I remove my gloves and take a sip of water, watching over the crowd. My hand goes to my necklace where I finger it with my thumb and forefinger. Just as I'm placing my glass down, someone leans into my ear.

"You got your gift then?"

A choked sound escapes me, thankfully hidden in the sea of people, and I hold my breath until he sits beside me—Lawry.

I can't find my tongue and words fail me. He holds out his hand, and I place mine in his. The table to our right is full, and their laughter is too loud for us to talk.

He stands. "Dance?" he asks (to my surprise) in perfect French.

I nod, and he leads us onto the dance floor where he pulls me into his body. "Breathe," he whispers in English.

I do.

"I was worried you might not have been able to come." His lips graze my ear, and my stomach jerks at the touch.

I pull back slightly. "What on earth are you doing here?"

"I have an assignment, and then you're coming back with me," he whispers.

"But you're a pilot," I reply, my eyes scanning those around us.

"Amongst other things," he says.

My heart is beating faster than it should, and my body sways into him even though I keep trying to leave a small space between us. We dance for another song until old feelings surface and begin to engulf me.

I stop dancing.

He brings my hand to his mouth and kisses my knuckles. His lips, although warm, are nothing like Reuben's, and I pull it free and walk back to our table. The other patrons have now left; we are obscured in the corner of the room.

"We received your letters," he says. The way he says *we* hurts.

He reaches up and wipes away my tears with the pad of his thumb. The gesture makes me want to break down even more.

"Now is not the time," I say, trying to compose myself.

"Who knows if we'll get the chance again," he replies.

He's right. I ran when they were married and again after Sami was born. And yet I'm still not ready for this conversation.

It's becoming increasingly claustrophobic in here as more people arrive, and I find myself looking out of the corner of my eye. I'm never truly able to let my guard down.

"Can we possibly do this somewhere else?" I ask.

He nods. Standing, he offers me his hand. I snatch up my gloves and purse and entwine my fingers with his. His hands are so much softer than Reuben's.

We weave our way through the bodies and out into the street. It takes a moment for my eyes to adjust—the moon, though full, is hidden behind a blanket of clouds.

"Come, this way," he says, holding onto my hand.

We pass some people and then turn onto a side street. It's empty and the echo of my shoes rebound off of the stone brick walls.

But then I notice the sound of other footsteps, maybe a second or two before Lawry. His hand tightens and he veers us down another street, moving faster with me matching his footsteps.

"I think we're being followed," he whispers.

The only way to find out for sure is to either turn around and see or dart down the next alley we come across. We dart down the alley.

It's a dead end.

He puts his arm in front of my waist and pushes our backs against the wall as we wait to see if whoever was behind us follows. I hear the sound of feet growing closer. A shadow falls over the entrance of the alley.

Lawry begins to push me with his shoulder, and we hug the wall, moving deeper into the darkness.

"I just want your money," calls a male voice.

Something hits the back of my legs, causing me to stumble, and I fall onto my rear end. Lawry turns to his side, crouching down to pull me to my feet.

Someone grabs hold of his shoulder. He immediately smacks the hand away and kicks out with his leg, still half crouching.

The figure falls but quickly scrambles back to his feet. The moon makes a break in the clouds; the glint of something silver catches my eye—a knife. I gasp and jump to my feet.

He slashes it towards Lawry with a *whoosh* and slices his arm before Lawry knocks it out of his hand.

I reach up the hem of my dress to my suspenders for my handgun. Lawry's back is to me. I can't see well enough to shoot, and I don't want to draw attention to ourselves.

The man punches Lawry, and he goes down.

"Stop, or I'll shoot," I say, taking my stance.

He lunges towards me, and I'm back in the woods. Before me is the face of the soldier I shot. My finger hesitates on the trigger just long enough for him to knock the gun from my hand and grab my wrist.

I have to think fast.

Forcing his thumb upwards, I manage to break his grip. But as I do, he swings his other arm into my side, and I draw in a sharp breath from his punch. I kick him hard in the groin. Grunting, he doubles over, and I knee him in the face, watching as he goes down and pulls himself into a foetal position.

Another figure comes rushing into the alley. I see Lawry rouse and go for my gun just as his face comes into view.

"No," I scream.

Reuben dives towards Lawry. There's a scuffle. I hear a crunch as knuckles connect with flesh and I rush to the heap where their bodies rolling around.

"Reuben!" I screech. "It's Lawrence."

He's on top of him about to punch him in the face. I grab his shoulder to stall him, but he shrugs me off.

I stumble back, winded.

I grab my side, a searing pain shooting through me. I claw at my side, something foreign sticking out—the handle of a knife.

I drop to my knees.

Reuben's head swings towards me. He jumps up and rushes to me.

"Don't—" Lawry shouts in English, but it's too late.

My fingers wrap around the handle, and I pull it free.

CHAPTER 48

"Come on. You need to stay awake."

The voice is distant.

A sting to my face rouses me. I draw in a deep breath. Crouching over me is Reuben, his eyebrows drawn into a V, face ridden with worry. And then I'm pulled into his arms.

"She needs a doctor." Why can I hear Lawry?

It comes back to me and I fumble, push at his hand.

"Stop it," he says, his hand pressed against my side.

And then I'm floating or flying. No...I'm in Reuben's arms. He says something over his shoulder, his breathing heavy.

I open my eyes...only this time, it's Lawry's face I see.

"Keep pressure on it," Reuben grunts out.

"What do you think I'm doing?" he replies, angry. "Just hurry."

Reuben says something under his breath, some kind of profanity aimed at Lawry. But I'm too sluggish now to even care.

"Annalise Rose, you open your eyes. Do you hear me?" Lawry says.

I do and it's the only time I have ever seen fear in his. It takes all my strength to stay awake. I begin to shiver.

He's looking over his shoulder saying something, and then something heavy covers me. It's warm and smells of Reuben.

"Just hold on, we're almost there," Reuben calls out.

I slip under, and when my eyes open, I'm staring up at a sky littered with stars. And then Reuben's eyes replace them, and I'm not sure which is more beautiful.

A dark pull grabs me.

I plummet into a pit of darkness.

My head thumps with shooting pain as I'm pulled from sleep by raised voices. "As soon as you realised you were being followed, you should have gotten her out of there," Reuben says, frustrated.

"What do you think I was trying to do? It's convenient how you just show up out of nowhere," replies Lawry, suspicion lining his voice.

"I wasn't going to let her meet a new source on her own. Of course, I followed her!" he exclaims.

"And a lot of good that did her," Lawry throws back.

A grunt followed by a loud thump forces me to open my eyes. Reuben has Lawry by the collar of his shirt, slammed up against a wall.

"Stop," I say, the words weak.

Lawry shoves at Reuben, and his hands lose their grip.

"I said stop, goddamn it," I force out and attempt to push myself up. I lose my breath and slump back down—a hand on my shoulder.

"Easy, you've just had stitches." It's a voice I don't recognise.

Lawry rushes over and takes hold of my hand, but my eyes seek out Reuben, his eyes on Lawry.

"Where am I?" I croak out.

Reuben comes over to my other side and wipes the hair from my brow. "My cousin, Franc's. He's a vet."

The stranger speaks again. "Don't worry, I know enough about the human anatomy," he says.

"You should have gotten yourself out of there," Lawry says. "You were stabbed because of me."

"No, it wasn't your fault," I say.

I search out Reuben again. He seems disappointed with me, and my heart squeezes uncomfortably in my chest. "Rest, I need to sort out getting us out of here. I can't risk anyone else getting caught up in this," he says. He nods in the direction of the door and Lawry lets go of my hand and follows him out.

"I've given you some plasma and penicillin, but you'll need to be careful until the stitches come out."

I nod.

He takes hold of my wrist between his thumb and forefinger. "You were lucky," he says.

Reuben must have lied about how much being shot hurt if this is what a stab wound is like.

Franc holds up a syringe; I cringe. "What's that?"

"Pain relief. It's not much, but it should make your journey from here more bearable. If it weren't for the safety of my family, I wouldn't let you leave until tomorrow but…"

"I understand. Thank you for helping me."

"I see now why Reuben is so taken with you."

His comment takes me off guard. "What do you mean?"

"The only other time I've ever seen him like this was when my cousin died."

"And by cousin you mean…Celine, his wife?"

He nods, and I flinch when the pinch from the needle goes into my arm.

Reuben returns, ending my conversation with Franc. He thanks him and shakes his hand. "I'm sorry, but we need to leave. I'll have to carry you to the truck."

He puts one arm under my back, the other under my knees. I grit my teeth to hold back from yelping.

"I know you lied to me," I say, hissing through my teeth.

"When?"

"After I shot you. You told me it didn't hurt that badly. But if this is anything to go by, I don't believe you were telling the truth."

His lip raises, and I think he's going to smile, but it drops into a firm line. "That was a graze, not a stab wound. You should have run."

Not him, too. "I did have hand-to-hand combat training, you know," I say defiantly.

Reuben shakes his head. "But you still got hurt," he replies.

"I'm sorry," I say and reach for his cheek.

He dips his head and gives me a hard, firm kiss and pulls away. I burrow into his chest. My body is heavy and aching.

~

I'm drowsy in the truck, slipping in and out of sleep but jerk awake every time the wheels hit a pothole. When I next open my eyes, Lawry's stare back at me. He has me in his arms. I try to look over his shoulder. I twist and turn, a strangled sound escaping me.

"Where's Reuben?"

"Hiding the truck, calm down," he says.

He moves us inside, and I know just from the smell, we're at the cottage.

I'm taken into the bedroom and carefully laid down on the bed. He reaches into a bag and pulls out a syringe, and I wait for the pinch. But it's hardly noticeable.

He leans down, his lips cover mine, and I gasp. They feel familiar, yet strange and unwelcome.

He pulls back, and I can't even look him in the eye. I hear a door close and the sound of footsteps. Straining to peer over his arm, I see Reuben and I can breathe.

Lawry scans between Reuben and me as though he's putting pieces of a puzzle together. And then he steps back, like he's just taken a physical blow.

He turns and begins to walk away. "Wait," I call out, but he ignores me.

Reuben remains as Lawry shoulders his way past him and out of the room.

I don't know what to think or feel in this moment. Reuben raises his eyebrows—a silent question—one I can't provide an answer to. I turn my face away. It's too much to comprehend—having my past and my present collide. I squeeze my eyes tight, willing the exhaustion and drugs to take me under.

CHAPTER 49

A weight in my bladder pulls me from my slumber. I need to go so badly, it's painful. I sit up, careful as I do, and lower my feet to the cold, wooden floor. It creaks under the pressure as I steady myself, hand on my side.

"Where are you going?"

My heart hits my chest. I almost stumble back on the bed but Reuben catches my elbow.

"What the hell?" I slap his hands away.

"Where do you think you're going?" His voice is low, almost a growl.

I grit my teeth. "To relieve myself, if you must know."

I take a step forward.

"Let me carry you."

Shaking my head, I continue my slow progress, but my bladder protests uncomfortably. "Fine." I don't have the energy to fight him.

He comes beside me and swoops me into his arms, bridal style. I let out a rushed breath and squeeze my eyes closed.

"Sorry," he whispers.

Lawry is asleep on the sofa, one bare leg over the top of the blanket, and I cast my eyes away.

It takes some coaxing for Reuben to let me take care of business alone. I sigh with relief, and once I'm done, I take stock of myself in the mirror.

There's a tap on the other side of the door. I see from the reflection in the mirror Reuben enter, closing it behind him, deciding he had waited long enough.

"What is it?" he asks, coming up behind me. "Are you in pain?"

"Not so much. I just look a mess."

His lips graze the top of my ear. A small flutter and a hot flush roll over me. "That's not what I see."

My breathing accelerates. "No?" I ask and continue to watch him watch me though the mirror.

"I see you. You're alive, and I've never seen a more beautiful sight."

His lips caress my throat. I lean into his body, tilting my head as he lowers his mouth to mine and kisses me. I don't kick up a fuss when he carries me back to the room and avoid looking at the sofa as we pass.

Once I'm in bed and I've had some water, I try to get comfortable. Reuben pulls over a chair and sits beside me. "So, he's the one?" Reuben asks.

I shake my head. "No, he *was* the one."

"Was?"

"Yes," I reply, staring up at the ceiling.

"Does *he* know that?"

I shrug a non-comital response and squeeze my eyes closed. His fingers wrap around mine, his calloused palms welcome. His question floats in the space between us. *Does he know that?*

CHAPTER 50

Reuben remained in the chair all night and most of the following day. I only woke to relieve myself and to drink. A waft of hot soup fills my nose, and I go to stretch but catch myself in time, the pain still profound. Slowly, I sit up.

Lawry comes in, carrying a tray with a steaming bowl of soup and some bread. "I never knew you could cook."

He smiles, but it doesn't quite meet his eyes. "It was the only thing Evie could keep down when we first moved in together."

Suddenly, I'm not so hungry.

"Sorry," he replies, sitting in the chair Reuben vacated to let Josette know what was going on.

"How are they?"

This time, his smile is undeniably full. "They're well. Sami is getting so big already," he replies. He adjusts my pillow behind my back and then lays the tray on my lap. "Eat."

I eye the soup and bring the spoon to my mouth to take a small sip.

"As soon as you're healed, I want you to come home."

I shake my head, dropping the spoon into the bowl. "No."

"It's not safe. Isn't this proof enough?" he asks, waving towards my stomach.

"You have no idea," I grumble and clench my teeth, pain radiating through me. The tension is doing nothing for my wound.

"Sorry, please eat."

And I do. He picks up a bowl and joins me, and I'm grateful for the quiet...other than the sound of us eating and the woods alive outside the window.

∽

Lawry doesn't push me on the subject of leaving over the next couple of days. But being trapped in a house with my past and present is awkward, the air stagnant. They continue to eye each other with silent hostility, as if they each have a claim over me. Is this my version of living in purgatory?

I've had enough and told Reuben I want to return to the house tomorrow. He agreed. Lawry needs to check-in and get back on track with his assignment.

"What is it?" I ask Lawry. He's pacing, the enclosed space becoming claustrophobic.

"What's going on, Ana?"

I shake my head, confused. "What do you mean?"

"You and him."

"It's complicated," I say, knowing the only complication is Lawry and me.

He walks up and takes hold my shoulders. "Am I losing you?"

How do I even begin to answer that? Why couldn't he accept my letter and let that be the end of it, the end of us?

"I'll do anything. Just tell me what you want me to do." His eyes are imploring.

"It's too late," I say. "I wanted you to choose me."

His eyes widen, and then he drops his hands and takes a step back as though I slapped him. "I didn't have any other choice," he replies, his voice hurt.

I shake my head. "Someone once told me there's always a choice."

His jaw ticks. A deep-set frown line appears between his eyebrows. "But that was our choice, Ana. We discussed it. We made a choice together."

I stare at him. His shoulders slump in a weird kind of surrender, acceptance even.

"Did we?" I ask, stepping closer, taking his hands in mine. "I don't think when it comes to love we have a choice," I reply, imploring him with my eyes.

"What do you mean?"

I drop his hands, shake my head, and turn away. He cups the back of my shoulders and coaxes me to look at him. "I kept my promise to you, Ana. I've been true to you, to us."

I can't stem my tears. My guilt consumes me in quicksand.

"Damn it, Ana. You're in love with him?" he whisper-shouts.

I shake my head, about to say no, but my lips betray me. "Yes."

And it's as much a revelation to me as it is to him.

I am.

I'm in love with Reuben.

He drops his hands and takes a step back, rubbing his palm over his face. "And what about him? Does he love *you*?"

I shrug. He cares about me, but is it love?

"It's infatuation, Ana."

I've never heard so much venom in his words before. I clench my fists, my nails digging into my palms. It's all I can do to keep from slapping him. "What's that supposed to mean?"

He crowds me. "I've seen the way you watch one another. I know he sneaks into your room when you think I'm asleep. The roaming eyes, the silent want." I've never seen him like this before, his jealously palpable.

"And so what? What did you think would happen? Did you honestly expect me to—what? Be your mistress?" I shout.

It's a low blow, my words sharp, cutting. I know I'm not being fair to him, but he's not being reasonable to me either. His nostrils flare with his ragged intake of air. I regret my words, seeing the pain they caused.

I reach out my hands to him, but he pulls away. I don't know what to do with myself. The room is charged, stifling. Wind rushes against the wood and rain trails down the roof.

He stops abruptly, turns back to me. His hands grab either side of my face. My hands instantly cover his, trembling, and then his lips are on mine.

CHAPTER 51

I wanted this—him—for so long. I kiss him back, taken to a place and a time when he was my everything.

But I'm not that girl anymore.

I'm not the girl he fell in love with.

Pushing on his chest, I turn my face to the side. "Stop."

But his lips find mine again, and this time I don't reciprocate. I feel the pressure ease off, and I know he's about to stop.

When he's yanked away from me with enough force, I stagger, almost falling over myself. A sharp, shooting pain erupts up my side.

Lawry is on his feet and rushes Reuben, punching him square in the face. Reuben stumbles but recovers quickly and retaliates with an uppercut and then a punch in the side of the jaw.

That's it, I've had enough. I throw myself between them, ignoring the fact my stitches may not withstand the sudden movement.

They rear back quick enough.

"She said, *stop*, goddamn it!" Reuben seethes, wiping his nose with his thumb, dripping claret on his shirt.

"It's none of your goddamn business."

I keep between them. Lawry's chest protrudes like a damn cockerel.

"Yes, she *is* my business!"

"Hardly. You don't even know her."

I shove Reuben's chest.

"Don't I?" He stares at me when he says, "you made your choice, and it wasn't her!"

I confided in him, and now he's using it as a weapon. "You've gone too far," I say, turning my back on him.

He storms off. The sound of the bathroom door slamming shut vibrates beneath my feet.

Lawry is in the kitchen, clutching the sink. I grab a cloth and run it under the faucet and bring it up to his chin. "Does it hurt?"

"Yes," he replies.

"Good."

His forehead creases at my lack of empathy, but right now, I'm beyond the point of wanting to appease him. "You say you love me, but it's not the same. Not anymore. I know you felt it… when we kissed. It wasn't right."

He looks like he's about to argue, but instead, he scans his knuckles. "That's what kills me…" He dips his head, looking me straight in the eye.

"Lawry, you need to let me go. I'm holding onto you, to the thought of us, by a frayed thread. Until we accept we aren't meant to be, my heart will continue breaking, and neither of us will be able to truly move on."

I've never seen him look so wounded, my words ones I never thought would pass my lips. The sound of something smashing draws my attention to the bathroom.

"You should go check on him."

His shoulders sag as he turns his back to me, and I panic. "Where are you going?"

"I just need to think. I need some air." He sounds defeated.

I nod as he opens the door. I can follow him and continue holding onto my past, or I can let go and live in the present.

I'm emotionally torn. But my body decides for me. I turn to the bathroom.

I enter without knocking. Closing it behind me, I take a deep breath as I face Reuben.

He's holding a flannel to his face, eyes cast down. I know he probably heard our whole exchange—the walls are thin.

I move toward him slowly, cautiously, and reach for the cloth he has gripped so tight, his knuckles bleeding. And without saying anything, I take my time cleaning him up. Thankfully, his nose isn't broken, just bruised like his ego. I remove fragments of glass from his knuckle from where he punched the mirror. His hand closes over mine, and my stomach flutters.

"Reuben, he would've stopped. You don't know him, he's a good man."

He closes his eyes and works his jaw. "Maybe, but he didn't stop quick enough."

"I can take care of myself." He raises his eyebrows almost to his hairline. "I cannot help it if trouble finds me," I reply, trying to ease the tension.

"He came for you, it's why he's here. Any fool can see that."

I shake my head. "It's partly why he's here, but it's a moot point."

I reach for his face, dabbing the last traces of dried blood. He takes hold of my wrist. "I don't doubt he loves you, Ana, but he sure as hell doesn't deserve you."

Groaning, I step away and lean on the edge of the bath. Reuben only knows a fraction of what my life was like before this. It's not fair for him to judge so harshly when he's biased.

"He's a good man, Reuben. We made promises to one another. And I was the one who broke my promise, not him. I'm not the victim. I gave myself to you."

He kneels in front of me and catches my chin between his

finger and thumb. Vibrant moss orbs hold my stare. "And why is that? He made a choice, Ana, and it wasn't you."

His words sting. Was it as simple as one choice? Or was it always fate?

"What and you choose *me*, do you? You don't even know me. Not really…"

Taking my hand, he pulls it to his chest, and the rapid beat of his heart vibrates against my palm.

"I know the things that matter. You might try and put on a façade, but I see you." His lips curve into a smile, his features warm.

I trail my finger along his jawline to his cheeks. He cups the back of my hand, leaning into my touch. My stomach comes to life with a flutter.

He brings his mouth to mine, and our lips move in sync. The kiss deepens, and my want for him increases—a throbbing ache between my legs.

I grab his hand and push it between my thighs. His fingers rub up against me in small, circular motions, but it's not enough. I reach for his crotch and undo his trousers.

His other hand tries to still mine, but when I wrap my fingers around his hard protruding arousal, he rumbles a sound of satisfaction. My thumb rubs over the wet tip. "Please," I whisper.

Breaking our kiss, he grabs a towel, throws it on the floor, and then folds another over three times. "Lay down," he orders, and I do.

A hot, pulsating need swarms low in my belly.

He pushes my dress up to my waist and slips off my knickers. Wrapping his hands around my ankles, he pushes my knees up until my feet are flat against the floor. Aware I am bare and open to him, I pulse with anticipation.

He peers up through thick lashes as he crawls towards my belly, raining a trail of kisses. My skin prickles until his lips brush against me and then his tongue darts inside.

I let out a cry of surprise and pleasure, pushing my head back into the makeshift pillow. His tongue is working in and out of me, slow and torturous.

"More," I say. I've never been vocal with him when we've been together, but I can't keep my mouth closed. "I need more," I breathe out, biting on my lip.

His tongue dips deeper, and he sucks, his finger joining in.

My back raises off the floor with a jerk. "Oh, my god."

The urge to clench my thighs around his head overwhelms me. My hand grabs a fistful of his hair, and I push his head closer, greedy for more.

He picks up speed, the sound of his tongue lapping up my arousal as it seeps between my buttocks. And then his teeth nip me. A sigh of a *yes* escapes my lips, the sensations building higher and higher. My head is thrashing from side to side.

My release comes hard and fast. The pulsing slows in soft, jerky waves. I'm out of breath, and yet Reuben was the one doing all the work.

I open my eyes and watch him move to his knees. Taking himself in his hand, he's never looked so big. He begins to pump his arousal. My hands reach out for him, my need for him still strong.

"I need you," I say.

He pulls his lower lip between his teeth, his breathing heavy, and nods, kneeling between my legs.

"I'll be gentle," he says, the words strained.

I feel the tip followed by his length and girth and let out a huff of satisfaction.

He holds his weight off of me, his hands either side of my head. I taste myself on his tongue when he kisses me.

Every thrust is slow and controlled. I stare between us and watch how perfectly we fit together. And then I'm coming undone again. I want to scream with pleasure. My hands are on his rear, pushing him into me harder, and I know it's an effort for him to continue going and keep his body from collapsing on top of mine.

I let out a strangled cry, and his hand moves to cover my mouth. He gives three more thrusts and shatters along with me.

He rolls over onto his back. My eyes follow and watch the rapid rise and fall of his chest. Fumbling for my hand, he links his fingers with mine.

CHAPTER 52

Once our breathing calms, Reuben takes a washcloth and cleans us both up, the act so intimate, my nose twitches with the urge to cry. Wiping my damp hair away from my face, he studies me. "What are you thinking?" he asks, pulling me into his lap.

I look away. My eyes train on the cracked mirror. "Are you sure you want to know?"

"I wouldn't ask if I didn't." Tilting my chin, his eyes probe mine.

"Lawry. I thought if he'd been with Evie, I wouldn't feel so guilty."

Sighing, he pulls me into his chest. "I'm selfish for wanting you the way I do," he says.

I want to ask him to elaborate, but the rumble of thunder followed by heavy rain cuts me off.

He sets me on my feet and straightens the straps of my dress. "You need to talk to him and resolve it once and for all."

He's right, regardless of what I feel for Reuben, I can't ignore the inevitable.

When we step out of the bathroom, Lawry is sitting on the sofa. His elbows are resting on his knees, head in his hands.

He peers up, his eyes trained on me, and what I see nearly kills me. He doesn't have to say anything. I know he knows. The sound in this house travels, and I was too far gone to care, caught up in the euphoria of the moment.

Reuben, however gruff and hostile he may be towards Lawry, knew this when he covered my mouth to try and avoid this on my behalf. My cheeks heat. I want to turn back around and lock myself in the bathroom. I'm hurting him, and I hate myself for it.

~

When we return to the farm, Lawry takes it all in but remains stoic. If he grinds his teeth any more, he'll need a dental examination. Josette rushes to me and hugs me as only a mother could.

And I don't know why, but I cry tears of happiness. She shoos the men away and takes me into the house where she provides me with a cup of tea. Knowing she bartered to get it for me only adds to my love for this woman. Vella sniffs me and licks my hand but doesn't jump, her instincts knowing to be gentle. I scratch her behind the ear when Lawry and Reuben enter.

Josette makes them sit at the table, their presence as they stand overbearing. They respectfully do as asked. Reuben sits beside me and Lawry opposite.

To everyone's surprise, Vella makes her way over to Lawry and circles his chair, then she sits beside him and shoves her head into his hand. He strokes her, and we all stare in disbelief. I peer over my tea to Reuben, who raises an eyebrow and shrugs. I can't hide my smile. Just like me, she knows he's a good man. And as much as Reuben wants to fight it, deep down, I think he knows it, too.

It's a relief when my stitches finally come out. Reuben spends his nights with me, but we haven't been intimate since the cottage. He offered Lawry his room, but Lawry opted to stay above the barn instead. We've been receiving sporadic radio transmissions but are still waiting on vital intel.

Isabelle keeps following Lawry with her eyes. I don't blame her. He does stand out in a crowd.

"He's married to my best friend," I tell her.

She sighs wistfully. Sometimes she seems so young in her mannerisms. "You know, I always had a thing for Reuben, but until you came, his eyes never wandered, not once."

I can't hide my blush or my smile.

"He's more like a big brother, anyway," she says elbowing me.

"No one else takes your fancy?" I ask.

She shivers. "Pierré has tried a few times, but something about him makes me uneasy."

I nod, remembering him in the barn when Vella went for him.

Reuben has to make a trip into town and offers to drive her back. She kisses my cheek and gives a cheeky wave to Lawry. His cheeks redden, and he waves back.

It's the first time we've been alone since we came here.

"I see why you're so taken with this place," he says, walking out of the barn. I wrap my arms around my middle and burrow my neck into my coat. The sun is setting, but there's a cold wind in the air. He wraps his arm over my shoulder and pulls me into his side. I rest on his shoulder as we watch the colours blending into brilliant reds and wild oranges.

"Evie loves to watch the sunset," he says, and I hear the smile in his voice.

I'm a little taken back at his mention of her, but I also know we need to put our past to bed and make peace with the present.

"You care about her?" I ask. My voice breaks, and I cough to clear my throat.

"Yes."

"You love her?"

"Don't ask me like you're questioning my love for you."

He's right. It's not a comparison you can make. Loving someone else and trying to cling to the remnants of what we had is useless.

"Would you change it if you could? If you had the foresight to see the present, would you go back and change your decision?" I ask.

He swallows, the veins working in his throat as he grapples for an answer.

I ask another question instead. "Would you change being Sami's dad?"

Turning his head to face me, he answers without hesitation. "No."

"Then I think you already know the answer to my previous question."

He nods and ponders this, searching my face. And I see the instant he gets it. "This was never meant to be our story, was it?"

I shake my head and try to hold back the wave of emotion working its way up my throat.

"Ana, you know my love for you was honest... My intentions pure?"

The tears come now, and he pulls me into his body, encasing me in the security of his arms. "Yes, and my love for you was, too. Don't hate me for being with Reuben?" I hiccup on his name. It's what would cripple me the most

"I could never hate you, Ana."

For the first time since Lawry arrived, I find myself no longer holding my breath in his presence. I can breathe without a crushing weight bearing down on my chest. And I now know why. He was the ripple in the tide but not the current.

CHAPTER 53

There is a heavy pounding at the door, and Reuben's name is called. It's Lawry. I sit up, and Reuben is already pulling on his trousers, his chest still bare. I reach for his shirt and pull it on.

"Stay here," he says more of a command than a request.

I don't.

I follow him to the back door as he pulls it open. Standing in his vest and trousers unbuttoned is Lawry. He looks past Reuben to me, and I pull the shirt tighter around me. It's to my knees, but I still see a glimmer of hurt.

"It's your mare. I think she's having her foal," he says, turning back to the barn.

Reuben pulls on his boots and rushes after him. I slip into mine, buttoning the shirt as I go.

"She's having difficulty," says Lawry.

"Know about horses, do you?" asks Reuben, but his question is void of hostility.

"A little," he replies.

"Good, because I might need your help," he says.

Reuben walks into the stable. Estelle is panting heavily,

anxious at his presence. He walks around her slowly and begins touching her stomach.

"It's okay, girl, *shh*, it's okay," he murmurs. "It's breech," he says.

Lawry rubs his palm over his face, and I look between him and Reuben.

"What does that mean?" I ask

"It means we need to help, or we could lose them both."

I gasp, covering my mouth.

"You going to reposition the foal?" asks Lawry.

Reuben nods. "I'm going to try."

Estelle is becoming more distressed, and I feel helpless. I reach out and stroke her nose. Her nostrils flare with her breathing.

"I don't think her waters have broken yet though," Reuben says, looking at the floor around her hooves.

I bite my lip. Reuben has worry etched all over his face, and Lawry's reflects this.

"What do you mean, reposition?"

Reuben comes back out and walks over to the bucket and then out to the well, pumping the lever. I follow.

"I need to help turn the foal."

Both him and Lawry wash their hands and arms as I watch on. "What can I do?"

Reuben comes over. "You can talk to her, stroke her, try to help us keep her calm," he says and kisses the top of my head.

I glance at Lawry who watches the exchange but says nothing. I don't see the hurt on his face this time. Reuben's open display of affection comes so naturally to him.

"Ready?" asks Reuben. Lawry nods his head.

Reuben walks behind Estelle, but I can't see what he's doing. All of a sudden, Estelle bolts forward.

"Woah, girl, woah," says Lawry.

"That's a good girl," calls Reuben.

I hear what sounds like a massive gush of water. I step to the side and see Reuben's trousers saturated. He shakes his head but continues.

"I can't get it to move," he says, grunting, his arm deep inside her.

I flinch as he continues fidgeting.

"Almost," he grunts but then pulls back. "Damnit."

Lawry steps beside him. "What's wrong?" he asks.

"The foal is big, and the more Estelle strains, the harder it is for me to reposition it."

Now I'm beginning to worry; he's almost resigned he cannot help her, and the thought terrifies me.

Lawry feels around the outside of her stomach and begins to push his palms in with effort.

"Try now," he says.

Reuben reaches in and grunts, sweat dripping down his face that contorts with the effort. And then he lets out a huge breath.

"I think I did it," he says, pulling back and waiting. I find myself moving to the side of Estelle now as Reuben steps back.

And that's when I see something, and cover my mouth. *Is that a hoof?*

Estelle continues to strain, and then it all happens too fast—a mound of legs and hooves drops to the floor with a thump. Although it's layered in straw, I flinch.

Nothing happens, and Lawry rushes forward.

A rope—no, it's the umbilical cord—is wrapped around its throat. Working swiftly, he untangles it but still nothing.

He looks up to Reuben, and he looks bereft.

"No, come, little guy, come on," says Lawry. He grabs a fistful of straw and begins rubbing the area around its mouth where there's a slimy residue. His fingers sweep the inside of its mouth and its throat muscle rolls. Then it makes a kind of mewling sound.

We all wait and watch in anticipation as it sits up. Lawry

steps back as Estelle's head comes down to nudge it. And then gradually, it pushes to its feet. Unsteadily and wobbly, it's standing, and then eventually begins nursing from Estelle.

I don't even realise I am crying until Lawry pulls me into his side.

"That was incredible," I say.

He smiles, looking down at me affectionately.

Reuben clears his throat. "Thank you," he says to Lawry and smiles.

I step away from Lawry and wrap my arms around Reuben, who holds his soiled arms away from me. "I'll go into town later this morning and have Franc come to check on them both," he says.

I step away and let him go wash up. It's only now, left standing alone with Lawry, I take stock of my appearance.

"I always did like your legs," Lawry says playfully and winks.

I feel my cheeks blush, but I can't hide my grin. "I should go and..."

His laugh echoes behind as I go back to the house. I hear the water running and go to the bathroom and tap on the door before entering.

Reuben is laying in the bath, he looks over, eyeing me with a smile—one much different than the way Lawry was looking at me. Reuben's stare burns into my soul and heats me from the inside out.

"Room for one more?" I ask, unbuttoning his shirt and slipping it from my shoulders, dropping it to my feet.

His eyes go dark as he holds out his hand to me.

"Always."

CHAPTER 54

Lawry and Reuben are tolerating each other a little more, but I can see the wheels turning, each trying to figure out the other.

At least they are civil, and there have been no more fights since we came back home—back to the farm. I have to keep reminding myself this isn't my home, but the longer I'm here, the more, deep down, it's become a part of me.

Reuben has become more distant. I try to stay awake, waiting for him to come to me, but I always succumb to sleep. Then when he does slip into bed beside me, he pulls me into his body, quickly followed by his soft snores. And then by morning, he's gone before I have a chance to talk to him.

I'm not too fond of this…whatever it is between us. Does he not know I chose him? That I want him?

"What's wrong?" asks Lawry when he greets me in the kitchen, Reuben nowhere to be seen.

"Nothing, why?"

He sips his coffee with a grimace. "You look tired," he replies.

I go over to the window and try to see if I can see Reuben.

"He went into town," says Lawry.

Josette nudges me to the chair and gives me a bowl of porridge. I smile as she dollops a spoonful of jam in the centre. She knows I have a sweet tooth.

"Did he say when he'd be back?"

Lawry laughs. "Like he tells me anything."

I stir the jam into my porridge, making it turn a light pink colour.

Lawry watches me and smiles, causing me to laugh. "What?"

"Nothing at all," he says. And it's nice just being together with no expectations. I never thought it possible, but it is.

"I need you to contact London for me," he says when Josette has left the kitchen.

He's already been here longer than he should have, and it was inevitable—his time here is spent.

Once we're both in the barn basement, I get to work on a transmission and relay the message back to him.

He has to meet a source who has some intel which cannot be passed any other way. I don't like the thought of him in the middle of Occupied France with limited French.

"You can't go on your own," I say.

"I have no choice, it's orders," he replies.

I throw my headset down and get to my feet. "You'll never get past the checkpoints. Do you even have any valid papers?"

He takes me by my shoulders to still me. "I'll get some, stop worrying. It'll be fine."

I cross my arms. "Easy for you to say."

I hear his familiar footsteps before I see him when he comes into view.

"Reuben, I need your help," Lawry says before I can acknowledge him.

I turn back to Lawry. "What? No."

"What is it?" asks Reuben.

He tells him he needs papers and has to meet with an informant. And of course, Reuben agrees to take him.

"We can go to the forger and then go straight to the informant," he says, like it's just a drive into town.

"I'm coming, too," I reply.

"No, you're staying here."

Is he kidding me? I scowl at Reuben. "Excuse me?"

"We have some important transmissions coming in, and you need to be here when they do," he says.

"How long do you think you'll be gone?"

Reuben gives a non-committal shrug. "A couple of days."

I don't like it. Not at all.

"Send Maurice a message. We'll go to him tomorrow."

I do as he says, but with trepidation. The idea of them both being gone and not knowing either is safe doesn't bode well with me.

After dinner, Lawry leaves us to go to the barn. I expect Reuben to make himself scarce like he has been doing, but he doesn't. And he doesn't even bother to wait until Josette retires for the night before he asks if I am ready for bed. I blush, and she smiles, her knitting needles tapping away with precision and timed stitching.

The warmth of his body follows me down the hall and to my room. I haven't been to his—not once—in the time I've been here, but then I remember it wasn't just *his* room, so I let the thought go. Vella is already curled up on a blanket. She squints out of one eye, acknowledging our arrival, then goes back to sleep.

I turn, words caught on the tip of my tongue, ready to take flight, when Reuben cups my face and kisses me. There is so much I want to say, but my thoughts become muffled. His hands trace the curves of my body, followed by his mouth. Laying me down on the bed, his body covers mine, and at this moment, the only thing that matters is the two of us.

He makes love to me as though it's the first time and the last, like it's hello and goodbye all in one and I don't know why.

Clinging to him, I wring him for everything he has to give, refusing to let go. Even after we've finished, I don't allow him to pull away. He stays inside me until he becomes hard again, and we continue where we left off. It's sweet and torturous. I am at the complete mercy of this man, and I never want to let go.

As I slip between wakefulness and sleep, he whispers to me, but I'm too far gone to pull myself back. My dreams are intense and vivid—Reuben always there, always watching.

I wake, stretching my muscles, weak but satisfied. My hand reaches for him, but all that remains is a cool spot where he should be and his scent on my pillow.

A fresh vase sits on my bedside table filled with lavender stems. And I know without getting out of bed, he and Lawry have already left.

It irks me. Why would he go without even as much as a goodbye?

CHAPTER 55

Isabelle arrives with a basket and a giant grin on her face.

"Morning," she says in a singsong voice.

"Someone's happy."

She plops down next to me and uncovers the basket.

I double-take. "Where did you get all of this?" I ask, looking at the contents.

"A friend," she replies, pulling out some chocolate and passing me a bar.

I take it and turn it over in my hands.

She shrugs. "I wanted to share it with you, and I thought Josette could put some of it to good use."

"Did someone mention my name?" asks Josette as she joins us.

"Here, I wanted to see if you could put any of this to good use," she says, handing her over the basket.

Josette's eyes go wide as she has a look through the contents. "We don't have money for this," she says, passing it back.

Isabelle waves her off. "It was a gift. Besides, it would go to waste otherwise."

Josette glances to me and then back to Isabelle.

"That's very thoughtful, dear." She begins to unload the contents, humming to herself.

I peel back the chocolate wrapper and snap it into pieces and pass some to Isabelle and Josette. Letting a square melt on my tongue, I close my eyes and savour the taste.

The last time I had any was when Reuben gave me some. Since he went, I've been left bereft. It's nothing like what I felt with Lawry when we were apart. This is a different ache entirely. One I can't even explain or put into words. But I do know this much—I love him, and when he returns, I'll make my feelings known. There is a hole in my soul without him.

Isabelle and I go to the barn basement as the others begin to arrive.

"Where did you say Reuben was again?" she asks.

"I didn't," I reply as Pierré stares between us, making me somewhat uncomfortable.

It's only when I frown that he looks away.

"What's his problem?" asks Isabelle, loud enough for him to hear.

"So, where are Reuben and Lawrence?" he asks as André and René join us.

I pick up the headset and try to act nonchalant. "They had business out of town, that's all I know," I reply, slipping the headset over my ears.

He chews on a piece of straw and gets to work on whatever contraption he's been helping René make.

We've received news that there are some parts on route to replace the broken machinery we hit at the factory. If we can't do something to intercept them and sabotage them, the hit on the factory will have been in vain.

"So what do we do?" asks Isabelle, fiddling with her hair.

I wait, but everyone seems to be waiting for me. "We'll have to intercept it, no question."

It's the first time me being here that I haven't had Reuben to aid in an assignment. He's a natural leader. He doesn't have to work hard to demand attention. He has a quality people are drawn to...well, most people. I think of him and Lawry being together, wondering how they've put up with each other. It's already been five days since they left. And that's five days too many.

"I think we need to get to them before they make it back to the factory. It will look less suspicious, like the parts are faulty instead of tampered with."

Pierré nods. "If we can find out where they'll be between now and their arrival, we can make it work."

We all agree, and I send a transmission. Someone in the resistance in Paris confirms an ideal location where we will be able to intercept.

"We'll have to split up," says Pierré.

I nod in agreement.

"Ana, you'll be with me and Isabelle you'll go with André and René."

Isabelle is about to argue but she shuts down quickly. I give her a look, and she shakes her head as we go over the details for tomorrow night.

As much as I dislike the idea of being with Pierré, he was the reason I didn't get caught at the factory, and since the incident with Vella, he hasn't made any other move to be untoward.

∼

My sleep was restless. I've been so used to having Reuben beside me, I forgot what it was like to sleep alone. I've sent out a transmission in hopes someone has any news on both him and Lawry, but by the time we're ready to leave, there's still no news.

Pierré is quiet at first, but then he starts talking—maybe to fill the silence, or perhaps just to be friendly, I'm not sure. "So, you and Reuben?"

I stare over at his hand resting loosely over the steering wheel.

"What about us?" I ask, attempting to keep any hostility at bay.

"You're together now. So, does that mean you'll be staying?" he asks.

"I have a job to do, but yes, I'd like to stay."

"You trust him?" he asks.

I cross my arms. "Of course, I do, why wouldn't I?"

"Because if I'm not mistaken, the other man he's set off with also has a thing for you. Are you not worried only one will come back?"

I swallow hard. Is he serious? "*Had* a thing, not has. And no. He knows it's nothing for him to worry about."

"Just making conversation," he says, innocently, and why I'm even indulging him is beyond me.

But what if Reuben doesn't know? We never were able to talk. What if Lawry tells Reuben he thinks what we have is lust like he did to me?

Was he saying goodbye the night in my room before he left without so much as a goodbye? Was there more to their assignment than either let on?

The thoughts unsettle me, and I bite the inside of my cheek. I need to focus on our mission—not on the two men who I love, albeit differently, but still, I love them.

CHAPTER 56

"Go!" Pierré hollers.

I stand still, holding the knife in my hand. Blood is dripping from the thin blade as I look at the man dead before me. As he tackles another, the heavy fall of footsteps is getting closer and shouting rings out.

"Please, just go," he grunts.

Gunshots echo, closer now. "I can't leave you," I say.

He manages to swing an uppercut to the other man who falls to the ground and hits his head on the floor with a thump. And then a pool of blood seeps out around him.

"Come," he says, grappling for my arm as he tugs me.

But he can barely hold himself up. His leg trails behind him, useless from the gunshot wound, oozing with blood.

"You need to go. We aren't both getting out of here." He leans his exhausted body against the wall.

I'm torn.

"Listen, you know I'm right."

And I do.

I look left and right and weigh up my options, but we only have one knife between us, and we're outgunned.

"I'm sorry," I say, and he nods.

"Go, I'll cover you."

I turn and break out into a run. My feet pound the pavement, my breathing laboured from the effort.

The street is poorly lit from the blackout, and the cloud cover is heavy tonight, leaving barely any illumination from the moon as I try to navigate my way back to the car. Even if I make it there, I can't risk being caught out with the curfews in place.

Every limb and muscle is aching by the time I find myself at the car, on the edge of town. As I start the engine, the noise pounds through my ears, and I worry someone will hear. I drive, the headlights hidden by covers, just enough to light what is right in front of me.

My ears ring, and my heart races furiously in my chest.

I arrive at the cottage and pull it into the spot Reuben hides the truck and cut the engine. Leaning my head against the steering wheel, I breathe in through my nose and out through my mouth.

Pierré could be dead now for all I know, and I have no way of sending a transmission until the morning when I'm back at the farm.

Climbing from the car, I strain to listen past the howling wind and creaking branches of the overlying trees. I grip the handle of the knife in my palm as my feet crunch over fallen leaves.

At the door, I lean my ear against the wood, reaching for the key hidden under the log. I bring it up to the lock and turn it until it catches with a *clang* and then lift the latch I push it open.

Closing it quickly behind me, I stand with my back against the door. The room is dark. I follow the wall until I come across a torch and switch it on, darting it all over. Shadows jump out from every corner but other than me and the furniture, the cottage is empty.

I go to the bathroom and scrub my hands clean before going

into the kitchen in search of food. Reuben came and replaced some cans from when we stayed here last. Opening a can of peaches, I sip the syrup while sitting on the sofa. I pull my feet underneath me on the couch and wrap myself in a blanket. I inhale. Oddly, it's a mixture of both Lawry and Reuben. I don't know where they are, or even if they're safe. And after tonight, I know my time here is jeopardised.

Dead eyes hold me captive. Souls evaporate into nothingness as their life is brutally pulled from them like a thorn from a rose.

The victims are both friend and enemies—some the faces of strangers. Some I know so well, down to the very last freckle.

A strangled muted scream tries to break free as I stand, watching as waves of blood coat Reuben, as hands grab and pull at him into a deep rich red pool until he is pulled under. When he surfaces, it's no longer his face I see, but Lawry's.

Evie stands beside a little boy, clutching the hem of her dress as dirt is thrown into an empty grave. The headstone reads *Lawrence Davenport, a beloved husband and father*. She's lost another man she loves, and Sami is now without a father.

Sylvette screams at me through a barbed wired fence, but I cannot make out what she's saying as she frantically points behind me.

I turn, a firing squad has their guns aimed, ready to fire. I hold up my hands.

The scene before me morphs into the farm. Pierré is pointing to Josette, who is now on her knees, head bowed as a gun is held to the base of her neck.

I can't move.

I'm frozen, the fear tangible.

Just as the trigger is pulled, I'm released and lunge forward. "NO!"

My stomach lurches as I crash to the floor with a heavy thump. I scramble to my feet, dizzy, disoriented.

My eyes are darting all around as I gasp for air—a nightmare, just a nightmare. My face is wet from tears, and my clothes stick to my body.

I splash my face with water. I need to warn her. I need to warn them all.

After last night, we are all compromised. The sun is only just peeping up over the horizon.

I need to go now, to Josette. Hopefully, it's not too late.

CHAPTER 57

I plough through the back door, raising a bark and a growl from Vella. She's on all fours, ready to attack until she sees it's me.

Josette is holding a dishcloth with a death grip from my intrusive entrance. I rush to her and pull her into my arms.

"Ana, where have you been?" she asks as I pull back.

"It's a long story, but I don't think any of us are safe," I say, bending down to pat Vella.

"We haven't been since the invasion," she replies.

I shake my head, hair whipping me in the eye. I stuff it behind my ears, ignoring the sharp pull of the strands from my scalp.

"No, we were compromised last night. It's why I didn't come straight here. I was worried I'd be followed."

She shuffles over and moves me to a chair. "Start from the beginning."

I shake my head. "The less you know, the better," I reply licking my lips, desperate for water.

I reach for the jug and pour myself a glass, then drink it down greedily.

She reaches for my hand, squeezes it between hers. "Now,

you listen to me good. I already know more than I should, so tell me."

So, I do. I explain how when we arrived, something wasn't right. It was as though they were waiting for us. Two soldiers jumped us, and we didn't even manage to hit our target. Pierré was shot as he fought off one, and I ended up stabbing the other. They had been waiting for us. It was more than a coincidence.

"I need to go send a message."

I stand, but I'm lightheaded have to sit back down again.

"Not before you eat something," she says.

I shake my head, but she cuts a thick slice of bread and smothers it with jam anyway. The smell causes my stomach to grumble and my mouth to salivate. I don't hesitate as I demolish it and wash it down with a glass of fresh milk.

I've been on the radio for almost two hours. There's hardly any information coming through. It's unsettling. I don't know if Isabelle, André, or René are captured, or worse…dead. Pierré wouldn't have gone down without a fight, but the fact that neither of us were killed straight away makes me think they wanted us alive.

Maybe I should get Josette and go to the cottage. When Reuben returns and can't find us, he'll know to go there. But I can't go yet. I'll wait until nightfall to see if any other information comes forward.

A rumble from high above vibrates into the ground beneath me. I disassemble the radio and hide them in their hidden sections of the basement before I ascend the stairs.

The sky is dark, unforgiving, as another rumble followed by lightning blasts the field in the distance. A storm is on the way. You can smell it in the air as the wind thrashes wildly against the barn roof. The horses are in the stable, brought in from the pasture. I cover the entrance and add an extra bale of hay for safe measure before I go to check on the young filly.

She's still all legs, happily beside her mum as she grazes her feed. I hold out my hand for her, and she comes over. Her nostrils flare as she smells my fingers before her rough tongue licks a path up my arm. I laugh, breaking out in goose bumps. Vella brushes against my leg, clearly getting jealous.

"You know I love you, girl," I say, leaving the horses be and heading for the house before the rain breaks through the clouds.

CHAPTER 58

There are moments in your life when you get this feeling—one you can't explain or decipher, but deep down, you have a sixth sense that something is wrong.

I should have made Reuben stay and not leave with Lawry. But I don't get to call the shots. An uneasiness settles into the pit of my stomach. It won't subside.

"I'm going down to the barn," I tell Josette, who is knitting in the rocker by the ager. She looks up with a smile, never missing a stitch. I leave the kitchen, Vella hot on my heels.

Approaching the barn, I notice the door is ajar, which is weird. I proceed with caution, listening to see if I can hear anything. The fur of Vella's back sticks up in a slim mohawk. It's the only visible sign she's not too keen, either, but she makes no move to bark or growl as she keeps close to my leg.

I push the door wide open and take a deep breath before entering. The same familiar smell of hay and straw reach my nose. The horse is still pasturing out in the field and will be brought back in later this afternoon.

Something tells me not to go to the trap door, which leads to the hidden basement of the barn. Instead, I walk to the tackle and run my fingers over the soft leather.

"Halt!"

The temperature drops in an instant and all the hairs on the back of my neck stand on end. Vella lets out a low rumble of a growl beside me, baring her teeth as a soldier steps out of a dark corner and into the light.

"Are you Annalise Delacroix?"

I nod. "Yes, what are you doing out here?" I ask, trying to keep the tremble from my voice, praying they don't know where the hidden door to the basement is.

"We have reason to believe a suspicious activity to be going on in the premises," he replies.

"You're mistaken," I say with confidence. "My husband provides produce, complicit with everything asked of him."

The soldier continues to stare at me. His eyes are too blue, his hair almost white, it's so blonde. The most Aryan man I have ever seen.

"You are to come with us," he says.

This is when I see out of my peripheral vision another soldier outside the barn with a rifle pointed towards me.

"Where?" I ask.

"For questioning," he replies.

Vella's growl grows louder, and the soldier eyes her.

"I don't know what you want from me," I say as innocently as possible as I try to run through scenarios in my head.

"What's going on?"

I turn to find Josette approaching the soldier by the barn door and my heart sinks.

"Who are you?" he asks.

"Josette, her mother in law," she replies.

"This is none of your concern. We just need her to come with us." He nods in my direction.

"It *is* my concern. This is *my* home. We've done nothing

wrong!" she exclaims, waving her knitting needles and ball of wool in the air.

My heart begins to race unsteadily. I go to step towards her, but I am grabbed around the wrist.

Everything else happens so fast:

Vella goes for the arm of the man who is gripping me tightly.

"Vella," I screech.

The man releases me but only because he has no choice as Vella shakes at him violently. I try to grab her off of him, but I can't get a hold of her collar.

I notice something to the right of me and turn my head just as the other soldier raises his gun and pulls the trigger.

"NO…"

I lunge forward as a high pitch yelp rips through the barn.

Vella's body falls to the ground with a hard thud. I rush to her side and cover the wound with my hands. She whines, and the sound ricochets all around us.

"Vella, it's going to be okay, you're going to be okay," I cry out as warm blood seeps between my fingers.

The officer who shot her yanks my shoulder and pulls me away; the other grips his arm where she had sunken her teeth only moments ago.

"You'll come now unless you want us to finish her off and the old woman," he says.

Josette rushes past us, untying her apron, and then holds it over Vella's gunshot wound. I don't know how bad it is. Her whimpering is unbearable. If I retaliate now, more soldiers will come, and I'll be putting everyone else at risk.

"Just let me help her first?" I plead.

His patience has all but evaporated. He strikes the side of my face with the butt of his rifle, and I fall to the ground. My eyes go to Josette and then to Vella. I feel helpless.

"Sorry," I mouth to Josette as the taste of copper fills my

mouth. I lick the cut on my lip. She shakes her head and rights her shoulders.

"You're making a mistake," she tells the officer who gives Vella a wide berth as he edges towards us, his temples dripping with sweat, the blood now caking the sleeve of his shirt, soaking it cherry red.

"Please, just let them be," I say and hold my hands in the air.

He shoves me in the back hard, and I stumble, but not enough to fall over.

Vella's heavy panting fills my ears as I walk away, praying Josette can save her. I didn't have any time to see the extent of the gunshot.

I wipe my bloody hands down my skirt, already soaked with dirt from the barn floor.

The truck comes into view around the other side of the house.

We've had thunderstorms, so no wonder I didn't hear the engine. But why were they in the barn?

I know someone has given us away, but why?

Even if they did venture into the basement, a partition hides what's left of our base. But it's probably not enough. If I had any inclination they would be coming, I might have had time to hide what was left.

I stare at my fingernails. Coated underneath, blood from Vella is already beginning to dry. I wipe the side of my cheek with my wrist—it's already starting to bruise.

Whatever happens, I need to stay strong. I can't—won't give up my friends or better still, my family.

CHAPTER 59

It's all very formal when I arrive at the police station. I find myself tucking my hair back into place, conscious of my blood-stained skirt and my filthy hands. I'm taken into an office where I'm greeted by two officers—one behind a desk and the other beside it. I'm told to sit, and the guards who brought me here are dismissed.

"So, Mrs. Annalise Delacroix. Do you know why you are here?"

I shake my head, clearing my throat, my fists tight in my lap. "No," I reply.

He eyes me for a moment without saying a word, his appraisal making me want to squirm in my seat, but I dare not move. I have to remind myself to breathe.

"We have reason to believe you may be working with an organisation, a collaboration of partisans."

I shake my head. "No."

"That's not what our source said."

Sweat beads on my lower back and the base of my neck. I want so badly to wipe it away, but I remain as still as possible.

"Your source must be wrong," I reply, trying to sound as perplexed as possible.

"Hmm, where is your husband? Reuben Delacroix, is it?"

"He went to visit a sick relative," I reply.

He stands and begins to walk around his desk, perching in front of me, appearing to be casual. But the smell of his cologne gets stuck in the back of my throat and I have to swallow hard to avoid gaging. It's almost toxic.

"And you stayed home?"

"Yes, we've been busy on the farm, and I stayed to help my mother in law."

His thumb and forefinger pinch his perfectly shaved chin. "His mother from his late wife?"

I nod. He knows too much.

He stands, the whiff whooshes past me, and this time, I cover my gag with a cough.

"Are you thirsty, Mrs. Delacroix?"

I shake my head, no. But the truth is, now he's mentioned it, I am dehydrated.

He signals for the Lieutenant who swiftly moves over to a tray and pours a glass of water from a jug, then brings it over and places it on a coaster in front of me.

"Please." He signals towards the glass, and with trepidation, I reach out and take it. Conscious of my slick palm, I cup it underneath with the other, worried I'll drop the heavy crystal glass.

I take a sip but can't hide my tremble. Innocent or guilty, this situation is enough to make anyone nervous. I take another sip before setting it back on the desk, my hand trembling.

"Thank you," I reply.

"You see, we're civil. We want the unrest to stop. We want rid of the partisans, the terrorists who care nothing for their fellow civilians or putting their own families at risk."

I nod.

"So, you see, we are reasonable. We will go easy on those who cooperate with us freely."

His eyes pierce into mine as he takes a seat back behind the desk, his presence overbearing. Everything about him has me on edge.

"If I knew of anything, I'd tell you, but I don't. I'm sorry."

He taps his fingers against the mahogany desk with perfectly manicured nails—hands unlike Reuben's. His have never seen manual labour in their life.

"I'm sorry. You leave me no choice."

He nods to the Lieutenant who stands next to me, gripping my shoulder.

"We'll give you some time to think about it."

"Think about what?" I dare to ask.

He slams his palm down so hard, I jump in my seat. A pen rolls off the desk and falls to the floor with a loud thwack.

"Don't be stupid, Mrs. Delacroix. You'll do yourself no favours."

And with that, he dismisses us.

"Come."

I get to my feet, my dress sticking to the back of my thighs. I tug at the hem and pull the material away from my skin.

He leads me out and down two sets of stairs, through a long, haunting dimly lit corridor with no windows in sight. We pass several heavily bolted doors. Stopping, he unlocks one, his keys rattling together as he turns one in the lock.

When he opens the door, I don't wait to be told, I enter. I listen as it's pulled shut behind me with a loud thud. The latch sliding into place makes my skin crawl, followed by the turn of the key—finality.

I drop to my knees in the middle of the room and let the tears fall. Next time I'm questioned, I doubt there will be anything formal about it. And no matter how much training someone has, that thought is terrifying.

CHAPTER 60

The sound of metal forces me from sleep, and I try to force myself awake as a heavy latch is slid open with an unhealthy *creak*.

Shivers roll over my body.

I've lost sense of time.

I don't know if it's morning or night. Disorientated, I grip the wall. My fingers trace over a crevice, and I squint into the darkness to see if I can make it out. It's a name, but it's too obscure to see.

The cold, damp air raises a cough from me, dry and hoarse from lack of water. I haven't had anything to drink since I arrived, and the hunger pains are setting in. I lick my cracked lips. The cut splits open, and a wet, metallic taste assaults my tongue.

I know what happens to women of war in places like this. What they might do to me in order to find out what I know. Will I succumb and let the others down? I genuinely hope not. I pray hard for God to give me strength, but I don't know what I can take before it is too much for me.

I want to be strong, but I'm consumed with a deep-rooted fear. I sink back to the floor.

A guard appears and overshadows the doorway. His presence does nothing for my nerves.

He points a gun at me. "Up," he says.

My limbs are heavy, but I manage to move and push myself to my feet.

He beckons me forward and out of the door. The corridor is faintly lit, and every so often, the lights flicker, followed by harrowing screams.

My steps falter.

"Move."

I do as I'm ordered and enter a room with a chair in the middle.

He forces me down into it.

The smell is sickening—urine and other things I don't want to even think about. My stomach rolls and I gag.

I attempt to cover my mouth, but my hand is pulled away and strapped down onto the arm of the chair.

I pull and tug at the restraint; it's no use.

Heavy footsteps get louder on approach, and then the guard stands to attention as three other soldiers enter the room.

It's now stifling, and I squirm in the seat.

I dare not look up, but I have no choice when a command echoes in the small enclosed space. I raise my chin.

"Name?"

I clear my throat. "Annaliese Delacroix."

Lights flicker aggressively overhead, followed by another bone curdling scream, and I flinch.

The man stares at me for an uncomfortable amount of time as he pulls at each finger of his gloved hands until he has removed them.

Slapping them against his palm, he walks around me until he is facing me again, the smell of leather strong.

Then it's question after question—always looping back to the same ones.

"Are you a spy?"

"No."

"Who are you working for?"

"No one."

"Tell us the truth and we'll go easy on you."

"I am."

My answers never waver.

I can see the frustration marring his face, and if I weren't so concerned about the repercussions of this, maybe I'd get some satisfaction.

He nods his head towards one of the other guards who stood to attention but said nothing—head up, staring past me.

He steps forward. He has something clutched in his hand, and I want to be anywhere but here.

Another guard grips my shoulder hard from behind, and I begin to panic.

"You leave me no choice."

My fingers, which are gripping onto the armrest are pried away and splayed open. The guard tugs on them painfully to straighten them, and no matter how much I try to clench them closed, it's no use.

The tool in his hand makes a weird sound when he releases the catch.

I can't watch. I force myself to close my eyes.

Cold metal hooks over my fingers and then tightens. I can't breathe.

A *crunch* and a *crack* precede a scorching heat as it surges through my hand—a piercing pain. Bright white lights up my vision, and then I vomit, choking on my bile.

I'm clammy but neither hot nor cold.

I'm not sure if I pass out because I'm brought to when a palm connects with my face, jarring me into consciousness.

And then another round of questions are thrown at me—same as before, I give the same answers.

I'm unable to ignore the earth-shattering pain in my hand as the restraints are released. I'm hoisted from the chair and thrown to the ground. I try to stop my fall, but I fumble feebly, trying to protect my already damaged fingers. The pain is now excruciating.

A rough taste of dirt coats my tongue where I face planted on the floor. I wipe at my face before a hand grabs my hair and drags me to what could be either a bath or a trough.

It's full of what once was likely clean water, but now it's muddy in colour. My face is held over the rim as the guard kneels beside me and whispers in my ear. "Admit to being a spy."

I shake my head.

Before I have a chance to take a breath, my face is plunged into the murky liquid, and forced its way up my nose. I try to blow it out through my nose. My hair is tugged backwards, and my face is pulled from the bath before being dunked back in again. I manage to get a tiny gulp of air this time to hold my breath.

It doesn't last. My hand is yanked, and a crushing weight falls over my fingers. I let out a strangled scream into the water, choking.

I'm pulled free and thrown into a puddle on the floor, spluttering as I hold my hand to my chest. I can't see who is in front of me, but those boots are so clean, I bet I could see my reflection if I moved an inch closer.

A foot connects with my ribs, and it burns from the force.

I see a long hose being pulled out and brace myself as a stream of ice-cold water attacks me.

I can't fight against the force to which I'm thrown back against the wall. Behind, something cracks, but I don't know what as I desperately gasp for breath.

I shiver, my teeth rattling uncontrollably. Pain thrums through my hand as I hold it to my chest.

"Take her back to her cell."

I'm dragged to my feet and stumble. I manage to find my footing, and then the same guard who brought me here leads me back into the hallway.

I want to run, but I have no idea where I am or even how to navigate the building. And I'd likely end up with a bullet in the back.

A noise catches my attention, a scuffling sound. Coming towards me is a figure being dragged by his wrists. As they get closer, I see the head lulling over the chest of a limp, lifeless body.

And I almost scream.

For a brief moment, I think its Reuben, but as the body is dragged past me, I see his face.

André.

My eyes follow his body. His legs are at odd angles, his feet bloody and butchered. I make out the words, *dispose of* and begin to hyperventilate. And then I lurch forward, not sure if I mean to run.

"Don't be stupid," says the guard so quietly, I barely hear him over my erratic breathing. "You just need to hold on."

I want to ask him what he means—is this a trick? Am I being tested? I say nothing, and he opens my cell door for me to enter. I don't turn around until I hear the latch bolt shut behind me.

When it does, I crumble to the floor and bring my hand towards my face to see the damage. I hold my breath. Three of my fingers are disfigured, and I gag when I see the tendon of one, unable to stop myself from dry heaving, no contents left in my stomach to expel.

CHAPTER 61

Every time the lights flicker, my body convulses involuntary. The sounds of screams echo through the halls and into my cell. This was nothing like when I first arrived, it was eerily quiet then, but now—the sounds are unbearable.

I'm taken into yet another room, and every time I leave the confines of my tiny prison, I think *this is it*. This is the day I'll die.

My concentration is limited. I don't know how long I've been here. It's the fatigue setting in—being woken and yanked from the cell at all hours. It messes with your mind. You become delirious.

My heart beats all wrong, and even my breathing is a struggle.

Is it my body's way of getting me ready for death? Or is this my subconscious making it so I won't be coherent when it finally does come?

They leave me in the chair for so long, my bum becomes numb, but I only fidget enough to ease the pressure of the cold metal slates beneath me.

A man is dragged into the room by his arms, legs dangling

behind him. They drop him in a heap in front of me, and it takes him a while to drag his body into a weird sitting position.

His eyes meet mine, and I can't look away.

Pierré.

His face is bruised, his lips split open. His eyes widen with acknowledgement when he sees me.

The officers leave the room, and I hear the click of the door behind me.

I scramble towards him and go to speak, but he quickly shakes his head—*no*—and brings his finger to his lip. He pulls my face so close, I hold my breath. I can smell his blood mixed with his own filth, and my stomach rolls. For a second, I think he's going to kiss me, but he pulls my ear to his bloody lip.

His breath is heavy as he whispers. "Say nothing, don't give them anything and you'll live. It's not you they want. Stay the cause."

He releases me.

Noise has me rushing back to my chair.

Footsteps approach me from behind until a figure stops beside me. I keep my eyes fixed on Pierré.

"Do you know this man?" asks one of the officers.

"No," I reply. My throat scratches, desperate for water.

They turn to him now. "Do you know this woman?"

He shakes his head. "No."

And it's only now I notice he is missing two of his front teeth.

"We know you're lying."

He signals to someone behind me who comes into my view and slaps me hard across the face with such force, my chair tips, and I fall to the ground with a heavy thud.

Pierré scrambles towards me and rights me with what little strength he has left, but he is yanked away and kicked in the ribs and face. I hear a crunch, and my stomach flips upside down.

He struggles to push himself back up. "What kind of man hits a woman?" he spits with a mouthful of blood.

The officer pulls out his pistol and points it to Pierré's temple.

"I will only ask you one last time. Do you know each other?"

Shaking his head, Pierré replies, "no."

His eyes are piercing into mine. *Keep the cause*. But I know we're both dead anyway.

I squeeze my eyes closed, but his eyes are all I see, imploring me to stay quiet. When I open them, I say the word which will most likely be a death sentence. "No," I breathe.

Pierré's eyes soften, almost as if he is saying thank you.

A click of metal is followed by a loud pop as the trigger is pulled.

I can't close my eyes quick enough. Pierré is shot in the head at close range. I gasp and heave, my body desperate to vomit, but there is nothing to bring up.

The officers leave the room—just me and Pierré—and his body twitches before it surrenders to the last traces of life it has left.

He could have given me up to save his neck, but he didn't.

∼

I don't know how long they keep me in the same room as his corpse, but when they come for me, I've soiled myself again. I'm beyond humiliation now; I don't know how much of my self-dignity remains.

I am half-escorted, half-carried out of the door, but they make me wait to see Pierré's limp body pass me as he's pulled down into the dark reaches of the corridor. What will become of his body? Who will mourn him now he's gone?

I try to pull away from the guard, but his grip tightens. "Don't do anything foolish. Just hold on," he says.

He shoves me gently back into my cell.

Is he trying to break me? Have me admit who I am?

"I don't know what you mean," I reply.

He nods once but says nothing more. He pulls the door closed and slides the lock into place.

I pull myself into a ball, even though it hurts to do so. I will myself to become invisible. To be anywhere but here.

Reuben's eyes find mine in the darkness.

His lips are moving, but I can't make out the words. He is frantic as he tries to call me to him. But it's no use.

I don't know how much longer I can survive this torment.

I kick off my shoe and drag it towards me. It takes me a while to pry the insole free with my one good hand. I blink until I see it, hidden.

My fingers tremble as I pull out the one in the rubber cover, the cyanide pill. I free it from the cover, hold it up, and stare at it.

All this pain and darkness can be over with this.

I roll it between my fingers.

Fifteen seconds, that's all it will take. And then no more suffering.

I bring it to my lips; the cold vial grazes my skin.

Squeezing my eyes closed, I inhale a deep breath. I'm so tired.

Reuben's singing rouses me from a deep sleep. His lips trace a path over my face, my lips, my throat. His touch heats my skin, sending warmth to every nerve in my body.

His mouth moves to my ear and he whispers. I tilt my head, unable to hear the words. He pulls back and I reach out, but my hand connects with something cold, damp.

I hiss through my teeth, reality setting in. I'm still in a cell, the pain from my hand, letting me know I'm still alive. Pressed firmly into the palm of my good hand is the pill. I scramble for the rubber cover and secure it inside before returning it to my shoe.

I'm not ready to give up on him, on us.

I pull myself into a ball and let the tears pull me into another state of exhaustion.

CHAPTER 62

"Up!"

Someone grabs at my arm, and I don't have the energy to recoil.

"You're being moved, but first you need to get cleaned up."

It's a female voice—almost familiar. My eyelids are heavy when I force my eyes open. Standing over me is a shadow. The light from behind makes it hard for me to see her face.

"Come on. Otherwise, they'll use force," she says, trying to help me to my feet.

I muster the remaining energy I do have and stagger into a standing position.

"What have they done to you?" she whispers under her breath.

I don't reply as I struggle to keep upright, my body soiled. Matted hair dried in blood falls over my face and my battered hand.

When my eyes finally move to her face, I don't know what to think.

It's Isabelle.

What is she doing here, and why is she helping me? No

guard follows us as we make our way to a washroom. When I see the bath, I flinch, causing pain to erupt through my ribs.

"I'm so sorry. I didn't know this would happen, you have to believe me," she says as she wets a towel and hands it to me.

And that's when it clicks. All along, she was the informant, *she* was the one who shouldn't have been trusted.

I rest on the bench and survey the room. Only one door and a small window on the wall at the far end, but it's not wide enough to fit out, and even if I could, I don't know what floor I am on. All I know is this is a higher floor than the lower level cell I have just left.

I take the towel and try to wipe at my face, but it's not an easy feat with my mangled hand. She takes it from me. I want to swat her away.

She begins drawing a bath, and my eyes dart everywhere. She walks over and bolts the door shut.

"Nothing will happen in here. I give you my word. I am just to help clean you up and then you're being moved."

How does she expect me to trust her?

And what other choice do I have?

She passes me a cup—it's warm, some kind of broth I think. I sniff and tentatively take a sip. And when it stays down, I sip some more until it's all gone. My stomach rolls and I wonder if it was poisoned or if I'm about to be sick.

The bath isn't deep. She helps me strip from my soiled clothes—no room for modesty now. She helps me into the tub while I keep my hand tucked in towards my chest. It takes me some time to sit without slipping. I know I must smell awful, but she says nothing about that as she reaches for my hand.

"Let me take a look?" she asks.

I shake my head, not wanting her to even look at it. She has a first aid kit on the counter and reaches for it.

"Ana," she says, and I relent, holding my arm out and resting it on the edge of the bath.

She gasps when her fingers gently try to examine my hand. I look away, reaching for the washcloth to try to wipe at my body.

"It's bad, you need a doctor," she says as she coats it with iodine. I let out a small groan in protest, the sting letting me know that feeling is not all lost.

"I'll wrap it the best I can."

I don't say anything and allow her to cover it in gauze and a bandage. The dressing is stiff, but it restricts me from moving my fingers involuntary, and for that, I am grateful.

"Do you know if they have Reuben?" I ask.

She shakes her head. "No, they are still searching for him."

I am momentarily filled with a small sense of relief. "They executed Pierré right in front of me," I say to her numbly, and look up into her eyes—bright as the blue sky, brimming with tears.

"And I saw André being dragged through the same corridor, too. It wasn't a coincidence. They wanted me to see."

She grabs a jug and tilts my head back enough to coat my hair and then begins to wash it.

"I'm sorry," she says.

"People are dead, Isabelle. Saying sorry won't change that."

"I had a family," she says as she massages the suds into my scalp.

"My little brother, Francois, was only five." She refills the jug and rinses my hair. "He wasn't meant to be there." Her eyes cloud over as she remembers something. "But he was, he was caught in the crossfire, but not by a German soldier—by a resistance fighter."

She grabs a towel and scrunches the ends of my hair between the cotton and her fingers. "My mama couldn't live with what happened, so she hung herself in our barn. When my papa found her, he took his hunting rifle and shot himself."

I grab her arm and squeeze. She looks at me—as if noticing I am still here—and reaches for another towel. She shakes it out and wraps it over my shoulders. We work together until I am out of the tub and back on the bench.

"And then I met someone. He was good to me. Made me feel less alone. He said he loved me and if I loved him, I'd join in the fight."

"But I don't understand why you informed on *us*," I say.

She shakes her head. "He was the SS, Ana, not the resistance."

It makes me gag at the thought, and I think the broth will make a reappearance, but it stays down. It all clicks into place now—Sylvette being arrested, the way she always tried to direct things towards Pierré, knowing my suspicions. She played on them, and well.

"I didn't care who died or who suffered. I didn't want to be on my own anymore and I wanted someone to pay for my family."

Tears stream down her cheek. "But not this, Ana. I never meant for any of this."

There's a knock at the door, and I startle. She looks to me and then the door. "Five minutes," she calls out. Rushing to me, she quickly helps me into some clothes and promptly runs a comb through my hair.

"Do you think God will forgive me for the things I've done?" she asks as she takes my arm in hers.

"I don't know," I reply. It's only now I see her youth. I always thought she was young, but it plagues me, so I ask. "How old were you when they came for you, Isabelle?"

She pauses and looks down at her feet. "Sixteen," she replies.

"So you're not twenty-one," I reply.

She shakes her head. "No, I turn eighteen next month."

Monsters.

"I'm sorry about your family," I reply and before I think better of it, I pull her into my body and hug her tight.

She lets out a choking sound and the floodgates open. It takes her a minute or so to right her composure.

"Do you want to know what the worst part is?" I hold onto her arm and wait for her to finish. "You all became my family."

"And what of this SS soldier you love?"

She shifts from one foot to another. "He has a different girl every week. He played me. I know that now."

I don't know what to say. Do I tell her it's all right? How she had no choice, and it's too late?

A heavy knock on the door reminds us our time is up. She covers her lip with her forefinger, and I nod as she slides the lock open. I take a deep breath and step out into the corridor.

CHAPTER 63

Separated from Isabelle, I'm taken to another holding cell. This one, although musky, doesn't hold the same lingering smell of death as my last.

I can't stop my body from silently shaking; this only adds to the throbbing pain in my hand. My hair is dry by the time my cell door is pulled open. It's the same guard as before. He doesn't need to tell me to move. I stand and walk towards him slowly as he leads me out into the corridor.

For the first time since I recall being here, there are no distant screams echoing in the background. Maybe they have finished with their interrogations for the day.

A light flickers, and I flinch, but there's still no sound other than that of our shoes as we move along the hallway.

"Be ready," he whispers.

I don't make any acknowledgement I've heard him.

He takes hold of my arm, reaches down to my hand, and drops something cold into my palm, closing my fist over it.

"Free France."

This time I look up and stare at his face. He nods, and I return it with one of my own.

"Sorry there wasn't more I could do for you," he says.

I feel tears brimming but force them away. Is this his way of telling me this is my last trip? That this will be the death of me?

"It's okay," I reply, not knowing how much I'm risking with my response. I finish with two words. "Free France."

As we exit large double doors, bright white light blinds me. I blink rapidly as my eyes adjust. The sun is high in the sky.

He leads me to a large truck with the back open and helps me up into the cab. He slams the door shut, and I shudder as the force vibrates through my aching body.

It's only now I risk opening my palm—a silver circle and unmistakably, my St. Christopher. My eyes shoot to the soldier and then back to my palm. I slide it into the bandage and hear the faintest clink as it touches the pill vial.

There's already a driver behind the wheel who I can't see, but there is no mistaking the uniform of the SS officer who has climbed into the passenger side. He's the one who has been interrogating me. One I haven't seen before joins us in the back of the truck and sits beside the French soldier, his head cast down. His eyes raise to meet mine as we are driven away.

Every bump in the road causes me pain. Every shake, every shudder, becomes intolerable, and I wonder how much longer I can stand it—the urge to vomit always there.

Out of nowhere, there is a huge bang, and the truck rises from the ground and drops back down with impact. I managed to steady myself and remain on the bench seat.

There's a strange hiss and a heavy *tchoump, tchoump, tchoump*, as the whole vehicle rattles.

The driver pulls to a stop. Unable to see much of what is happening outside, I try to remain calm and ready just in case. But I'm weary and staying alert is an effort.

The SS officer orders the SS guard and the French soldier out of the truck and they quickly comply. The unmistakable sound of a gun being fired causes me to drop to the bed of the truck, covering my head.

Shouts. More gunfire.

The back door is ripped open, I can see a silhouette, but can't make out the figure.

"Ana?"

I crawl toward the sound—Reuben.

His hand reaches for me, and I stumble out of the doors.

Gunshots continue to rain so very close, but I have no idea from which direction.

Reuben's eyes go wide when he sees me, his jaw clenched tight. With his arm under mine, he tries to get me to move along with him, and for the most part, I'm able.

Isabelle appears out of nowhere, gun raised. I stagger back but realise her gun is pointed behind us. Her eyes meet mine with so many things unsaid as Reuben continues past, leading me towards another vehicle.

A loud thud and boom erupt. Reuben and I fall to the ground; he tries to catch the brunt of my landing but isn't very successful, and an ear splitting scream leaves my lips.

We manage to pull ourselves back to our feet, and I turn back. Isabelle is laying at an awkward angle, her body contorted, and her eyes wide open—void of life.

The soldier who escorted me at the police station is also laying on the ground alongside the SS guard.

A shot rings out and whizzes past my ear so close, the buzz remains even as I strain to open my jaw to dislodge the sound.

Although I feel like Reuben and I are moving with speed, I fear we are no closer to the other vehicle than we were moments ago. He begins to half-drag, half-carry me.

I see René jump out to pull a pin and throw a grenade. Shards of earth and debris rain down over our heads, and a dust cloud settles.

More shots. More sound of screams. Who they belong to, I do not know.

Close enough to the windscreen of the vehicle, I glimpse who is behind the wheel.

Lawry.

His expression pained, he leans out of the window with a pistol in his hand, shooting past us.

"Hurry!" he screams in English.

Just as we approach, Reuben moves behind me, and we are both thrown forward. We scramble to pull one another to our feet awkwardly.

His face, usually tanned, has gone a pale colour. I stare between us as a stain begins to spread over his clothes.

My heart is thumping so hard I can hear its urgency.

Thump Thump, thump thump, thump thump.

I cover the patch with my hand—sticky, wet, thick. But he pushes my hands away and reaches for me in the same area.

And then I am hit with searing pain.

His hand can't stop the blood from seeping through his fingers. The patch on his clothing continues to spread, and I try in vain to cover his, too.

We've been shot.

René is beside us and his lips move, but I can't make out his words. My body becomes too heavy, and I begin falling.

The sky spins above me.

Faces come in and out of view, but they are muted, and I can't make them out.

The last thing I register is the sound of the faintest whisper.

"Hold on, don't give up."

And then all the pain, sight, and sound evaporate, and I fall into nothingness.

CHAPTER 64

I must have the flu. My head and body are too heavy, and my eyes protest angrily as I try to open them.

I'm thirsty, so very thirsty. It hurts to swallow. Even breathing is a struggle.

Voices come into focus, both familiar and not.

"You're okay, Ana. You need to wake up now."

I force my eyelids open. They are so dry, they sting. I blink, but it does nothing to ease the stabbing dryness.

"Ana, it's me."

Lawry.

I go to answer, but it's almost impossible.

He leans over me, and I see what looks like a cup and a straw. He holds it to my mouth, and I suck until fresh liquid coats my throat. I splutter but continue to suck.

"Slowly," he says patiently and pulls it back ever so slightly, only allowing me to take a small sip at a time. The exertion causes my heart to race, and I barely raised my head from the pillow.

"Where am I?" I manage, my throat still rough.

"Hospital," he replies, wiping my brow.

"What happened?"

As I ask, a montage of memories come flooding back. I try to sit up, but his hand is firm against my shoulder.

"Calm down. You were shot, you need to stay calm. *Please.*" His plea is enough for me to obey.

I look from side to side, but I don't see him.

"Reuben, where's Reuben?"

His eyes hold something I have only ever seen one other time, and it's when he told us about Samuel dying.

A cruel sound works its way up through my chest and out through my mouth. I try to ask if he's dead, but I don't want to know the answer if he is.

"Ana, you need to breathe for me, okay? You need to breathe, and I'll tell you everything."

It takes me what feels like forever to calm enough for me to hear him over the pounding in my head and the erratic thumping in my chest.

He takes my hand in his. It's familiar and yet foreign. My first instinct is to pull it away, but I don't. "What do you remember?" he asks.

"Isabelle, dead. Reuben was shot. I was shot?" It's more of a question. I don't know how much of my memory is credible.

He nods in agreement.

And then he begins to tell me what happened when they returned to the farm to find I'd been arrested. Reuben lost his mind, trashed the basement before he carried Vella and buried her in the meadow. My tears fall silently because we had a bond, her and me, but I know she's with Celine now, wherever she is.

Josette was beside herself, and René arrived with news André had also been picked up. It was enough for them to make Josette pack a bag, and they went to lay low at the cottage.

A French insurgent was the one who sent the news of where I was, and it was Isabelle who met with Reuben and confessed everything. Lawry had to hold him back, worried he would physically hurt her, unable to comprehend it was her all along. She was leaking information about them to the Germans.

She was able to get enough intel about me being moved by the Gestapo and insisted she come and help in the rescue mission in any way she could. She wrote me a letter which he leaves on the bedside table.

When I was shot along with Reuben, René and Lawry managed to get us both into the vehicle and rushed us to the nearest hospital. It was the only thing he could do to save me.

Reuben's wound was terrible but not as bad as mine. He knew we wouldn't have long before the Gestapo caught up to us and René was able to get me and Lawry papers to get us into Northern France and onto the boat which got us back to England. It was dangerous, but there was no other option.

This was five days ago.

CHAPTER 65

I wasn't fit for service—not back in the field, anyway. I was offered a job again as a radio operator, and I immersed myself in my work, always with an ear open hoping to hear anything which might tell me what happened to Reuben, Josette, and René. I saw everyone else's lifeless bodies. The corpses haunt my dreams, screams I can't ignore.

I write when waking from the nightmares. It's the only thing which seems to calm me when my body is released from paralysing fear, and I reach for Reuben, but the spot where he should be is cold and barren.

Evie and Lawry gave into their feelings, and I'm glad they did. The thought of them being together no longer fills me with loathing or bitterness. If anything, it gradually eases the guilt I still felt for being with Reuben.

But I would never change what we had. I cling to the small note he gave to Lawry wrapped in a gold band with a diamond encased in the centre. It was a silent promise, a question. I wear it on my necklace. I don't know what happened to Celine's ring.

My hand never was the same after what they did to it. My fingers set almost wrong, and the skin on my finger where my tendon was showing is too taut, but I can move them. And for the first time since being ridiculed as a child because of it, I'm grateful I write with my left hand, not my right.

Sami Junior grows so much every time I see him. He becomes more and more like his father in looks but his Dad in mannerisms. So much like Lawry.

Evie never forces the issue, but I know she wishes she knew what happened to us in France.

But I can't tell her, not any of it. She doesn't even know about my miscarriage, only Lawry does. He was the one the doctors told, and he told me.

He wasn't sure if he should, but he did anyway.

I wasn't far along, and although I only found out after the fact, the knowledge is devastating. I was assured it shouldn't affect me conceiving in the future. The thought made me physically sick. There is only one man I would want to have children with, and I don't know if he is dead or alive.

I unroll the small piece of paper, the writing bold like Reuben, each word holding so much hope.

I will love you until my body leaves this earth, after that, forever and always.

I've memorised these fifteen words, and yet every day, I stare at it, willing for news of his safety.

I remain true to him and what we had, even though we never made promises. We never had to. I was his from the moment I gave myself to him. It just took me longer to understand it was why I wanted to wait to be with Lawry. I was only ever meant to give myself to one man, and it was always Reuben.

If I get to see him again, I want him to read all the words I wrote while we were apart, of the ache which resided without him by my side. Deep down, I believe he is alive. I know I would feel it if he wasn't.

I admitted my feelings for him to Lawry but never to him. I

wonder, does he know? When he closes his eyes, does he see me, saying the words I so desperately want him to hear?

"I love you, too, until my body leaves this earth, after that, forever and always."

It's almost a prayer I say out loud each night before I close my eyes in the hopes we will meet again. I often wonder if Samuel made it to America to his wife, and was able to meet his child. One day I hope to find out; I like to believe he did.

"As soon as the war is over, I'm going back to France to look for him," I say to Evie as she rushes after Sami on the fresh lawn.

"Where will you start?" she asks, swooping Sami into her arms.

"Be careful," I say, taking him from her and tickling him like crazy. He lets out the cutest roar of laughter.

She rolls her eyes and covers her protruding stomach. I ache to carry a child of my own.

"You'll have this one day, Ana. I promise you will. Samuel is looking out for you. I know he is."

I smile at her words which hold so much conviction—so much hope. It wasn't easy for her to accept her ever-growing feelings for Lawry. We talked about it before she finally gave in to them.

They are two sides of the same coin and on the other is Reuben and me. Every path we take leads us to the exact destination meant for us.

CHAPTER 66

War has changed the town, the people. Everyone is trying to rebuild as best they can. Homes turned to rubble, bodies to ash.

In the aftermath, all that remains is the journey of the survivors. Some see it as luck, others a curse. Jewish survivors are returning to cities they called home their entire lives to find out their whole family were wiped out by mass extermination, many not wanting to accept or listen to the harsh reality of what happened during those times.

My steps are weighted as I make my way towards the farmhouse. I even have to stop and catch my breath, not from the exertion, but the force of anxiety penetrating my chest cavity. I close my eyes and tilt my head towards the sun. The warm glow across my skin calms me enough for me to draw my shoulders back and carry on.

A distant bark catches my attention, and at first, I think it's a mirage or a memory. A dog comes bounding towards me. I crouch down.

It can't be.

A puppy—all wobbly legs—knocks me onto my backside as she manically sniffs, licks, and pushes into my hand affectionately. I can't help my tears; she looks just like Vella, only younger. She licks away my tears and I grab hold of her and pull her into my lap and rub her belly. Her back leg bounces up and down, tail going wild.

"Well, I'll be damned."

My head shoots up at the familiar voice—one I haven't heard in years but is warm and inviting as it ever was. I gently nudge the puppy from my lap and jump to my feet.

"René."

I can hardly believe my eyes. He pushes his glasses up on his nose and holds open his arms for me, greeting me with a hug.

"You're alive," I whisper.

"So are you," he replies, pulling back to look me over.

"Your hair grew," he says.

I can't help but laugh at his comment, but the puppy soon has enough and jumps up, her paws on my leg prying for my attention.

"Come on, there's someone who'll want to see you," he says, offering me his arm.

I swallow, afraid to ask who it is, wanting to, but unable to even form the words.

"What happened to you after..."

"After you were shot?"

I nod and eye him as the soil crumbles beneath our feet.

"It was mayhem. But all he cared about was getting you out."

I know he means Reuben and I spin the ring on my finger, my stomach jittering uneasily. A small figure in the doorway catches my eye, and before I can stop myself, I am propelling my legs forward, arms pumping.

Josette.

She turns her head at the sound of my feet. Only it's not her. I stagger as I come to a stop, breathing heavily. René comes up beside me.

"This is my wife, Rosaline." He waves for her to come out.

Now I see her. It was only her height, petite build and similar braided hair. How could I have mistaken her for Josette?

"Rosaline, this is Ana. What's it been, almost four years?" he asks in disbelief that I am actually here.

I nod and she reaches for my hand. I have to wipe away the sweat before I take it in greeting.

I look to René a silent question. He stares at the doorway as if willing her to appear but shakes his head.

"No, she didn't make it," he says, the pain evident in his voice.

I cover my mouth and breathe in through my nose, the smell of fresh manure floating past.

"Come, you must be thirsty," says Rosaline. The sun is high, and the temperature continues to soar.

René takes my hand and leads me to the kitchen—a room I remember so much as if it were my own. My eyes roam the space. It seems the same and yet different.

"What happened?"

I sit, and Rosaline pours some freshly made lemonade.

"She had a stroke a week before they declared victory in Europe."

Sipping the sour drink, my eyes water, not from the bitterness of the lemon but the surge of emotion.

"Where was she when she died?"

"Right here. Rosaline and I took care of her," he replies, covering her hand with his. She smiles softly, her eyes a rich chocolate.

"I'm glad she was home and not alone," I reply. The fears which haunted me of her being sent to a detention camp don't bear thinking about.

The pup comes to sit at my feet expectantly. "She looks just like Vella," I say, trying to hold back tears.

René nods. "She's from the same breeder."

"What's her name?"

"Poppy," he replies

I smile, scratching her behind her ear.

A roar of an engine catches my attention, and I turn my head towards the kitchen window, standing but unable to see who it is.

My body begins to move closer, and I see a familiar silhouette getting out of the driver's side.

Heart racing, I move to the back door. He's on the other side of the truck now and ducks down, reaching for something, no, *someone*. A female with long brown locks. He stands to his full height, and I'm able to get a good look at him. His hair is a little longer, his chin a shadow of hair. His face weary. He's lost weight, but otherwise, he seems the same.

As if sensing me, forest green hues pierce into me. His mouth gapes. I didn't hear a noise, but I may have taken his breath away. *Reuben*. The girl is saying something, but he is fixated on me. She turns, and that's when I see the swaddle in her arms followed by a mewling sound.

I have to grab for the door frame to support my weight.

A physical blow hits me.

I force air into my lungs. His eyes do not stray from mine. I watch on as his hand goes to the small of her back, and they begin to walk towards me.

But it's too much.

Déjà vu.

I've seen this before.

Letting go of the wood, I do the only thing I can think to do.

I run.

CHAPTER 67

I race from the house and out into the field. My name is heard behind me, but I don't stop, I just keep running. I only come to a stop when I reach the meadow. Struggling to catch my breath, I put my hands on my knees.

At the sound of pounding feet behind me, I straighten and spin towards him. I step back as he ascends on me, but he doesn't stop until the toes of his boots are touching mine. His scent washes over me in a wave. His hands reach for my face, and then he's kissing me.

Reuben is kissing me.

I struggle to process everything and pull back.

"What is it?" he asks, breathless, in English, his French accent thick and warm.

"I just…the baby… I—"

His eyes crease, squinting at me. Leaning closer, his lips kiss the tip of my nose. "Not mine," he says, his lips moving to my cheek. "Rosaline's sister."

His lips brush over mine softly.

"Oh," I say on a sigh before my lips press against his.

We kiss as if it's the first, the last, and every time in between.

His hand doesn't stray from my face. He holds the back of my neck firm beneath his palm.

When we do stop, he rests his forehead against mine.

"You're alive," I whisper, unable to keep my tears at bay.

"So are you," he replies.

I rest my cheek against his chest, and the sound of his heart is exactly as I remember.

"I am now."

His body relaxes. When he's sure I'm not going anywhere, he pulls back to survey my face.

"What's your name?" he asks.

I smile, staring up at him. "It's Ana," I reply.

He cocks an eyebrow. "Ana is your real name?"

I nod. "Ana Dubois."

He lets out a satisfied sigh. "I always wondered," he says.

I stroke his cheek, needing to know he isn't going to disappear.

"You thought I found someone else?"

I shake my head but then nod, and my cheeks heat. I honestly don't know what I thought.

"I'm yours, Ana, until the day I die. Forever." His gaze penetrates mine.

"And always," I reply, looking into pools of forest green.

"And always," he whispers back in French, lifting me into his arms.

I wrap my legs around his waist. "You came home," he says into my neck, his tongue sweeping over my collar bone.

I throw my head back. "You are home," I groan.

"I want you," he says, almost pained.

"Then take me," I reply.

From the words passing my lips, everything else happens so quickly, and then he's buried deep inside me, and we both sigh in unison.

"Home," he breathes.

Neither of us last long. We're brought to a fast, rapid climax, and I wouldn't have it any other way.

After we lay there, his fingers trace lazy circles over my skin, over the scar from the stab wound and to the bullet wound. I reach over, and my finger runs over his matching one.

His hand goes to my hand with the ring, and he brings it to his lips and kisses it.

"So is that a yes?" he asks.

"What?" I reply coyly.

"You'll marry me?"

My smile reaches my ears. Even if I wanted to act unaffected by his touch, his lips or his words, it's impossible. I don't want to wait. Not after being apart from him for this long.

"Yes."

He kisses me with reverence and covers my body with his.

As turned on as I am right now, there is still so much we need to discuss. "We need to talk about what happened…"

His lips stop me. "And we will, but right now, I want to get lost in you some more." He slides into me excruciatingly slowly, and I let out a consented mewling sound.

I wiggle, satisfied I can feel him everywhere.

His eyes bore into mine—the lust, love, and admiration I see are a reflection of my feelings for him.

It's impossible not to feel overwhelmed; tears of joy roll down my cheeks.

As he moves inside me, his hands reach for my face. "I love you," he says.

"Je t'aime," I reply.

∽

Wrapped in his arms, underneath a tree, we talk until the sun sets and my skin gooses with bumps. He dresses me, and I dress him. We are never not touching.

He tells me of his arrest—how they caught up to him about two months after we were shot, how he spent the remainder of the war in a prisoner of war camp. He was luckier than most; he bartered and helped other inmates where he could. But I know it took a toll on him, I can see it—etched deep in his eyes, stories he'll never be able to tell.

The basement never was discovered, Isabelle never told them. And when the Germans ransacked the house, they found nothing incriminating. They took Estelle but left the filly.

René managed to stay off the radar, undetected, and moved in to look after Josette. He kept helping with the resistance where he met Rosaline.

Her sister, the woman I saw with the baby, was visiting from town. I'm embarrassed by my behaviour. I'll apologise when I see her, although he says it's not necessary.

"I still can't believe it," I say.

"Believe what?" He pulls me into his arms, rocking us back and forth so softly.

"That you're safe and alive."

He kisses my temple, "I hated that I couldn't get you out when you had been arrested," he says with self-loathing.

I shiver. Memories wash over me; I don't think I'll ever forget.

"I dreamt of you when they had me in prison. You kept calling out to me, but I couldn't hear your voice. I hated not knowing what happened to you and Lawry."

He takes my hand and gently examines my damaged fingers; his face turns into a grimace. "I hate that I wasn't able to stop this," he says, kissing the back of my hand.

"It could have been worse." I shudder. "Pierré was shot right in front of me. He saved me, did you know?"

His face is solemn. "I heard he was captured so you could escape."

"It's true. He was a good man. I saw them drag André's lifeless body right past me."

I can still smell the damp musk mixed with urine, faeces and blood, it's one you can never forget.

"They didn't…you weren't?" he struggles to find the words.

I lean back, my hands lay over his chest. His heart beats rapidly. "No, they didn't touch me, not like that."

And even if they had, I'd never tell him. Some secrets are best buried deep. His eyes soften, but I can see he carries so much weight over what happened.

"It's not your fault, Reuben. You saved me."

He shakes his head. "No, it was Larry." His finger trails over my cheek.

I can't help but chuckle. He smirks, he knows it's Lawry. I slap at his chest.

"He kept his promise," he says.

"And what was that?" I ask, wanting him to tell me.

"He kept you alive, and he gave you my message."

My thumb spins the ring on my finger. "I lost Celine's ring," I say, unable to keep eye contact. "I'm so sorry."

He turns my chin with his index finger. "No, I took it. When I gave this to Lawry." The unease in my stomach abates. "René made sure Josette was buried with it."

A twinge in my chest tightens.

"I hate that I never got to say goodbye to her. Where is she?" I ask

"She's buried next to her husband and Celine."

I sit up and stare back at him. "Maybe I can visit them, leave some flowers," I say.

"Of course." He pushes my hair over my shoulder and kisses my throat.

"I was pregnant!" I blurt out.

His hand stalls before he pulls me into his lap, facing him. "You and me?" he asks.

I nod. "Yes. I lost it. I didn't even know."

He kisses me with a tenderness I have never experienced before. "God willing, maybe we'll have them someday," he says softly, tears pooling in his eyes.

I nod, knowing he feels the loss. Some might say you can't miss something you've never had, but I do, every day. I wonder if it was a girl or a boy. What colour hair and eyes would he or she have had...

Overcome with nostalgia, I fear I'll never know.

But being back with Reuben, anything is possible.

"Come, you must be ravished," I say and climb out of his hold.

"You have no idea," he replies, still managing to raise a blush from me.

"I'm staying at a Bed and Breakfast in town, I should get back."

He shakes his head once. "No, we'll go get your stuff. I'm not letting you out of my sight," he says with a wicked grin.

∼

It turns out he moved to the cottage and René and Rosaline stayed on at the farm. It was only right—without them, it would have gone to shambles. We didn't wait to marry; as soon as we were able, we had a small ceremony and now he's mine in every way possible.

"And you're sure? About making this our home?" he asks as we drive up to the familiar cottage. I smile, stepping out of the truck. I breathe freely.

He comes to stand beside me.

"I'd love that," I say and stand on my tip toes and kiss him.

He swoops me into his arms; I let out a *whelp* sound and laugh. He carries me up to the threshold.

Looking down on me, his eyes smile with passion and promise.

Home.

EPILOGUE

Present

What happens when we die?

No one truly knows, and if we do, it's a distant memory. One we have no recollection of from one life to the next.

I often dream of being with Reuben again. I ache for it daily, and yet here I am—waiting.

He visits my dreams. Sometimes it's a memory of us making love or the smell of his freshly brewed coffee; other times, it's nightmares he never survived the war. But mostly it's of our reunion.

His shirt still has the faintest scent of him, and I inhale as I drift off into the deepest crevices of my mind—where my body doesn't always ache or creak with every movement.

And I can breathe without effort.

"What took you so long?" he asks.

I turn and find Reuben, patiently waiting. I leap into his arms and bury my face into the crook of his neck.

"Anyone would think you missed me," I reply.

"Always, mon amour, je t'aime."

I soak in his voice, and my heart races to sync with his as it always does when we are together.

"And I love you," I reply.

He kisses me, and when we come up for air, he twirls me once, and then we begin to dance to a silent melody, one only we can hear.

Bringing my hand up to his lips, he turns it over and kisses the inside of my wrist.

"Are you ready?" he asks.

"For what?" I reply, scanning every feature of his familiar face.

"Our next adventure."

I nod, and my eyes gaze past him to row upon row of wild lavender which reaches my knees. The open meadow is full of wildflowers, alive with wonder. He captures my eyes, and silently, we share a thousand words.

I peer between us as he entwines my hand with his—no longer stained by old age, or plagued with arthritis—once again youthful and vibrant.

In front of us await our friends who have long since passed. I take one step and then another, with him by my side. Just as it was in life, we move together as one, continuing our journey together.

Our hearts found one another in war and once again in peace.

This may or may not be a dream, but for now, it is right where I want to be.

The End

LETTER TO READER

Thank you for making it this far and joining me on this journey through Hearts of War. I can't begin to express how much your support means to me.

This was always meant to be my first novel, but it became the prequel to Where the Heart Is and Dysfunctional Hearts. It was a long time coming and really was a labour of love.

I do hope Ana resonated with you as much as she did with me. This era holds a special place in my heart, and I hope to share more books in this genre with you in the future.

If you enjoyed it, please consider leaving a review for Hearts of War on Amazon. It doesn't have to be much—one sentence will do—but I would be forever grateful if you'd consider doing so. Reviews are extremely important for authors as a way for people to find out about our books. And we can't make that happen without you, thank you!

ACKNOWLEDGMENTS

Mum, thank you doesn't seem enough. You are my sounding board, my rock, my biggest support system and my best friend. I love you.

To my family, I love you to the moon and back.

Dad, thank you for sharing your love of history with me.

Carlie, thank you for always cheering me on, love you skin 'n' blister, first my sister, forever my friend.

Cassie—Soul sister, lobster, best friend. You are an inspiration and I'm so damn proud to know you. Thank you for the power of your edits, your patience, for always supporting me and pulling my head out of the sand. I wouldn't be able to do this without you. I love YOU!

Crystal—my beautiful, funny and loving friend. Thank you for proofreading and always having my back. No flocks given, love you and miss your face!

Dusti—thank you for always being so beautifully you and beta reading when my novels are at their roughest and loving them anyway.

Julie—I love your guts, always.

Kirsten—Beta Bitch girl you rock, thank you for always being honest and your endless support.

To my fellow tribe and PLN authors, especially Amber, Ruth, Heather, Lindsey and Kayleigh, I love you. I wish I could name you all. Thank you, Tarryn Fisher.

To my famalam, I love you guys. Dave, Grace, Tam, Alex and Niki, Covid has really messed up our shenanigans, we have a lot to make up for. Jon, we miss you every damn day.

Friends who are my family, and embedded in my soul. Victoria, William, Laura, Andy, Evie and Zach, and my mountain goat, Ethel. I love and miss you all. I can't wait for our next adventure.

To all the people I've met along the way who continue to support me. Beverlina, Donna, Andrea, Michelle, Simon and Arek, thank you!

To those who support me whether you read my books or not, I see you.

To my most loyal companion, Harley, gone but never forgotten.

ALSO BY L.S. PULLEN

Where the Heart Is

Dysfunctional Hearts

Hearts of War

Burning Embers

ABOUT THE AUTHOR

L.S.Pullen aka Leila, is a daughter, sister and proud aunt. Hearts of War is her third novel. Born and raised in North London, she recently relocated to Peterborough, England. Her passion is reading and writing. She also enjoys art, photography, film, and theatre. In true English fashion, loves afternoon tea. No longer working the corporate life, she is currently writing full time. As well as managing a small craft business Wisteria Handmade Crafts and Indie Author's Book Services offering multiple services to other aspiring and self-publishing authors.

Visit her website to find out more:
https://lspullen.co.uk

Join her Facebook reader group:
LSP's Stargazers

facebook.com/lspullenauthor
instagram.com/lspauthor
twitter.com/lspauthor
bookbub.com/authors/l-s-pullen

Printed in Great Britain
by Amazon